THE
WILD
GIRLS

THE
WILD
GIRLS

A Novel

PHOEBE MORGAN

WILLIAM MORROW

An Imprint of HarperCollins*Publishers*

P.S.™ is a trademark of HarperCollins Publishers.

THE WILD GIRLS. Copyright © 2021 by Phoebe Morgan. All rights reserved. Printed in the United States of America. No part of this book may be used or reproduced in any manner whatsoever without written permission except in the case of brief quotations embodied in critical articles and reviews. For information, address HarperCollins Publishers, 195 Broadway, New York, NY 10007. HarperCollins books may be purchased for educational, business, or sales promotional use. For information, please email the Special Markets Department at SPsales@harpercollins.com.

Originally published in the United Kingdom in 2021 by HQ, an imprint of HarperCollins UK.

FIRST U.S. EDITION

Library of Congress Cataloging-in-Publication Data has been applied for.

ISBN 978-0-06-314483-5

22 23 24 25 26   LSC   10 9 8 7 6 5 4 3 2 1

Praise for Phoebe Morgan and *The Wild Girls*

"Sublimely dark." —*Woman & Home* (UK)

"A wonderfully atmospheric thriller of secrets, lies, and betrayals, *The Wild Girls* is a heart-stopping roller coaster of a read with a dark sense of menace and hugely relatable characters."

—B. A. Paris, author of *Behind Closed Doors*

"Well-paced. . . . Morgan has a particular skill for creating a vivid sense of place." —*Daily Mail* (UK)

"When three estranged friends set off for an all-expenses-paid trip to Botswana, you just know it won't be long before they discover the catch—and what a terrifying one it is! Tense, well-paced, and featuring a cast of relatable flesh-and-blood women, *The Wild Girls* is an exhilarating, read-in-one-sitting ride."

—Louise Candlish, internationally bestselling author of *Our House*

"A spine-chilling tale." —*The Sun* (UK)

"A cracking page-turner."

—Cara Hunter, bestselling author of *All the Rage*

"Morgan knows how to ramp up the tension." —*Woman* (UK)

"Dark, twisty plotting, compelling characterization, and an ending I didn't see coming at all."

—Harriet Tyce, bestselling author of *Blood Orange*

For my agent, Camilla,
for always believing in me

After

The police tape looks unnatural in the lush green surrounds of the safari lodge complex. The doors are all open now, as the forensics team come in and out, their clinical white uniforms catching the light of the sun as it burns down on the empty, parched plains. Dotted on the wooden walkways and inside the five lodges are numbered yellow markers—that's where they found the first body, that's where they found the second. Over there is where one of the more junior officers uncovered the first victim's shoe. On the edge of the Limpopo River, in among the sticky, thick mud and the shiny-backed insects, that's where the blood spatter was, bright and viscous. They were lucky it didn't get washed away.

Above, a helicopter circles, the drone of it loud and relentless, a harsh man-made noise disrupting the constant hum of the cicadas. From the cockpit, you'd be able to see the whole site, in all its glory—here, the main lodge, able to sleep twelve people. At each corner, a smaller lodge, set up for one guest, alone.

The four glistening plunge pools, one of which contained the missing knife, the blade of it circling lazily around the drain. The wooden walkways that connect the lodges look like a maze from this height—or an elaborate board game, designed to catch you out.

In this game, though, half the players are dead.

The forensic officer thinks this place will be shut down now, forever haunted by the events of one hot, dreadful weekend in March. He feels the loss; it seeps from the windows of the lodges, rises up from the river, rustles with the wind through the gum trees, whispering a warning to anyone who might come near Deception Valley. Briefly, a white butterfly lands on his arm, weightless against his uniform, but just as quickly, it is gone. He stares at the patch on which it landed, remembering the imprint of its tiny limbs.

How easily beauty can be destroyed.

PART ONE

Prologue

Grace

The invitation lands like a grenade on my doormat early on Friday morning: *You are invited to celebrate Felicity's 30th birthday. Date: March 28. Place: Botswana, Southern Africa.* I stare at it for a few moments; the swirly, smug font, the thick, expensive card it's printed on, the way her name sits elegantly on the page. The edge of the invite is embossed with gold foil; it must have cost her a fortune. I imagine them shooting through letterboxes all over the country, pretty missiles just waiting to detonate. Her friends scooping down to pick them up, fingers slitting open envelopes, eyes running over the words. *Who else will come?* I think to myself, *Who else will be invited?*

My watch beeps, signaling to me to get up even though I'm well awake now. My eyes flicker across the date—of course, Valentine's Day. Sending out invitations to arrive today is so very *Felicity* that I almost want to laugh, despite the curl of anxiety percolating in my stomach. Although I haven't seen her for almost two years, I still know Felicity inside out. At least, I think I do.

"Grace?"

Without warning, the letterbox is rattling and I take a step backward, heart pounding, as the front door to the flat swings open, letting in a blast of cold February air and a rush of London noise; the scream of the traffic, the faint wail of sirens, a maelstrom of voices, people going about their busy lives. My fingers clutch the invitation as I step backward, pulling my dressing gown around me, my feet bare and freezing on the tiled floor. Someone is coming in.

"Grace? What are you doing up?"

My flatmate Rosie is panting in front of me, and I let my breath out, relief flooding through my body as she shakes her head like a dog, sprinkling tiny droplets of water. She's dressed in running gear, purple lycra clinging to her, the embodiment of fitness as always. Her dark hair is wet, flattened to her skull, but her eyes are bright with the glowing look of someone who's just burned 500 calories before I've even had breakfast.

"What's that?"

She pushes past me, nodding at the invitation in my hand as she does so.

"An invitation," I say, swallowing hard, and she laughs, groans. Her soft Irish accent is lilting, effortlessly light.

"Not another one. Jesus. I'm still out of pocket after Jess and Jamie's. Why do these people think everyone can stump up to afford it all? I bet they want you to buy them a fancy toaster on top of it, too. Whoever invented the idea of wedding lists should be shot."

"Not a wedding," I interrupt, closing the front door behind

her, shoving the invitation into the pocket of my dressing gown. "A birthday party. In Botswana."

She's in the kitchen now; I can hear the sound of the fridge opening and shutting, her quick, confident little footsteps scurrying about. Getting on with her day as though nothing has happened. Because for her, it hasn't, has it? The invite is for me, and me alone. Unwanted, a memory flashes into my mind: Felicity, laughing on another Friday two years ago, her mouth wide, the top of her blouse falling slightly open to reveal the lace of her bra, the gleam of her skin. The strange, smoky smell of the courtyard; the sense that something bad was coming. The cold metal of the fire escape stairs. A disconnected phone call that came the day after. Always, the taste of tequila, sharp and dangerous on our tongues.

I push the images away.

"A birthday party? Whose? I didn't know you had any friends in Africa," Rosie asks as I follow her into the kitchen. She sounds a bit awkward, perhaps thinking that she could have stopped after *friends*. It's true that I never have anybody around. After what happened, I find it harder to go out, and more difficult to have people in my own space. Strangers frighten me, though I don't like to admit it. Taking people at face value has become something of a challenge.

I breathe in deeply to clear my head, try to make my voice sound normal. Already, it's as though I've lost the ability to act casual, forgotten what I'd usually say in this situation. The invitation has heightened everything; raised the stakes. Brought back the past.

"An old friend," I say at last. "A girl I went to school with."

"Nice." She nods, accepting the half-truth, gulping water

down quickly and easing off her trainers. "Pricey, though. The flights alone won't be cheap, will they? Still, I'd love to go somewhere like that. See the elephants, that sort of thing. Don't get many of those in Dublin, nor here." She laughs, slams down her glass on the counter, the sound making me flinch. Sweat is glistening on her brow; small beads of moisture that she dabs with the back of her hand. "I'm going to hop in the shower. I'm out with Ben tonight for V day. Are you . . . ?"

Her words tail off and I can see her flush slightly with embarrassment, the blush creeping up her ivory throat.

"I'll be in," I say flatly. "I don't have any Valentine's Day plans, Rosie."

"All a load of nonsense anyway," she says, grinning at me, and then she disappears, leaving me alone in the kitchen, the invitation still in my hand and my thoughts whirring. Felicity wants to see me. After all this time. But the question is, has she forgiven me? Have I forgiven *her*?

And who else will be invited?

Alice

"Babe? You're using all the hot water again. Hurry up, will you? I'm late for work."

Alice sluices the last smudges of apple conditioner out of her dark hair, pulling a tangle out with her fingers, a little bit too hard—there is a tug of pain—and reaches for the shower dial, turning the water off with a hiss. Her skin feels warm and tingly, but already she is dreading the cold tiles of the bathroom floor, the icy rush of air that will come as soon as she steps outside. She and Tom are rationing the heating: Alice hates it.

Tom is hovering impatiently, naked, and his sleep-smudged eyes don't meet hers as he steps past her and into the shower cubicle. *Happy Valentine's Day*, Alice thinks but doesn't say.

She towels herself off quickly, avoiding her reflection in the mirror, brushing her teeth as fast as she can. There are tiny trails of blood in among the mint froth when Alice spits in the sink; she wipes them away with the tips of her fingers, runs the cold water until the porcelain is clear. She is late for work, and Year Six are like animals if left alone in a classroom for too long. Alice can just picture them careering into the school, their parents (the ones that turn up, at least) casting disapproving eyes at her empty desk—*Ms. Warner, running late again . . .*

There's no time to blow-dry her hair and so she shoves it up in a bun, drinks a quick glass of water standing at the sink, and grabs her leather rucksack. There isn't time for makeup, either; she's slathered some tinted moisturizer across her cheeks and wiped the mascara smudges from underneath her light green eyes, and that will have to do. It's not far to work, a fifteen-minute walk through deepest darkest Hackney and then she's there. Quicker and cheaper than taking the bus, and less chance of seeing a pupil. Since that time Alice saw Liam Donoghue from the senior school on the number 43 and he insisted on sitting next to her, she has steered clear. No one wants the boundaries blurred. Least of all Alice Warner.

She crossed a line once before, and she won't let herself forget it. Alice knows how easy it is to lose everything, how rapidly mistakes can spiral into more.

Alice's hand is on the latch when she sees the envelope,

wedged in the letterbox, half in and half out, hovering above a pile of junk mail, none of which either of them can ever be bothered to open: red and yellow flyers, laminated promises with no meaning; a Hackney newspaper full of bad news, the edges already ripped and tatty. Her heart sinks as she takes in the fancy handwriting on the front, addressed only to her. A wedding invitation, she'd bet their flat on it. Not that she's got the money to place a bet right now, far from it. Quickly, Alice grabs it and stuffs it into her bag to read later, yanking the door open and stepping out onto the rainy London street. Water immediately drenches her left shoe—*Great*, she thinks, *a good start to the day.*

It's lunchtime when she remembers it. Her fingers graze the cool paper as she is searching for her phone, having spent a busy morning trying to teach Year Six the basics of fractions, a subject Alice is rustier on than she'd thought. She is slumped at her desk, drinking a cup of instant coffee that's been cold for an hour already. She knows she should pop to the M&S on the high road, but she can't face the thought of spending eight quid on a sandwich and some crisps; buying the flat with Tom has cleared out every last penny in her account and she has promised herself she'll be good for the next few months. Cut out any unnecessary expenditure, that's what they had said. The plan was to start bringing in a packed lunch, but, well. She doesn't see Tom doing that.

Alice pulls the envelope out of her bag and uses a pair of slightly gluey scissors to slit it open, already wondering who it'll be this time. She is thirty—still prime time for summer weddings and expensive hen-dos. It's never-ending, really it is. She won't have anything to wear—she's put on weight recently, feels curvier than before, as Tom has pointed out more than once.

And then she sees the name, and she has to put the scissors down because her hands begin to shake. *Felicity's birthday.* And she wants Alice to come.

Hannah

Hannah is in the baby's room when Chris brings the post in. Of course she is—where else would she be? He's just about sleeping through the night these days, which is something Hannah could weep in gratitude for to whoever might be listening, but still he wakes up at around five every morning and she sits with him, feeding and stroking, calming and shushing, as the hours tick by and the dark becomes light. It feels like the two of them are the only people left in the world in those moments, as she listens to his breathing, feels the beat of his heart against hers. Her eyes always feel gritty with tiredness; the shadows of the cot bars make strange shapes on the wall: a tiny prison. During those dawn hours, she forces herself to feel grateful, to remember how much she wanted this, how far they have come to be parents. She must remember that. At all times.

"Morning," Chris whispers, keeping his voice soft—he usually does nowadays for fear of Hannah flying off the handle at him if he doesn't. He's clutching a mug of coffee and the smell makes her want to rip it out of his hands, but she is still breastfeeding and has had two cups already today, so of course she doesn't. He pops the stack of mail down on the ottoman next to Max's cot and peers down at their sleeping baby boy, whose blue eyes, the mirror image of hers, are squeezed shut (although Hannah doubts they'll stay that way for long). Chris is dressed in a suit and tie, all sharp angles and clean-cut corners, and she feels a sharp pang of jealousy as she pictures him leaving the house, popping his earbuds in and hopping onto the tube to work, interacting with other adults. Most of Hannah's conversations these days are pretty one-sided.

"Is he okay?" he asks her, and she nods sleepily, a yawn stifling her reply, and brushes a strand of her dark-blond hair away from her face. It feels dry and frizzy to the touch; she hasn't paid any attention to it for weeks.

"He's fine, we're all good. Have you got a busy day today?"

Chris nods, takes a slurp of his coffee. The noise grates on Hannah slightly but she forces herself to ignore it. Chris is a lawyer, working in commercial law but wanting to make a move to family. "Commercial law is so boring, Hannah," he tells her all the time, and she wants to scream at him to try being cooped up with a baby for twenty-four hours a day, with nobody to talk to except Peppa Pig on the screen. Hannah hates Peppa Pig. She has started to dream about her; her rounded pink snout, the high-pitched sound of her voice. She taunts Hannah; in nightmares, the pig's mother blinks her long eyelashes directly into hers, tickling her skin.

But of course Hannah never says that.

"Remember the Clarksons are coming over tomorrow night," Chris says, and Hannah's heart sinks like a stone beneath her nightie—naturally, she'd forgotten. Most of the time now, her brain feels like a sieve with extra holes. The Clarksons are Chris's colleagues, invited for a hideous double-date dinner in an attempt to rally Hannah's spirits, give her some company. Chris doesn't understand why she hasn't been in touch with the girls in so long, why their close-knit friendship has become so distant. She hasn't yet found the words to explain it to him. Every time Hannah thinks about it, she feels a weird mix of emotions, but mainly she feels so guilty that she wants to disappear, hide under the baby's cot and never be found.

As Chris reaches down to kiss Max goodbye, Hannah gets a whiff of his aftershave—it smells different, new.

"See you later," he tells her, kissing her on the mouth, and she puts her hand on the back of his neck, trying to re-create the old passion, find their spark. *Who are you wearing new aftershave for?* she wants to ask him, but she knows she's being ridiculous—this is *Chris*, for God's sake, and so Hannah says nothing, just waves and smiles at him as he backs out of the baby's room.

Max has miraculously stayed sleeping, so she takes the opportunity to sift through the mail her husband has left on the side, noticing the messy, chipped polish on her nails as she does so. There's never time to replace it. She doesn't understand the mothers with neat nails. A bill, addressed to Chris, a Boden catalog (is she really that old?), a flyer advertising some Valentine's Day lingerie (chance would be a fine thing), and something else. A stiff, square envelope, addressed to her. Briefly, Hannah wonders if it's from his mother—she often sends cards, her little way of checking how they are (read: checking how *she* is coping with Jean's longed-for grandson), but her latest was last week and this feels a bit soon for a second, even by Jean's standards.

Hannah rips the paper, and the invitation tumbles out—nice, thick card, expensive. Someone with money—not his mother, then. Hannah thinks it must be a work thing, and then she sees the name and it's as though she's been dunked in cold water. The memory flashes back through her like a bolt of electricity. The cold of the wall against her jeans. The darkness of the sky. An unfamiliar hand rubbing her back.

Guilt crawls up her throat, and Hannah puts her fingers to her neck as if she can stop it in its tracks. She can't change the past; she should know that by now. Her necklace, a thin gold chain from Chris, is cold underneath her fingertips, and she rolls it against her skin, pressing down harder than she needs to, imprinting herself with its tiny interlocking pattern.

Just then, her phone, caught in the folds of her nightie, beeps loudly with a message. It's a familiar name, but one she hasn't seen in months: Grace Carter. There are only three words, and Hannah cannot work out the tone—hesitant, or accusing?

The message says: *Are you invited?*

Chapter One

February 14
London

Grace

I'm working from home today, so I spend most of the morning on my laptop, googling photos of Botswana. I don't even bother with a shower or my contact lenses, just sit there in my scrubby white dressing gown, glasses on, scrolling through the pictures. It says the temperature over there is eighty-six degrees, even in February, and it only gets hotter in March. Felicity always hated having a March birthday, said she wanted to be born in the summer when everyone was in the mood to drink rosé at any time of day. I continue scrolling through the websites, lose myself slightly in the images—imagining the hot sun on my back, the rustle of the grass underneath my feet. It's been so long since I left London. Sometimes, I feel like I'm destined to be in Peckham forever, as though my soul will wander the busy streets for years after I die.

Botswana would be something different. It would be an adventure. And I'd get to see the girls again, after all this time. Girls—it's ridiculous to call them that, now that we are all women in our thirties, but that is what we've always been. That silly nickname: *the wild girls*. Old habits die hard, after all. The thought of seeing them makes my stomach twist. Memories spin in my mind, like tricks of the light that I cannot quite catch.

Perhaps I don't want to.

I picture them; Alice Warner, her long black hair trailing down her back, her wide smile, the smell of her musky perfume as she leans in close to me, sharing a secret. The look on her face after she's had a few too many glasses of red wine—which, let's face it, used to happen more often than not. The way her eyes glow when she's got gossip. And Hannah Jones, God, Hannah. The sensible one—the one we all needed the most. The mother hen—a real mother now, judging by her latest Instagram photos that I look at sometimes on long, lonely evenings but am too scared to like. The one who'd tuck the covers around you after a night out, be first up in the morning making tea and toast. Those big blue eyes that made you think everything was going to be all right; her clean, calm home; that pale English rose skin that she didn't even have to do anything to. Like an advert for serenity, was Hannah.

And Felicity Denbigh. The one who kept us all together— until she didn't anymore. I conjure her up—that bright, almost white-blond hair that she smoothed down twenty times a day, a surprising, infectious cackle of a laugh that strangers always thought she was faking. The silver rings on her fingers, the way they glinted in the light. Her bright red lipstick, no matter what. Felicity the fun one. The popular one. The one you want around.

Only she hasn't been around—not for two years. Suddenly, as I think of them, the way we were, I am struck with a visceral pang of longing that almost makes me gasp. The room seems starker, shabbier, even more lonely than it already is. Without their energy, their friendship, my own life has dwindled even further somehow, lost its shine. It's not that the flat isn't all right—it's okay in the summer, when the sun beams into the living room and we don't have to worry about the heating as much. Rosie does so much exercise that she's always boiling, but I can't say the same for myself.

I moved to this flat two years ago, after everything happened and I stopped seeing the girls, and ever since, my life has been . . . I don't even know what the word is. Static, I suppose. I thought I was doing the right thing by keeping my distance from them all, and of course, I couldn't go near Felicity. But maybe I was wrong.

I exhale. It's taken me a long time to admit it to myself, but it's true. As everyone around me moves forward—having babies, getting married, buying houses, moving, in Felicity's case, to New York—I have stayed still. Worse than still—sinking.

And this invitation has got to be the thing that gets me out. I check my phone, and my stomach lurches as I see the little red notification pop up, like a finger tapping me on the shoulder, impossible to ignore. One new message.

Hannah has replied.

Hannah

Hannah doesn't respond to Grace's message straightaway. She needs some time to think. For Felicity to invite them now, after all this time—it feels odd to her. Is it a peace offering? A sign that she wants things to go back to how they were? Or is it simply another chance to show off—to tell the world how much better her life is than the rest of theirs?

That's the thing about Felicity, Hannah thinks. Everything about her life has to be *the best*. The best job, the best boyfriend—although actually, she's not sure whether Felicity and Nathaniel are still together anymore—the best incredibly glamorous apartment in central Manhattan. On forgiving days, Hannah thinks it is because of what happened to her, what her father did—and on other days she is not so sure. She hates thinking about Felicity's father; Michael Denbigh has been known to pop up in her dreams and she quickly pushes the thought away.

When Felicity first moved to New York, two years ago, so soon after the night everything fell apart, she promised them all that she'd keep in touch. Hannah thinks of the message she sent telling them about the move, how sudden and abrupt it felt. But in it, she did say she'd call, Hannah knows she did. She'd even sent Felicity flowers. Lilies, for her new flat. She remembered afterward that Felicity always said they reminded her of funerals, but she'd only meant them as a nice gesture. Or an olive branch, perhaps, after that night. Felicity had never acknowledged receipt. She probably thought she didn't owe her anything, after what Hannah had done. Or perhaps she'd sent them to the wrong address; Felicity didn't give them many details about where she would be living, or who she'd be living with over there. Hannah wonders whether Nate went with her, or whether their love story burned out in the way Felicity's often did. She has imagined Felicity's life many times over the past two years; picturing a spacious, shiny flat on the Upper East Side, Felicity swinging her legs in and out of bright yellow taxis. She's no idea what it's really been like, because Felicity hasn't been in contact.

Felicity always used to be the one who kept them together—made the effort to see the three of them regularly, kept the invites flowing. She made it fun, too—constantly laughing, pouring more drinks, lightening them all as the weight of their lives grew heavier and heavier. It's only looking back that Hannah can see a kind of desperation in Felicity's neediness, a darkness shuttered up behind her eyes. When they were teenagers, it was Felicity's house they gathered at, clustered together up in the attic, playing endless games of truth or dare while her father stalked around downstairs, the house empty after the death of her mother. Hannah used to wonder whether her own mother would have put a stop to the games they were playing; their dares growing bolder and bolder, pushing themselves to see how far they would go. They called themselves the wild girls, after Alice overheard Felicity's father calling them "feral," with more than a hint of despairing anger in his voice. Hannah closes her eyes, remembering the sensation of the attic—the candles flickering, the dust motes glowing in the air. An open window, a glimpse of the night sky. Felicity's voice telling her to jump. Her arms, spread-eagled in the air as she fell, landing winded in the garden as the others peered down at her from above. Looking back, it was dangerous. She could've broken her neck. Felicity's dad had helped her up, in the end, his hand too far down her back. Even now, she can remember the sensation of it—an uncomfortable churn that she tries not to think about. The bruises smattered her skin for days. She'd been lucky not to face serious injury.

The games were always instigated by Felicity. She was the

flame; the other three were the moths, gray and unpalatable in comparison. When she left so soon after that night two years ago, the group floundered, sputtered out. None of them knew how to *be* anymore. And so they stopped—their little friendship group abruptly cut off, after so many years together. Hannah began to lose herself in the fertility details, the painful ins and outs of them, all the while clinging to Chris like a life raft. The closeness they'd all had had come to an end. The wild girls were no more.

Only now, it turns out that maybe it was all just on pause.

Beside Hannah, Max stirs in his cot. He'll want feeding soon, but if she is lucky and quick, she might be able to have a shower while he's still sleeping. The idea of hot water pounding onto her shoulders, easing the ache in her muscles, is seductive; a moment of peace, a chance to think, just for a few minutes. She'll leave the door open, so that she can hear him if he cries.

Before Hannah can think about it too much longer, she taps out a reply to Grace. *Yes. The invite came this morning. I don't know if I'll go yet.* A pause. She could leave it at that, turn her phone off and pretend nothing ever happened. Go back to her day, back to the endless routine of nappy-changing and breastfeeding, of trying to seem interesting to her husband as her breasts throb uncomfortably beneath her blouse and her son's blue eyes watch her, following her around the room in case she does something wrong. But Hannah's fingers carry on writing, as though she is not in control at all. *Will you?*

Hannah hits send, and leaves the phone in Max's room as she heads for the shower. She hears it beep instantly again, but this time she ignores it, continues stripping off her clothes, steps into the hot steam of the water and tilts her face upward into the stream. Her body feels cumbersome, loaded with weight and with worry, and she runs her hands over her stretch marks and her hips, squeezing the flesh a little bit too hard. Hannah forces her mind to go blank. She doesn't want to know the answer to her question. Not yet.

Alice

They did a class project on Africa once, at school. The kids drew pictures of the animals—elephants, gazelles, leopards, strange four-legged creatures dotted around the pages of their workbooks, the sky above them a bright line of blue, simple and opaque. They wanted to paint their faces; Alice had said no and felt guilty for the rest of the week. Most of these children will never go to Botswana—most of them will probably never leave Hackney. Would it really have killed her to let them wear a bit of face paint? Tom would say she is too strict, that the way she always plays by the rules stifles the children's creativity. What he really means is that it stifles him.

On the way home from school, she pulls the invitation from her bag again. Red ink has furred onto the edge, a leaky pen to blame. As she walks, Alice rereads it, properly this time. It's only then that she notices the small print at the bottom, like a little afterthought: *all expenses paid*. She blinks, stops in the middle of the street. A group of teenagers pushes past her, hoods up, gum on their breath, and a woman with a raffia shopping bag tuts loudly, but Alice ignores them all. *All expenses paid?* God. Is Felicity really so rich that she can pay for her friends to come on holiday? Alice thinks of her own dwindling bank balance, and for a moment, the hot, blind panic that has threatened to overtake her recently rises up, climbing her throat and creating pins and needles in her hands. But while Alice exists on discounted sandwiches and tap water, thanks to the massive weight of their mortgage that hangs over her head like an ax, Felicity rents an apartment in New York yet can somehow afford to fly her friends out to Botswana to celebrate her birthday.

In what world, Alice thinks to herself, is that fair?

Chapter Two

Grace

In the end, it's my flatmate Rosie who acts as the catalyst. Well, Rosie and her boyfriend, Ben. I can't say I like Ben; he's just one of those people that are hard to get on with. It's obvious what he thinks of me—he thinks I'm in the way, that if I would just go ahead and move out, he and Rosie would be able to have this flat all to themselves. But it's my name on the rental agreement, and there's nothing he can do about that. I was living here before Rosie even met him.

They came in late, on Valentine's Day night. I was in my pajamas—if I'm honest, I hadn't changed out of them all day, I didn't see the point. I could tell they were a bit drunk—well, Ben was, Rosie always watches it because of all her gym work—and Ben leaned toward me slightly, a weird smirk on his face. There were lipstick marks on his cheeks and chin, as if they'd been kissing, and for a second, something had hung in the air as I stared at them. Then Rosie started talking.

"We had a lovely meal, didn't we, Ben? Honestly, Grace, it was so delicious. Sexy Fish, the place was called. I bet you'd like it."

I nodded, pushed my glasses up my nose, just for something to do. I felt awkward in my own flat, which in turn made me feel irritated; irrationally so.

"I don't know if you *would* like it there, Grace," Ben said, and he grinned, started laughing a bit at his own joke. He had a sort of choking laugh, staccato and mean.

I felt the muscles in my stomach clench in preparation.

"Come on, Ben, let's go to bed," Rosie said, but she was a bit giggly too. I could tell she was on his side.

I decided to be brave. "Why wouldn't I like it there, Ben?"

More sniggering. He's good-looking, is Ben, there's no two ways about it—attractive in that macho, stereotypical way. The sort of man Felicity would like. Very symmetrical, like her old boyfriend, Nathaniel. But in that moment, he looked ugly. Further proof that appearances can be deceiving.

"Well. Sexy Fish." He gestured at me, his eyes roving over my unwashed, mousy brown hair, my slightly coffee-stained pajamas. My glasses. Everything.

"Doesn't sound like your scene, that's all. *Sexy* Fish."

The humiliation was rising up my cheeks, but with it a sort of anger. Bubbling up, closer to the surface. The skin underneath my arms felt wet, damp with embarrassment and sweat.

"Ben! God, sorry, ignore him, Grace," Rosie said, and she grabbed his arm, started tugging him toward the bedroom. They disappeared into the corridor, out of sight, but I could hear them laughing as they went, Rosie shushing him frantically but not properly. I only caught snatches of Ben's words—*lonely, spinster, weirdo. Leech.*

I sat still in the half-light of the kitchen after they retreated, thinking about my life, how small I had let it become, and how it had to change. I thought about the all-expenses-paid note, how crazy it would be. How much *fun*, too. I thought about the past, about my three best friends—letting myself remember them all, as they really were, not as I wanted them to be. The wild girls. The thought almost makes me laugh—I haven't left the house for almost a fortnight, *wild* is the last word anyone would use to describe me. I imagined us all, together again— what might happen. What might come to light. I thought about who might be there, and what that might mean for me. Would it be worth the risk? I considered it, carefully, the way I would a mathematical equation at work.

Then I reached for my phone, and messaged Hannah.

Yes. I'm going.

As I say, Rosie was the catalyst. And then, there was no going back.

Hannah

So Grace is going on the trip. Hannah's fingers hover over the keyboard. Part of her is desperate to go—let's face it, an all-expenses-paid holiday is pretty amazing—but then the other part of her keeps imagining turning up there, seeing them all, them looking at her post-baby stomach, the huge gray bags underneath her eyes. The woman they used to know was child-free, thin, and in general a lot more fun. Is she afraid of what they'd think of her now? Felicity used to have this way of looking at you, a once-over, her gray eyes sweeping you up and down. Alice and Grace said they never noticed it, but Hannah did. It always felt as though she was assessing you, checking if you were fit for purpose. If you lived up to her standards.

And after that night, it was clear none of them did. Least of all Hannah, but she has only herself to blame for that.

Hannah's indecision is broken by the sound of Max crying. She waits, poised—sometimes his cries snuffle themselves out quickly, but at other times, times like today, they rev up and turn into full-blown wails. Sure enough, it begins, and the sound cuts through her like a knife sliding through fruit, piercing her heart like the stone in the center. It is impossible to ignore. Underneath her T-shirt, Hannah's breasts ache, heavy with milk. As she gets to her feet, she feels tears prick her eyes. It's late now—what has she achieved with the day? Chris brought her home some flowers earlier, red roses for Valentine's Day, but they didn't go out or anything. They didn't have a fancy dinner—not even a sneaky glass of wine. Chris said he was knackered from work, and slumped in front of the TV, like he was fifty, not thirty-three. Hannah put her roses in a vase, pricking her fingers on one of the thorns, a tiny scarlet globule appearing on her skin. She wiped off the smear of blood on one of Max's muslin cloths. It's not as though he'll notice—all he does is vomit on them. Thin, wet white strands that smell of nothing.

"Max, Maxy," she says now, picking her son up, nestling him close against her chest even as the sound of his cries echoes through the flat, buzzing through her skull.

"He all right?" Chris mumbles from the living room, but Hannah can tell from his voice that he's still watching TV—he's got that disengaged, distracted tone that drives her up the wall. She can't afford to be distracted. Max won't let her be.

Her son begins to quieten a bit. She can feel the quick thump of his heart against her chest, and immediately she starts to feel guilty. She shouldn't resent her family. She wanted this so badly, didn't she? Her little family—sometimes she thinks they're all she's got. She supposes in a way, they are.

Hannah used to have more of a life. The four of them: her, Grace, Alice and Felicity, they used to drink and laugh and stay out late into the night, their arms around each other as their high heels clattered on the pavements of West London. They used to wake up together, mouths dry, desperate for bacon sandwiches, and squeeze into one room to look at the photos from the night before, taken on someone's blurry iPhone, or before that, on clunky digital cameras. Hannah used to be able to tell what each of them was thinking just by making eye contact. She doesn't think she has ever felt as close to anybody as she used to be to them, not even Chris. She looks down at her son. Not even Max.

Isn't that kind of bond worth salvaging?

Before she knows what she is doing, Hannah's hand reaches for her phone again. It waits in her palm, patiently. *Make a decision, Hannah. Yes or no.*

OK, she replies to Grace. *I'm in.*

The second she presses send, her son begins to wail, as though he already knows what is going to happen. He knows she is going to leave him.

"I'll come back," Hannah whispers. "I'll always come back to you, Maxy. I promise."

The words echo around the room, bounce back to her like a curse. She doesn't always keep her promises, no matter how hard she tries.

Alice

She wouldn't be able to go, even if she wanted to. Alice can't take time off work—she's not like Grace or Hannah, she doesn't have their freedom. She teaches in a state school in inner Hackney—there aren't exactly supply teachers queueing up to cover her shifts. Most sensible teachers avoid this place like the plague.

When she gets home from school, Tom surprises her by thrusting a bunch of red roses into her face.

"Happy Valentine's Day," he says. "I'm sorry I forgot this morning."

When Alice looks at him, he seems younger somehow, as though she can see the boy he used to be shining through his features. She feels a rush of affection toward him as he leans toward her, kisses her on the lips. He tastes of coffee, but she doesn't mind. He's one of those people who can drink coffee at all hours of the day and still sleep like a log every night—not a privilege Alice has. *Guilty conscience*, she thinks, before pushing the thought away and taking the flowers from him, raising them to her face. They don't really smell of much—they're probably cheap—but she pretends they do because it will please him.

"Thank you," she says, meaning it, and puts the roses in a nice, tall vase retrieved from under the sink, stands them in the middle of the kitchen table.

They have dinner together—nothing fancy, pasta and sauce out of a jar, but Tom's bought a nice bottle of red and Alice drinks two big glasses more quickly than she'd planned. She loves the weight of a wineglass in her hand; it relaxes her, softens her edges, even if the glass is from a pack of six that they'd gotten from Ikea. It's always been Alice's weak spot, wine, *your Achilles heel*, Felicity used to say. She was the first person to give Alice alcohol, actually—smuggled from her parents' drinks cabinet; they sipped it up in her attic. Every week, a little bit more, Felicity's eyes watching her friends carefully to make sure they drank. It became a game—who could handle it, who could drain a glass without vomiting. Felicity's father never stopped them; in fact, Alice can remember him laughing as she stumbled down the stairs, can recall his breath on her face as he leaned in to smell the alcohol. Her own parents would have gone nuts, but Michael never did. It was almost as though he liked seeing Felicity drunk, as though it was one big joke.

Alice can remember the unease in her stomach, the pressure of Felicity's gaze on her as she raised the bottle to her lips, inhaled the sweet, sticky scent of it. Some mornings, she'd black out, be unable to remember the evening in the attic before. Other nights, her memories were fragmented, incomplete, but always, there was the sound of Felicity's laughter, wild and unsettling. But familiar.

"How was school?" Tom asks, and Alice shrugs, tells him about little Sabah in Year Six who never has a proper packed lunch. Alice has started stockpiling bananas to give to her, keeping them in her desk drawer then giving them to the ten-year-old at breaktimes, or first thing in a morning, when the sight of the hunger on her face is more obvious. Tom thinks she should speak to social services.

"It's always such a fine line," Alice says, "and it's not as easy as that. There are rules we have to follow. Procedures. Getting the authorities involved isn't always the right thing to do."

Tom laughs, swallows a mouthful of wine. The corners

of his mouth are stained mauve. There isn't much left in the bottle now.

"You and your rules." He rolls his eyes, and it stings. "D'you know what I like about you, Allie? You're so . . . predictable."

Her cheeks burn. Their little kitchen is hot. The red roses seem to glow a little bit brighter, their thorns sharpening under her gaze. She knows he is saying it deliberately. To hurt her, in that funny, subtle way that he sometimes does. That funny, subtle way that nobody else would even notice and that she tries so hard not to think about. Almost subconsciously, Alice's fingers go to her upper arm and she rubs it, remembering the night that his actions weren't so subtle after all.

"Actually, Tom," she says, making a split-second decision, "I'm going away soon. I'm going on holiday."

He blinks, taken aback. "You, a holiday? But it's not Easter. Not your six-week summer jolly yet, either."

"I'm going to Botswana," she says, relishing the look on his face. He looks absolutely stunned, and it strikes her how long it has been since anything she did surprised him, since she didn't act in exactly the way she is supposed to, exactly the way he wants her to act. Good little Alice. Perfect girlfriend, teacher, homeowner. Living in a flat that she wishes they hadn't bought, with a man who is sometimes, just sometimes, a little bit cruel to her.

He doesn't know about the night she broke the rules.

"You're going to Botswana? When? What for?"

"I told you, a holiday. Next month. Yes, I'm going to Botswana, for a birthday party." Alice rolls the words around her mouth, enjoying the way they feel, little pearls between her lips. Pausing, she watches him, and picks up her wineglass. "I don't think you're invited."

Alice gets up, a few remnants of the pasta congealing stickily on her plate, and leaves the room still clutching her wine, closing the door behind her—not slamming it, she never slams doors, but shutting him out nonetheless. She goes into their bedroom, pulls out her phone and scrolls through to WhatsApp. Alice deleted their old group eventually, the one the four of them used to have, but she still has their numbers so it's easy to create a new one.

Group name: *Felicity's birthday.*

Members: *You, Grace, Hannah, Felicity (NY number).*

You: *Botswana. Party time. Who's in?*

Grace: *I am.*

Hannah: *Yup.*

You: *I've just told Tom, so no backing out now.*

Grace: *Do we think Felicity still uses this same number?*

Hannah: *Well, time difference, remember. She probably hasn't seen the messages yet.*

You: *It's the only number I have for her now.*

Grace is typing . . .

Hannah: *It's odd seeing all your names pop up on my phone. It's been a while.*

You: *I just thought a group would be easier. That's all.*

Grace is typing . . .

Hannah: *Yup. Makes sense. Sorry, gotta go. The baby's crying. But I'm going to book flights soon.*

You: *OK. Me too.*

Grace: *Me three.*

You: *Night, then.*
Hannah is offline.
Grace is offline.
Felicity: *Sorry girls, I've just woken up to all your messages from last night. YES! YES! YES! I'm so glad you guys can come. Don't book flights, it's all on me. Will email you details now. Just get yourselves to the airport on March 27. I'm so excited. We have a lot of catching up to do. It's party time, ladies.* 🍾🖤🍾🍾🍾🍾

Chapter Three

March 27
London

Grace

It's a drizzly March day when I take the tube to Heathrow Airport—the day before the party. Felicity suggested a long weekend, Friday to Monday, so we ought to get back late Monday night and be ready for work on the Tuesday. Her birthday is the Sunday, but she said she wanted us there a few nights before, to make it worth our while. She said she would be heading out there a couple of days earlier, to prepare for the party. I've spent the last three nights scrolling through her social media, searching for clues as to whether she and Nathaniel are still together, but he doesn't feature anywhere. She appears to have started a new account recently; none of her older posts are there at all—the first one is of her in New York, an iced latte held up against a bright blue sky. As if her old life never existed.

Perhaps they have split, then. The thought of seeing him, even on a screen, makes my stomach churn with anxiety, but I try to push down the uncertainty. I scroll back up through her feed, double-checking to make sure he's definitely not there, exhaling when I reach the end. Botswana will be fine; it has to be. I made the decision that I wanted my life back, so this is the price I have to pay. I'm stronger now. I know I am. If he was still a part of her life, there would be evidence online.

It's a long way to come! Felicity texted, *And I so appreciate it!!!* She always was a bit over the top, Felicity—queen of the exclamation mark. Her messages are as though nothing has ever happened, as if no time has gone by. I picture her sitting in New York, deciding to reach out to us—what prompted it? Was it the split with Nathaniel, or did that happen ages ago? I can't let myself hope. Perhaps, I wonder, it's of less relevance to her than it is to us—maybe she barely thinks about us, added us to the invitation list as an afterthought. Let bygones be bygones, and all that. It's the sort of thing she might do, I suppose.

The three of us—Hannah, Alice, and I—have arranged to meet at the airport; time was when we'd all travel there together, but nobody suggested that and I'm happy going on my own. This way, we're all on an equal footing. I spend longer than usual on my appearance—straightening my hair, which I haven't done for ages, putting on eyeliner, which I have always been categorically terrible at. Someone once told me it makes me look like a pigeon, and I think they were probably right. I've been so used to hiding myself away, deliberately not attracting anyone's attention, that daubing on lipstick and blusher feels completely unnatural now, but I force myself to do it anyway. This is all about moving forward, after all.

I burn my hand on the hair straighteners; my fingers are shaking.

I pack strategically—Felicity always looks amazing, and surely two years in New York can only have strengthened the range of her wardrobe. I wince, imagining all her other friends—sophisticated, rake-thin Americans sipping champagne and eating nothing. I feel so out of my depth already. The temperature is over ninety-five degrees out in Botswana this weekend, Felicity sent us a screenshot, and the thought of exposing my body to everyone makes me feel slightly sick. Oh God, will it be a pool party? I shove a wraparound into my case, reassure myself that nobody can stop me wearing that if I want to. I don't want anyone looking at my body. Not anymore.

Since we all agreed to go, Felicity has kept up a constant stream of information to us, and for just these few weeks, it's almost felt as though I have friends again. I become accustomed to my phone pinging at all times of the day and night, as gradually, the coldness between us begins to thaw, at least via WhatsApp. None of us has actually spoken on the phone, and I'm certainly not brave enough to be the first person to do so. Felicity emails us all details of our flight: the 10:30 a.m. from Heathrow to Botswana on Friday, March 27, and she's told us a car will pick us up from the airport.

My stomach fizzes with excitement at the thought of it all—the humidity, the heat, a chance to escape London. And, of course, the chance to see the girls.

In the end, I have to sit on my suitcase to force it closed because I've packed so much stuff; insecurity packing. I bring a swimming costume, just in case, a one-piece, and Rosie lends me a couple of long dresses, which she says will keep the mosquitoes off my legs. I think she's a bit jealous that I'm going; she keeps looking at me strangely, out of the corner of her eye. As though perhaps she is seeing me properly for the very first time. It gives me a splash of confidence. At last I am doing something, getting out of my rut—because I can admit it now, I have been in a rut. And I don't want to be in it anymore.

The tube rattles through West London; I count the stops on the Piccadilly line with my eyes, rubbing at the shiny red weal on my hand from the straighteners. It's been a little while since I've even got the tube, and only now do I realize how very small I've let my world become. Everywhere feels so busy, so colorful, so loud.

My carriage starts off packed but thins out as we leave the center of the city, so that by the time we reach Acton there is only me and a family sitting across from me. There are two teenage boys, both on their phones, a harangued-looking father holding two large rucksacks, and a woman with what looks like a two-year-old on her lap, its eyes plump with tears. None of them catches my eye, and for a moment I feel as though I really might be invisible, and the thought of it fills me with a desperate kind of panic that I have to breathe through. I picture myself growing older in the Peckham flat, Rosie moving out to be with awful Ben, and the windows getting dirtier and dirtier until nobody can see inside and I cannot see out. It would be all too easy to let what happened set the tone for the rest of my life, but by doing this, by going to Botswana and facing them all, I am conquering my fears.

My therapist would be proud.

Just as suddenly as the dark thoughts arrive, we rattle around a corner and the sunshine comes out through the clouds, filtering through the dirty windows of the tube, illuminating the dust motes floating above the faded blue seats. My phone pings as it regains signal, and I see that Felicity has sent a series of picture messages to our WhatsApp group.

I actually gasp as the first of them loads—it's a photo of a safari lodge, set against a brilliant blue sky, surrounded by gum trees and luscious green grasses. The second picture shows a great wide plain, and in the foreground is a baby elephant, beautiful and strangely endearing, her gray head bowed to the ground, leathery trunk searching for sustenance. The third photo, by contrast, is of Felicity's hand, her long, glossy pink shellacked nails wrapped around a tall glass of champagne. She looks like she's in a hammock; I can see the ropes of it in the background, and the yellow and red stripes underneath her tanned knees.

Can't wait to see you all! her message says. *Safe flight!!!*

I picture Alice wincing at the overuse of exclamation marks, it jarring with her teacher's mindset. Hannah replies straight-away.

That looks amazing, Flick!

I'm surprised to see her using the old nickname, Flick—despite the growing warmth of our messages over the last few weeks, this is the first time anyone has used it. For some reason, it feels like a turning point, and for a few seconds I allow myself to hope. I hope that this trip makes everything go back to normal. I hope it brings us back together. I hope it gives me back my friends. I hope it allows us all to forget why we've been apart.

Most of all, I hope it gives each of us what we deserve.

The family sharing my carriage gets out at Heathrow too, all of us blinking into the light and looking around for the exit. It's been so long since I got on a flight—in fact, I think the last time was at university, the skiing trip to France that I couldn't really afford but didn't want to miss out on. I follow the signs to the terminal, and the crowd becomes busier; I scan the faces, looking for Alice or Hannah, wanting to see them but at the same time feeling the anxious butterflies in my stomach fluttering madly. At a sign for the toilets, I duck in and reapply my makeup, my fingers shaking slightly. It's just adrenaline, I tell myself, the adrenaline of being somewhere new, out of the flat, out of the usual routine of my boring, boring life. It's a good thing. It proves I'm alive. That I'm not broken after all.

I smear foundation over my cheeks even though I already have lots on, and dab lip balm on before washing my hands with the weird, slimy, colorless soap they tend to have in airports. I stare at my reflection in the mirror, trying to see myself through their eyes. My light brown hair that hangs to my shoulders, my muddy brown eyes, small upturned nose, and slightly thin-lipped mouth. There are lines on my forehead that weren't there before. What will they think of me now? It's been two years, almost to the day, since I saw them. We will all look a little bit older, a little bit more tired. Apart from Felicity, of course. Judging by the photos, Felicity will look better than ever.

"Excuse me, can I get past?" There's a dark-haired woman trying to move behind me and I start, realize I've been standing there dumbly, staring at myself in a daze. She looks at me, impatient almond eyes waiting for me to respond.

"Sorry," I mumble, and there's nothing for it now, no more time to procrastinate. I leave the toilets—"How was your ex-perience?" asks an automated voice, and I mindlessly press the happy face. May as well start as I mean to go on.

My phone beeps as I reenter the terminal. It's Hannah: *Come*

to the champagne bar in Terminal 5. Have checked in already.
Will get you a drink. Alice here too.

So they're together already. Insecurity creeps up my stomach—
did they travel here together, after all? What are they talking
about? Are they discussing me? I had imagined us all meeting
at the exact same time, on an even footing; I hadn't pictured
the two of them cozying up in a champagne bar without me,
my having to play catch-up. The last one to join the party. The
tagalong, again. A memory flashes back to me, of hot tears
running down my face, the sound of their laughter in a cold,
smoky courtyard, filtering through a small toilet window as
I crouch breathless on the floor. I push it away: now is not the
time to go down that road. Not when we've come so far.

I give myself a little shake, tell myself I'm being ridiculous,
grab my case and hurry toward the security gates. I've got the
electronic boarding pass that Felicity sent through on my phone
and the queue isn't too bad—it is a random Friday in March,
after all. I take off my boots and coat and walk through the
body-scanner. When the machine beeps and a security guard
steps forward to pat me down, I realize it is the first time I've
been touched in over a week. The thought shames me; I think of
Ben and Rosie, laughing at me, my perceived lack of sexuality.

"Are you carrying any metal, any dangerous items?" the
guard says, and I shake my head, impatient. I want to catch
up with the other two. I don't want them talking without me,
catching up, sharing secrets over a glass of airport champagne.
Not when I'm not there to join in.

Or to defend myself.

"Clear," the woman says, and I step forward, relieved, collect
my bag and head through the gates. The smell of duty-free hits

me; expensive perfumes, the sticky fizz of sweets, a whiff of alcohol as I pass a whiskey-tasting pop-up. There is too much choice, too many colors—prices leap out at me, overwhelming in their number. I hurry through, resisting the urge to down one of the dark, potent shots of whiskey, my shabby little case catching slightly on the trail of a stranger's scarf, and then I see it: a round champagne bar, brightly lit, surrounded by high, faux-leather stools.

And there they are: my oldest friends. Alice and Hannah, bags by their sides, heads together as though they are conspirators. Exactly as I remember them. Thick as thieves.

Chapter Four

March 27
London

Hannah

It's really difficult holding her stomach in while sitting on these stupid high stools. Hannah had arrived at the airport first, and thought this might be a good way to break the ice; it seemed like a better alternative than sitting having a smoothie in Pret for two hours. She hasn't told the others, but she had a glass of champagne before either of them even arrived—she knows it's early, but surely holiday rules apply, and to be honest she had needed something to settle the nerves. Hannah hasn't drunk any booze for months and months, firstly because of what happened—the thought of alcohol made her guilt even worse—and then because of the baby, so the bubbles have immediately gone to her head. Her boobs are still sore because she'd used the breast pump so much earlier, but at least the fridge is full of milk for Max, and once that runs out Chris will have to fend for himself and go to the pharmacy.

It'll be good for him, Hannah thinks. A chance for him to see what her life is actually like, tending to the baby 24/7. When she comes back, he might start helping out with Maxy more.

Ha! Perhaps it's the champagne talking now. *Don't get ahead of yourself, Hannah.*

"Are you going somewhere nice?" the bartender asked her earlier when she'd arrived on her own.

"Botswana. A safari lodge," she'd told him, and he'd whistled, nodded.

"Very nice. Gonna be hot out there, even this time of year. Hope you've had your jabs. You'll have to keep your wits about you, you look like the type who might burn. A proper English rose."

Hannah had found herself blushing, even though he might not have meant it as a compliment. It has been so long since she has sat in a bar, even a fake, stand-alone one in the middle of a noisy, busy airport, and so long since she's had a conversation with a man who isn't Chris. She touches her arm, the small indent in the skin a reminder of the vaccinations they all had before coming. Even going to the clinic felt exciting, a promise of adventure to come. The nurse had handed her a clutch of brochures, warned her of typhoid, cholera, hepatitis A. Hannah had nodded and smiled. It would have sounded strange to say that even the mentions of disease excited her—the words sounded exotic, otherworldly. For months she had thought only of mastitis, colic, postnatal complications. Of motherhood, in all its guises.

Felicity's photos look amazing. Hannah sips her drink, wondering who else will be there. She doesn't know for sure, but suspects that Felicity and Nathaniel, her old boyfriend, may have split—she hasn't mentioned him, and there is nothing on her social media that indicates their relationship anymore. Perhaps that is a good thing. Shame burns in Hannah's stomach at the thought of seeing him, given what a state she'd been in last time. Remembering his kindness, the follow-up calls, she feels guilty all over again.

Who else, who else? Presumably, friends she has made in New York—Hannah shudders at the thought of them seeing her in her bikini. None of them kept in touch with anyone else from school, so she'd be surprised if anyone like that turned up—it was always just the four of them. Felicity's college friends—Deb and Andrew maybe? Her family? Hannah feels a shiver of unease at the thought of seeing her father. She doesn't know how any of them would be able to look him in the eye. He'd always creeped Hannah out, since they were kids, long before he did what he did to Felicity. She doesn't relish the thought of spending an evening in his company. Felicity's mother passed away when they were younger, but clearly, she's going big with this birthday so perhaps she has invited extended relatives to come along. Hannah feels a pang when she thinks about Felicity's mother, Diane—turning thirty without her must be painful. Perhaps that's why Felicity has decided to make the most of it, surround herself with other people to make up for the one person she is lacking.

"Another?" The waiter is in front of her again, smiling, and Hannah is surprised to see that she's finished her glass already. She wonders briefly if he's used to this—the great British public downing booze before lunchtime, propping up the bar at all hours of the day.

"I'm meeting some friends, so I'll wait," she says, reluctantly, and as she says the words she realizes how long it's been since she really felt they were true. Since Max was born, the only people Hannah sees or speaks to are colleagues of Chris's that he insists on inviting around, or her parents, or acquaintances from her work who text every now and again about nothing. None of them are her *friends*. None of them are the women who have known her since she was five years old, who have cried with her and held back her hair and slept in her bed with their arms around her waist.

Her real friends have always been the girls. And despite everything that happened, despite Felicity leaving, she wants them back. She wants that feeling of *us* back. The question is, do they feel the same?

"Hannah!"

At the sound of her name, Hannah spins around on her stool, almost toppling off it in the process, and suddenly, there she is. Alice—her long dark hair swept up in a ponytail, her eyes bright and sparkling, a bright purple suitcase by her side.

For a second, they stare at each other, watched by the barman, and then Alice steps forward and wordlessly embraces Hannah, enveloping her in the piquant scent of her perfume and an overwhelming sense of familiarity.

"It's so good to see you," she says, and her voice sounds sincere, genuine. A lump rises in Hannah's throat, and quickly she swallows it down, annoyed with herself and with the champagne. Alcohol makes her needlessly emotional, it always has, sometimes with catastrophic consequences. Chris always used to say he thought it was sweet, but she's not sure now that he was telling the truth.

"It's good to see you too," Hannah says, sounding even to her own ears a little wooden, but Alice being Alice doesn't seem to notice, she simply sits down on the stool next to her and orders two more glasses of champagne, pink this time.

Hannah watches her as she moves, adjusting herself on the

stool, tightening her ponytail, fiddling with her bag as she hooks it underneath the bar. Alice—*her* Alice. Out of everyone, the pair of them were perhaps the closest—she'd be the one Hannah would text first, the one she'd call if she was sad, the one she'd rely on the most. Sometimes, Hannah thinks about what might've happened if she *had* told her the truth two years ago, instead of keeping it to herself—how the events of that evening might have played out differently. But it's pointless to speculate; what's done is done.

Alice has always been pretty, but somehow she looks even more so than Hannah remembers; there are no bags under her eyes and she looks healthy, fit, almost muscular. She doesn't have children—at least, she didn't two years ago, and when Hannah glances down at her finger she can't see a ring so she and Tom obviously haven't got married—if they're still together, that is. It strikes her how little she knows about Alice's life now, when once they knew every detail of each other's days, lived in each other's pockets.

How times change.

"Funny how things change," Alice says, as though she has been reading Hannah's mind, and Hannah sees that she is gesturing to the champagne glasses. "Time was these would've been shots, but there's no way I could handle that now. *And* I've stopped smoking!" She laughs. "I'm a changed woman, Hannah. I'm surprised you recognized me."

"God, shots—the thought makes my stomach heave." Hannah shudders, remembering their sixth-form days. Alice was always the biggest drinker; she'd drink the rest of them under the table, then bounce back the morning after, raring to go again. Her hangovers never seemed as bad as Hannah's—she must have developed a tolerance for it. Hannah hasn't had a shot since that night—even now, the thought of tequila makes her feel physically sick, conjures up images of her bare feet on tarmac, her head on Nate's chest—and later vomit, acidic in her throat, splattering the bathroom floor back at home.

Their drinks arrive and Alice raises hers aloft.

"To Felicity," she says, and the toast takes Hannah by surprise. "For bringing us back together. At last."

Hannah nods and echoes Alice because she doesn't really know what else to do, and Alice takes a long sip, setting the glass back down on the bar top and smiling. Her face, when Hannah looks closely, seems almost triumphant.

"So," she says, "you had a baby!"

Hannah thinks of the day in the hospital bed, Chris white-faced by her side, her grunting and groaning and pushing and that weird moment when she had looked around the room, past the doctor and the midwife, and thought of Alice. Her closest friend—not there at the birth of her child. Hannah didn't text to tell her—Alice didn't call to ask. Hannah had buried the sadness with an Instagram account and a Mommy and Me group and her husband, but it was still there. Hidden, but there. Like a shameful little secret: *I miss you.*

Alice is staring at her expectantly. It's the first thing anyone will ever think about Hannah now. It is her status: mother. Wife.

But it's easy, familiar territory, at least, and so she pulls out her phone, starts showing Alice photos of baby Max—of her and Chris leaving the hospital with him, her own expression pale and shell-shocked, of Max swaddled up in his cot, wearing a cute little duck's outfit that Chris's mother bought him even though Hannah had clearly said that she hated the kind of parents who dress their children up as animals. He stares back at her: her baby boy, and for a few seconds Hannah's heart seems to contract.

Alice coos and ahhs and makes all the right noises, but Hannah can hear her own voice bouncing back at her and she knows she must sound boring. She wonders whether Alice wants children now—she didn't use to, when they were younger, but things change. Hannah wonders whether she and Tom have talked about it, but she doesn't feel as though now is the right moment to ask. Maybe later, once they've spent a bit more time together, gotten used to being around one another again. The barman has his back to them now; her talk of babies must bore him.

But gradually, as they drink their champagne and watch the flight time grow closer and closer, Hannah starts to feel her body relax. This is Alice, after all—Alice whose house she used to go to for fish and chips on a Friday night when they were still in school uniform, Alice who sat next to her in math and helped her write notes to the boy she fancied, Alice who held her hand and listened to her cry when the first time she and Chris tried to get pregnant didn't work out, before Hannah closed herself off and things got too painful and intense to share. There is nothing to be afraid of.

Is there?

It's a while before they think to message Grace. It's Alice who does—Hannah has gotten a bit swept up in the moment, reminiscing about the past, but Alice whips out her phone and squeals at the time.

"Grace is cutting it a bit fine, isn't she? Do you think she's still coming?"

Hannah feels her heart give a little lurch. This holiday only works if the four of them are together, like pieces in a game. The players can't be imbalanced.

"I'll text her," she says quickly, and taps out a message, orders an extra drink so that it's ready and waiting for when Grace arrives. Best to start things off on the right foot. If she's anything like Hannah, she'll be feeling a bit on edge—and Grace has always been a bit of a panicker. She's the one Hannah worries about the most—well, used to worry about anyway. Lately, she hasn't felt as though she has the right. Or, to be totally frank, the inclination. It's hard to open up to people who won't open up to you.

"God, the photos Felicity sent through looked amazing, didn't they?" Alice says dreamily, and Hannah nods, feels a shiver of excitement run up her spine as she thinks about the place they're going to—the heat, the wide African plains, the beautiful skies.

"I can't wait for some sun," she tells Alice. "A proper break from it all."

"It's so nice to see you, Han," Alice says suddenly, and she reaches out and grasps Hannah's hand, holds it for a second in hers. Her palm is dry and warm, and the whorls of her skin feel familiar. Memories of the four of them in the attic at Felicity's surface—they used to sit in a circle, holding hands, a stolen bottle of wine in the middle of their ring. Sometimes Felicity would light a candle, and in her mind's eye Hannah can see the flicker of her gaze on them all, daring them on, controlling the game. If Hannah ever felt nervous, Alice would squeeze her hand.

Now, the tips of Alice's nails graze against her wedding ring and she taps it, lightly, as though reminding Hannah that it's there. Hannah and Chris had gotten married just before Max was born, in a small, private ceremony. The truth was, Hannah hadn't been able to bear the thought of a big party without the girls there. So they invited hardly anyone, pretended it was what they wanted. But now, all this time later, Alice's hand is tight on hers.

That's how Grace finds them: locked together, holding hands, best friends all over again. For now, at least.

Alice

Alice doesn't know what it is that makes her reach for Hannah's hand, and after she has done so she feels embarrassed. But it's nice, somehow, and when Grace appears Alice is disappointed to let go. Now that she is actually here, now that they've committed to this trip, Alice just wants to feel close to Hannah again, to all of them. When they were kids, they'd weave themselves brightly colored friendship bracelets, lock their pinkie fingers together, and swear to be best friends forever. If only it were that easy now.

Grace looks a bit tired, if Alice is being completely honest. She's got lots of makeup on, a bit too much, and her smile looks strained. She's wearing a long, knitted dress and little black heeled boots, which isn't what Alice would really call traveling gear but each to their own.

Alice can tell that Grace feels odd being the last one to join the group, but she quickly pushes the worried expression off her face and Alice stands up to hug her, wrapping her arms tightly around her in the way she did with Hannah. Grace feels thin, a little bit too thin, and Alice can almost feel the nerves radiating through her body.

"Grace," she says, "we were worried you weren't coming."

Hannah smiles at her; Alice can tell the champers has already gone to her head a little. She always was a bit of a lightweight and Alice is guessing she hasn't had a drink for a while if the baby's still only small. What was its name? Miles? She must remember by the time they get on the plane, especially if they're sitting together.

That's a thought.

"What seats are you both in?" Alice asks them, and Grace checks her phone.

"26C. You?"

It turns out that Hannah and Alice are sitting together, 19B and 19C, and Grace is farther back on her own.

"Ugh, that's a pain," Alice says, "maybe we could ask someone to swap?"—but Grace shakes her head and says it doesn't matter. By the expression on her face though, it looks like it does.

The three of them sit in a row around the curved bar, and Alice can tell Grace is anxious. She feels bad for her, she's always been such a nervy person, and so when neither of them are looking she reaches into her handbag, her fingers finding the familiar silver foil packet, and slips a tablet into the remains of Grace's drink. Nothing bad, of course—only a little something to help her chill out a bit. Alice takes one every time she flies, just to relax herself, and it looks like Grace could use the same. Not that she or Tom have flown for ages—they can't afford it anymore. Speaking of, the champagne bill probably isn't going to be cheap.

"I'll get these, shall I?" Alice says, but on cue, Hannah shakes her head, pulls out her credit card like Alice knew she would if she offered first.

"No, no, this was my idea, I got here first. I'll get them."

"Are you sure?" Alice says, relieved, and Grace looks embarrassed, but Hannah nods and smiles at the barman as he brings over the card machine.

Some people never change, after all. Alice thinks of Tom, their Valentine's dinner, and feels her stomach curl. Now who's predictable?

In the end, they are the last ones to join the queue for their flight. Hannah and Grace have become a bit giggly, and Alice almost wishes she was the one with a seat to herself on the plane. She texts Tom, sending him a photo of the plane on the runway, stark against the gray English sky, and it's a few minutes before he replies. She fiddles with her phone, pretending to herself that she doesn't care, but when his reply does ping through, she feels a whoosh of relief.

Have a safe flight, he says, *and come back soon. Xx*

Just enough, Alice thinks, just enough to show her that he does still care. That's how they always play it, she and Tom—there's always just enough to keep her holding on, to keep her coming back for more. Sometimes, Alice wonders how things would be now if she'd left Tom that night two years ago, or if he hadn't come to join them at all. She wonders what might have happened if they hadn't all stopped seeing each other, if she'd told the girls the truth about their relationship and let their little support network curl around her, protecting her. Alice pushes the thought from her head, reapplies her lip balm. There's no point thinking like that—what's done is done.

They've bought the flat—they're in it for the long haul, now. She fights how claustrophobic that sentence makes her feel and focuses on the present, on the line of people in front of them, all of them double-checking their passports and fiddling with their phones, heads down and robotic.

Alice thinks about work as they board the flight, of what she'd be doing now if she wasn't here. The school wasn't particularly happy when she announced that she needed the time off, but Alice had pretended her father was ill, said she was heading home to Cornwall to make sure he was all right. Nobody could really argue with that. Besides, she thinks to herself as they shuffle through the narrow aisle of the airplane, doesn't she deserve a few days off? She works hard at her job; she's good at it. St Hilda's isn't an easy school; they don't have a great reputation. They need people like Alice to show up and do the work—and most of the time, she does. But everyone needs to relax every now and then, and without Felicity's generosity, there's no way she'd ever be able to go on a holiday like this. The trip of a lifetime. She's going to make sure of it.

No matter what.

Hannah and Alice tell Grace they'll see her on the other side and make their way to row 19. They are next to a man on his own—he's quite good-looking actually, and Alice nudges Hannah and pulls a silly face, like she would if they were twenty-five again. Hannah snorts with laughter, and Alice notices her licking her lips a bit, combing a hand through the ends of her hair. She needs a trim; too many split ends. Some highlights wouldn't go amiss either.

Alice wonders what Chris is like now. She never used to get much out of him—always thought he was so corporate. A bit boring, if she is really honest. But still, Hannah seems happy. Relatively so, anyway. Certainly happier than the last time Alice saw her, but after all, that's not saying much.

Hannah was in a terrible mood that night.

They order gin and tonics as the plane takes off, and Alice pops a tablet on the edge of her tongue to try to drown out the whirr of the plane. She wants to be able to get some sleep—wake up feeling refreshed and ready to see Felicity and whoever else is there. Hannah pulls a guidebook out of her bag and Alice has to stop herself from rolling her eyes.

"Do you think we're going to get much time for sightseeing?" she asks her, and Hannah shrugs, not picking up on Alice's sarcastic tone.

"Well, wouldn't you like to, a bit? Do you not think Felicity will let us?"

Alice laughs. "She's not a jailer. I just think the party will be the focus, you know. And we're not here for that long—only a long weekend. Four days."

"I'd like to see the animals, though. Wouldn't you? I've always wanted to go on safari. It's exciting."

"Well, we're not actually going on safari, are we? We're just staying in the lodge. Which looks phenomenal, don't you think? How can she afford it all? God, I'm so jealous."

The words are out before Alice can stop them, the gin loosening her tongue. She didn't mean to admit that.

"Nathaniel used to make a lot, too," Hannah replies, not seeming to notice. "Remember, his hospital used to pay for his apartment, in London? He was in the private sector. She probably got used to a certain kind of lifestyle, even afterward. I doubt she's dealing with the kind of mortgages we have."

At the word, Alice feels the gin swirl in her stomach. She doesn't want to think about their mortgage right now. She doesn't want to think about how really, she shouldn't even be ordering a £6 gin and tonic when there is so much money going out of her account and so little coming in. She wonders how much Hannah earns these days. She must be on statutory pay if she's on maternity leave, surely, but as a lawyer Chris probably earns a packet. Being corporate and boring does have its upsides.

"Have you bought Flick a present?" Alice says, and Hannah nods.

"I was early to the airport so I got her a little something. Just earrings—nothing huge. And a card. It is her birthday, after all."

"Of course," Alice says, her mind whirring. Maybe she could get her something from the plane? One of those duty-free things. Perfume. That would look a bit shit to Hannah and Grace, though. More proof that she's a bad friend.

Not that the evidence isn't already out there, just waiting to be found. But Alice doesn't want to think about that. There is no point in torturing herself.

She can feel herself getting a bit sleepy, so she yawns and tells Hannah that she might close her eyes. Hannah seems happy with this—a chance for her to get back to the guidebook—so Alice leans back in her seat and lets the tablet work its magic. She'll think about the lack of a present later. For now, she just wants to relax.

Chapter Five

In transit: London to Botswana

Grace

I know I shouldn't care that they're sitting together but I do. I know it can't be intentional, that Felicity just booked all our flights at once and that they'll have been randomly assigned, but somehow this isn't the way I wanted this trip to start. I've already been last to the airport, now I'm separated from them again on the plane. It feels as though a barrier has come up, as if events are conspiring to keep me apart from the others. It's typical, really; I've spent so long keeping myself apart from the world, and now that I want in, I'm being shut out.

It's not a big deal, I tell myself, the main thing is that we're all here, we're together, and so far everything has been fine. It was a tiny bit awkward when I first saw them—it almost looked like they were holding hands at the champagne bar, but I think I must have imagined it—and by the time we boarded the plane it almost felt like we were back to our old selves. I'm not naive enough to think that everything will have been forgotten, but as always, Felicity's positivity and her enthusiasm—her photos, the messages, everything—have ignited something within the rest of us, a friendship that has been lying dormant for the last two years.

Sometimes I wish I was the kind of person who had the ability to do that for others—make them feel wanted, special. I don't think I inspire that in anybody.

As the plane ascends through the clouds, though, I start to think properly. Light filters through the window, yellow tinged with pink, falling on the little tray in front of me, a gentle kind of magic. I need to make plans. I need to use this trip as a chance to change direction, to alter the way my life is turning out. I'm only thirty, after all; there's still time. I could move house when we get back, see about finding some new flatmates. Stop enduring Rosie and Ben's excruciating mockery of me. Go back on the dating apps, even—try to meet someone new and forget about the past. *What would Felicity do?* I think to myself, but it's hard to conjure up the image of her now, and my mind feels as though the edges are becoming a bit blurry. It must be the champagne, although I didn't actually have that much—not as much as Hannah and Alice. There's a couple next to me, probably in about their forties, and they smile sympathetically when I inadvertently let out a huge yawn.

Embarrassed, I stifle it with my hand, but the man grins at me.

"Try and catch some sleep now if I were you," he says, with a warm accent. "I'm jealous—I can never sleep while I'm traveling."

"Neither can I, usually," I say, which is true, but gosh, I do feel weirdly tired now. Exhaustion threatens to overwhelm me, and I smile at the couple and let myself sink back in the seat. It's not very comfortable, but I can't seem to care—I feel as though I'm floating upward, as the lights on the plane flicker on and off, and the low hum of the couple's chatter fades into nothingness. Then, everything goes black.

Hannah

Alice is asleep, and when Hannah gets up to go to the bathroom she notices that seven rows behind them, Grace is too. She looks much younger in her sleep, innocent somehow, and Hannah has a sudden urge to get her a blanket, wrap it around her and make sure she's comfortable, like she used to do if Grace was hungover when they were teenagers. Hannah used to like taking care of people, making herself feel useful, but now that that's her sole purpose in life with Max she resents it a lot more than she did before. Why is that? What's wrong with her? When she had first started going to NCT classes, some of the other women said they were worried about being mums—but now that they all are, they universally appear to be loving it, according to the endless Instagram pictures and gloating Facebook updates. How can Hannah admit to them that sometimes she has her doubts? The simple answer is that she can't. Not after everything she went through—she has to be grateful for Max. To not be would be shameful, a disgrace. She knows that.

But maybe she could talk to the girls, to Alice and Grace at least—maybe they are the ones who might understand. Hannah feels a flicker of hope in her chest at the thought of unburdening herself, of being honest for once. The four of them always used to understand everything about each other—until they didn't anymore. The last time Hannah told anyone how she felt, it didn't end well. Does she really want to run that risk again?

When she gets back to her seat, she feels guilty for having these kinds of thoughts about motherhood and so she pulls out her phone, flicks through the photos of Max. Hannah took a selfie of them together the other day, pushing her face up close next to his, breathing in his baby smell as she smiled and pressed the button to capture the image. She even thought about posting it to Instagram, but then she looked at it properly and the idea of strangers on the internet seeing it made her want to gouge her eyes out. She looked dreadful—there was no way anyone could see it. She looked nothing like the insta-mums that clog up her feed—they may as well have been a completely different species. Hannah ended up deleting that photo altogether—Chris always says she shouldn't keep things that make her feel bad about herself. He used to say that about the girls, actually, especially in the weeks and months after Felicity left, when Hannah kept trying to get in touch—that if they were no longer making her feel good, she ought to cut the friendships off. In the end, that is what happened, but it wasn't really her choice.

Hannah steals a glance at Alice as she sleeps. Her long dark hair has slipped out of her ponytail and is falling down her shoulder, almost brushing Hannah's arm. She thinks about reaching out and touching it, but she doesn't want to wake her. Hannah closes her own eyes, hoping to get some sleep herself—there are still hours of the flight left to go. It's ironic, really—she spends the majority of her life longing for a bit of time to herself, desperate for an unbroken night's sleep, one in which Max doesn't wake her up crying, but now that she is thousands of miles away from her baby she finds she cannot sleep at all. Her mouth feels stale, and her legs ache from being sedentary for so long.

Instead, Hannah thinks about Felicity. She imagines her preparing for the birthday party. If Hannah knows Flick, it'll be a fairly lavish affair. She has brought a selection of dresses—black if it's really formal, a bold printed maxi-dress if they're all going colorful, and a jumpsuit, which she already knows she won't have the courage to wear. Oh, and she has also brought her Spanx, because she can almost guarantee that none of Felicity's other friends will have had children, and even if they have, they'll be the glossy insta-mum type that they've already established Hannah has no hope of ever being. If Felicity is single again, she'll be going all out with her appearance, too. Or perhaps she'll have a surprise for them, some new American beau. Hannah smiles to herself at the thought. That would be typical Felicity.

She is about to start having a look through the in-flight entertainment to see if there's anything she can relax with that isn't Peppa Pig for a change when the seat belt lights come on and the flight attendant's voice comes over the speaker.

"Ladies and gentlemen, we may experience a little bit of turbulence over the next twenty minutes or so, and the pilot has advised that you fasten your seat belts and do not get up from your seats until the seat belt lights go off. Thank you for your cooperation."

No sooner has she finished speaking than the plane gives a big jolt and Hannah is swung sideways, hard into Alice's shoulder.

"Sorry," she says, but to Hannah's surprise Alice doesn't stir. Hannah notices the man next to them looking at her, too, and he catches her eye and smiles.

"Your friend's a good sleeper, eh?"

"So it seems," Hannah says, feeling oddly put out that Alice can sleep peacefully through this turbulence while she has to endure it. She glances at her watch—thinking about the time in the UK: Max will be wanting a feed and beginning to grizzle. She wonders what he and Chris are doing, and how many times Chris has phoned his mother. Hannah knows Jean thinks she is the devil incarnate for going on holiday—her most recent card implied as much. The inside was quite a contrast to the flowers on the front.

The plane bumps again and Hannah's stomach clenches—she has never liked turbulence, although she knows it's harmless, she's read all the articles. From what she can remember, Grace hates it—though they've actually never been on a plane together before, but she told Hannah about the university ski trip where she vomited in a paper bag. Hannah hopes Grace is all right. She twists her neck, trying to crane her head backward to see whether she's still asleep too—she can't imagine she is—but the plane gives another shudder and she is forced to turn back around.

"What brings you to Africa?" the guy next to Hannah says, perhaps noticing her anxiety and trying to distract her, and she tells him the truth: a birthday party.

The words sound a bit childish when she says them like that, but he chuckles. He has got a nice face, actually, Alice was right—his eyes crinkle at the sides when he laughs, and he's got the kind of sandy-colored hair that makes you think of beaches and surfing and warm fish and chips.

"You?" Hannah asks him, and he tells her a mate of his has started a company there and is trying to persuade him to invest.

"It's a beautiful country," he says, and his voice softens when he speaks about it, as though he's remembering a person, not a place. "Challenging, though. It has its drawbacks. Very different to the UK."

"Of course," Hannah says, but she feels a flicker of unease in her stomach, picturing poverty, wilderness, the unknown. Something about the way he describes it makes her feel uncomfortable, as though she is part of the problem.

They chat for a little while—he asks what she does, and Hannah tells him she's in human resources, keeping it very top-line for now. It's on the tip of her tongue when he tells her that she's lucky to get time off to say that actually, she is on maternity leave, but somehow the words just don't come. Hannah finds herself enjoying it—pretending just a bit, to be someone she is not, and once she's told one lie (well, a lie of omission really) it becomes easy to tell another. She plays a little game with herself in her head, begins egging herself on.

When he asks if she is married, she tells him she's recently separated, has yet to take her ring off. When he asks about her friends, Hannah says that they all live down the road from one another, that they see each other all the time. When he inquires about children, she looks the other way, laughs, and tells him not yet. A flight attendant stands up at the front of the plane, catches Hannah's eye, and for a strange moment she feels sure the woman can tell that she is lying, even though she is meters away, her focus on the turbulence. On cue, the plane gives another jolt, and Hannah's stomach roils.

"I've still got a lot of the world to see first," she says, gesturing at the little electronic map of the plane, which is replicated on both their screens, tracking their progress as they move across the globe, closer and closer to Botswana and to Felicity.

He smiles at that, and when the seat belt sign flicks off and the flight attendant comes back over toward them, he orders two gin and tonics, "and make them doubles."

The turbulence is calming down, now—Alice still hasn't woken up, and the stranger and Hannah both put down their trays and balance the drinks on them, he downing his fairly rapidly while she sips away at hers, the ice clinking against her teeth. She doesn't know what's come over her, telling all those lies, and finds herself hoping against hope that Alice doesn't wake up, because what if she mentions Max or Chris in front of this man? He will think Hannah is totally insane. Perhaps, she thinks as she stares past him out of the small rounded window into the blackness, perhaps she is.

The plane is in darkness now, and there are only two hours to go. The stranger tells Hannah his name is Adam, and when they begin their descent into Botswana, he hands her a thick paper card with his name on.

Adam Draper, Hannah reads, of Draper and Sons. A law firm. She almost wants to laugh. Here she is, miles from home, pretending to be someone else, another version of herself, and she ends up chatting up a lawyer. She's already got a lawyer at home.

Alice wakes with a start as soon as the plane touches down. Hannah starts talking immediately, still anxious to ward off any comments that Adam might pick up on, but now that they're here she is starting to realize that it doesn't matter. It's not as if she is ever going to see him again, is it? So what if he knows she's a liar—Alice doesn't, that's the main thing, and besides, it was only a bit of fun. A way to pass the time during a turbulent patch on a long-haul flight. Plenty of women would have done exactly the same. In fact, it's exactly the sort of thing that Felicity would do. She might even find it funny—maybe Hannah will tell her about it when they arrive. Use it to break the ice.

Chapter Six

Botswana

Grace

The heat hits me as soon as I step off the plane. It feels thick, like a heavy blanket, and utterly all-encompassing, filling my mouth and drying my eyes so that they feel gritty and small. The sky is inky black—it's late here now, we're one hour ahead of London—and above us, the stars glow silver, little jewels in the dark. It feels otherworldly, and totally magical. I felt groggy when I woke up, as though I'd been hit on the head or something, but now, excitement pulses through me like a hot rod down my spine and actually I'm grateful that I was able to sleep the whole way, all eleven hours, and that I didn't get sick. That would have been embarrassing, to be honest. Hannah says there was a bit of turbulence, which I'd have absolutely hated—I'm such a baby about things like that.

I pull off my cardigan, tie the sleeves of it in a knot around my handbag, and wait on the tarmac for Hannah and Alice. It feels tacky beneath my feet, as though if I trod too hard I'd sink into the ground, be swallowed up by this strange new land, never to be seen again.

The two of them appear within minutes; Hannah looks a bit odd, all keyed-up somehow, but Alice looks as though she's only just woken up. Her mascara is a tiny bit smudged under one eye, and I make a gesture to her to let her know but she doesn't seem to notice me. *Fine then*, I think. I won't tell her again.

We follow the signs to the baggage carousels—Hannah and I have brought hand luggage only but Alice's other case is huge—and once we've got everything, we head into the glassy white of the terminal, following the instructions Felicity has sent over. The air-con washes over us, calm and cool, a contrast to the sticky heat of outside.

We're here! I WhatsApp Felicity excitedly—Alice and Hannah are both texting their partners, but I haven't got anyone else to text so I may as well be useful, let her know we've arrived. It's not as if my flatmate is bothered about whether I've gotten here safe; she's no doubt relishing having the flat to herself with Ben. My message goes through, but I don't get the blue ticks that show she's read it. She must be getting ready for us to come. I wonder if she's feeling the same odd mixture of nerves and anticipation I was feeling earlier about seeing everybody again. It must be even worse being the hostess—the pressure is on.

But Felicity always did well under pressure, from what I remember. Some might even say she relished it. In my mind's eye, her face flashes angrily at me; her words echo and bounce off the iron fire escape steps, sharp arrows of pain that pierce my skin over and over again.

The airport is smaller than Heathrow, but quite full. I look around, wondering for the first time if anyone here is coming to the party—whether some of them might even have been on our plane. She might've invited others from the UK, after all, or perhaps it'll mainly be Americans. Now that she's got her shiny new life, she might not want too many people from the past clinging on. Apart from us, of course. Her old best friends.

I think of the flat in Peckham. God, I'm so glad we're here.

"Ms. Carter?"

A man's voice interrupts my train of thought and the three of us all spin around. He looks like a chauffeur, and is holding up a piece of white card with our names printed on in black type. Grace Carter, Alice Warner, and Hannah Jones. It feels like we're on a school trip.

"Yes, that's me, that's us," I say excitedly, and he nods solemnly, not smiling.

"Excellent. Won't you please come with me?"

We exchange looks—Alice seems a bit more awake now, and Hannah grins at us both.

"First-class service, this," she says, and the three of us follow the man outside, back into the heat. Lights from the terminal illuminate the space in front of us, and I look around, trying my best to take it all in. Oddly, the stump of a tree greets us, sprouting from a patch of red earth laid into the tarmac; behind it are round banks of succulents, dotted between large umber boulders. Above us, the sky feels wide and endless, freeing somehow, and I feel the smile spreading across my face, have to fight a sudden urge to laugh out loud. I can't believe we're here.

We follow the man to where a bank of taxis and buses are lined up, white in the overhead lights; there is a cacophony of horns honking and people talking. I see a quite good-looking man with sandy-colored hair staring at us in the line for the taxis, catch the whites of his eyes in the darkness, and I frown, then realize he's not actually staring at us, he's only looking at Hannah. I nudge her.

"That guy can't take his eyes off you!" I say, thinking it's funny and that she will be pleased, but instead she frowns and grabs my arm, pulling me along with her, hurrying to keep up with our rather mysterious chauffeur.

"Probably a weirdo," she says, and I see Alice steal a glance at her, as though there is something between them that they know and aren't saying. I feel the old fears stir in my stomach. I don't want to be the odd one out. I don't want to be left behind. Not this time. Not ever.

We're moving away from the taxis and the airport, the sounds and lights of it fading slightly. The air is so deliciously hot and so still, a world away from rainy, windy South London with its traffic lights and billboards and discarded takeaway boxes that blow up and down the streets. It feels as though we're in another world.

"Please."

We have stopped in front of a shiny, sleek black car, and the driver is gesticulating to Alice to allow him to take her big case. She obliges, of course, and smoothly, the man pops open the boot with a silent hiss and puts the luggage inside, before opening the doors for us to get in.

Hannah goes in the front, and I'm in the back with Alice.

"This is very fancy," she says, staring at the tinted dark windows, running a hand over the smooth black leather upholstery of the back seats. There's a drinks holder in the middle, and a row of USB portals complete with thin white iPhone cords, ready for use.

"Typical Felicity," I say, lightheartedly, and Alice nods.

"I suppose. Hey, I wonder how everyone else is getting there. Do you think she's putting on this kind of show for all the guests, or d'you reckon her oldest and dearest are getting a bit of special treatment?"

"I hope it's the latter," Hannah says, as the car engine starts—a soft, expensive-sounding burr, not the choking, loud engines that roar past the Peckham flat at all times of the day and night at home, crisscrossing London like persistent, polluting flies. I twist around, looking out of the rear windshield, and see the sandy-haired man who was staring at Hannah climbing into a taxi behind us, his face caught in the lights of the cars. I watch as we begin to drive and the airport disappears behind us, growing smaller and smaller until I cannot see it at all.

The driver doesn't speak to us again, and when Hannah volunteers to give him the address he merely shakes his head, taps at the glowing sat nav to indicate that he already has it. I wonder if he speaks much English other than the essentials; I realize I know not a word of Setswana and feel immediately guilty.

"Felicity really has thought of everything," Alice says, and I think I can detect a note of jealousy in her tone, though of course it could just be wonder. Admiration. All of us have always admired Felicity, on some level, anyway. Though my own view of her has been tainted, somewhat.

"It's not too far a drive from here, apparently," Hannah says, squinting at the address on her phone and reading it aloud to us anyway. "Deception Valley Lodges, Botswana."

"Deception Lodges! Weird name," Alice says, and I privately agree with her—I can't help but wish it was called something else. "It's a shame it's so dark," Alice continues. "I can't see a bloody thing."

"We'll be able to in the morning," I say. "Perhaps we can just have some dinner tonight. I slept all the way through the flight, missed out on all the food. Though I don't suppose it was particularly good."

"No," Hannah agrees, "I didn't like the look of it so didn't bother either. I've only had crisps since lunch—I'm starving, now you say it."

"Felicity will have thought about all that," Alice says confidently. "I reckon she's got this whole weekend planned down to a T." There is definitely an edge to her voice this time; I'm not imagining it.

"What time does the party start tomorrow?" Hannah asks, and I check on my phone to see what Felicity's said.

"Drinks from seven, guests arrive from eight. Oh. So maybe we are the only ones actually staying over? Perhaps the others have all rented their own places nearby. Do they have Airbnb here, do we think?"

"D'you think Nathaniel will be there tonight?" Alice asks suddenly, interrupting my question, and I bite my lip too hard, taste the iron of blood. I've been trying not to think about that, about the tiny chance that we've got it wrong and that actually, they are still a couple. I take a deep breath, in through the nose, out through the mouth, and start running through some of the CBT affirmations my old therapist gave me. I told myself I could do this, and I can.

"I don't think they're still together?" Hannah says, her voice twisting upward, making it into a question. "I have been wondering, but surely she'd have said if he was coming. He hasn't popped up on any of her channels lately."

There's a brief silence in the car.

"We don't really know much about her life now, do we?" Alice says, drily, and none of us can think what to say to that so none of us respond. Felicity isn't the only one keeping her life a closed book these days—Alice's statement could apply to us all.

"Has anyone texted to say we're en route?" Hannah asks, breaking the moment.

"I have," I tell them, glancing at my phone. The screen is resolutely blank—Felicity hasn't replied yet. Licking my lips, I run my tongue over the slight indentation I've made with my teeth. It will be sore, come the morning.

We lapse into silence as the car purrs along, and gradually, the streetlights that surrounded the airport and the main highway, though dimmed by the tinted windows, begin to disappear completely. We have been driving for about twenty-five minutes by now, at a guess, and I wonder how far away from the airport the lodge actually is. We must be almost there. Felicity said it was quite remote, on the edges of one of the plains, near the Limpopo River, but it is starting to feel like the complete middle of nowhere, that's for sure. I hadn't realized we'd be quite so isolated.

But just a few minutes later, we come to a stop.

"Your lodgings," the driver says succinctly, his low voice cutting through the silence, and I wait as he gets out of the car and comes around to open our doors. I feel uncomfortable doing so—surely I could just get out myself—but I sense that this is all part of what he's been paid for, and I don't want to seem foolish or odd.

We clamber out, and now that we're out of the car, I can finally take in our surroundings properly, illuminated by the glow of the headlights. We are on a smooth tarmac road, and in front of us stands a huge pair of tall wooden gates, with an electronic buzzer and keypad to one side. The chauffeur unloads our cases in silence, and I begin to worry about whether we ought to be giving him a tip. I haven't even taken out any money—I didn't think. I so rarely go anywhere that I haven't thought it all through, and I feel suddenly stupid, woefully underprepared. But Hannah of course saves the day, reaching into her handbag and proffering a couple of notes to him with a cautious smile. To my surprise, he waves her away, shaking his head, and I worry then that we've misjudged the whole thing and been rude.

"Thank you," we all chorus awkwardly, and he moves forward, punches four numbers that I don't glimpse into the keypad. The gates begin to open silently, sliding smoothly apart, and the driver retreats, climbing back into the car without so much as a single word.

I watch, we all do, as the red taillights of his car disappear into the darkness, leaving the three of us and our luggage standing alone in the middle of the road. Fleetingly, I have to fight the urge to run after the car, cling on to the last vestige of home. The road is too still somehow, and the high gates look a little bit foreboding in the half-light. I wonder if Felicity has felt lonely, out here on her own.

There is a pause, then Alice breaks the silence.

"Well, he was a bit weird!"

"Maybe he just didn't speak very much English," Hannah says. "Not everyone has to, you know."

"I don't need a lecture, thanks," Alice snaps back, and I feel my stomach clench slightly. I don't want us to fall out. Not over something like this.

"Come on," I say, picking up my bag and grabbing hold of my case, "let's go find Felicity. This place looks incredible, doesn't it?" Inwardly, I give myself a shake—I'm being ridiculous; there is nothing to be afraid of out here.

And it does look incredible. It really, really does. As the gates swing smoothly open, a set of bright silver lights come on and illuminate a long, wide sandy path that stretches through the spindly thorn trees that are dotted on either side. We follow the track, and turn the corner to see the Deception Valley Lodges come into view. More soft, rounded floor lights are dotted along the sides of the path, showing us the way, and as we get closer a larger floodlight comes on, shining a big white circle onto a huge wooden lodge, raised up from the sandy ground by short wooden struts. There are what look like gas lamps fixed to the sides of the buildings, too, glowing gently and casting a flickering orange light across the space. Through it, I can just about make out the water, cutting through the sand in neat straight lines, like man-made streams that must feed into the nearby river. In front of the first walkway is a wooden sign, and I use the torch on my phone to read it aloud.

Deception Valley Lodge Complex
Main Lodge →
Zebra Lodge ←
Gazelle Lodge →
Lion Lodge ←
Cheetah Lodge →

"Cute names," Alice says. "Hey, do you think all those animals are actually here? Roaming around?"

"Of course not, not in the complex itself!" Hannah says, rolling her eyes, but I see her look quickly from side to side, as if checking that nothing is about to sneak up on us. I feel a little pinch of unease; I don't mind gazelles, they're beautiful, but I wouldn't fancy coming across a lion out here. I wonder how close they really are though, picture them out on the plains, perhaps a hundred meters away. Their ears pricking up at the sounds of our arrival, their eyes glinting in the gloom at the thought of fresh meat. *Stop being ridiculous*, I chastise myself.

The place looks exactly like the photographs Felicity has sent through—the big wooden lodge is in the center of a sort of complex, with four smaller buildings at each of the four corners, separated from the main lodge by wooden slatted walkways that stretch across the sand, grasses, and water underneath. As we step forward, more floodlights shoot upward from the floor and illuminate our way, and I can see tall green fronds dipping forward, forming a little crisscross half canopy overhead, covering us, or trapping us in. The walkways are surrounded by grass, and though the night is still, our movement makes them rustle slightly. Beyond the lodges lie the plains—stretching out into the flat, limitless African landscape, bisected by the Limpopo River.

"Wow," Alice says, as we make our way toward the central lodge, "she wasn't joking, was she? This is really something."

"Oh my God!" Hannah shrieks, and I spin around, but she's smiling, pointing to a glistening blue plunge pool that stands outside one of the smaller lodges, brightly lit by more footlights.

"There's one for each lodge," Alice says, squinting in the dim light to the next lodge in the far-right corner of the main house. "Imagine that, a pool each! D'you reckon they're heated?"

"They don't need to be here, silly," Hannah says, and she's right; I can feel my knitted dress sticking to my back and wonder what on earth possessed me not to get changed into something lighter at the airport. Sweat is starting to coat my upper lip and I wipe my face self-consciously, not wanting my first meeting with Felicity to be when I'm covered in perspiration. All my foundation will be long gone, no doubt. Why didn't I freshen up at the airport?

The lights are on in the main lodge and we reach the front door—me first, Alice next, with Hannah bringing up the rear. We hesitate suddenly, all of us frozen on the doorstep, and for a second, I feel a strange prickling sensation on my neck, as though someone, or something, is watching us. The air seems very still, save the belching of frogs, the hum of insects. I feel something land on my arm, the burr of orange wings, and jerk away rapidly. The three of us wait, and I have the odd sensation that the lodge is holding back too, its doors pulsing with anticipation.

"What are you waiting for?" Alice says sharply, and at the sound of her voice I shake the feeling off, lift up a hand, and knock. As I do so, a sense of foreboding washes over me, sudden and inexplicable, as though a voice in my ear is telling me not to go any farther, not to enter the lodge. But it's too late: the wheels are in motion, and the game has begun.

Chapter Seven

Alice

Nobody answers the door when Grace knocks, so Alice steps in front of her and tries again, louder this time. Honestly. She's got the presence of a mouse sometimes, has Grace. There's the sound of cicadas in the air, humming madly, and Alice is in such desperate need of a shower that she is going to jump into one of these pools if Felicity doesn't answer the door pretty sharpish.

"Give her a call," Hannah says when there is still no reply, and Alice whips out her phone, relieved to find that she has a bar of signal—her data roaming must have kicked in—and WhatsApp calls Felicity. The phone rings out, the tinny sound cutting into the night air.

"Flick!" Hannah calls, her voice echoing slightly, but there is no sound apart from the gentle rustling of the grasses and the whisper of the insects. It all feels a million miles from Hackney.

"Ugh, where is she?" Alice groans, and sends her a message: *We're here! Let us in.*

"Does anyone have Nathaniel's number, in case he is here after all?" Grace says hesitantly, but Alice doesn't anymore, and Hannah says she hasn't either. The expression on her face is odd when she says so; Alice would call it defensive, if she didn't know better, but she doesn't push her on it. After all, she herself hasn't exactly been forthcoming about why she no longer stores his number on her phone.

Alice gives the door a little push with her hand, not expecting anything to happen, but to her surprise, it gives.

"Hey, it's open!" she says, relieved, and she pushes again, properly this time. Sure enough, the door swings back, and they are immediately met with a screen of wooden beads, presumably to keep the insects out. They rattle loudly, breaking the tension, and Alice half laughs, batting them away with her hands. The scent of pine is strong in the air.

"Brilliant," Hannah says, stepping forward through the beaded curtain and cupping her hands around her mouth to shout. Her nails are short and stubby, chewed down to the edges. Alice wonders, briefly, what she stews over—her baby, probably.

"Felicity! We're here!"

Hannah's voice bounces back at them, a little bit too loud.

"Maybe she's in the shower?" Grace suggests, but she looks a bit uncertain. She pulls her knitted dress down farther, so that it covers her knees, and her hand goes to her collar, making sure it's straight around her neck, as if she doesn't want anyone looking too closely. She's mad—she must be sweltering. Alice's own top hangs low; she's never been one for covering up exactly, but even so she can feel beads of perspiration gathering between her boobs, which isn't exactly pleasant.

"There must be other people here if it's open," she says, and she dumps her case down on the tiled floor and kicks off her shoes, relishing the feel of the cool floor against her hot feet. "Ah, that's better. Bloody hell"—she looks around, taking in the surroundings properly for the first time—"this place is amazing."

She walks forward, the others following, down a cool, dimly lit hallway with framed photographs hanging on the walls, depicting a variety of animals in the wild—Alice catches sight of a lion, close-up, his jaws wide open, and a zebra, spindly legs moving so quickly that they are almost a blur, black-and-white stripes against the dusty red of the earth. There's one of a mother elephant standing with what must be her baby, their trunks touching sweetly, the Botswana plains burnt yellow in the background. Each photograph is surrounded by an ornate gold frame, making the pictures feel as though they are almost 3D, as though the animals could jump out at them through their wooden cages. Farther inside, the hallway opens up to a vast living room, with walls painted a deep red and beautiful African paintings and sculptures dotted around, giving the place a vibrant yet traditional feel. Three plush sofas are set against the walls, stacked with plump, squashy cushions, artfully decorated with throws across the back. Everything looks completely pristine—trust Felicity to have gotten somewhere that comes with a cleaner—and presumably a driver, too. Even if he is a bit on the quiet side.

Tall bronze lamps stand on either side of each sofa, and in the center of the room is a large, low table with a glass top. Through it, you can see the oriental rug that covers most of the floorboards, patterned with black, yellow, and green triangles. Heavy floor-to-ceiling curtains hang at the windows, tied back with thick gold ropes complete with tassels, their fronds stretching down toward the floor, still and flat against the clay plaster of the wall.

Up above them, the high roof is made of wood and thatch, woven together into a point that stretches up into the sky. Beneath the rugs, the dark wooden floorboards shine in the lamplight. The whole thing feels opulent and very, very expensive.

"Jesus," Hannah says, "this place must be costing her an absolute fortune. Isn't it gorgeous?!"

She turns to stare at the others, a huge grin on her face, and her joy is infectious because soon Grace and Alice are smiling too, unable to believe what a luxurious place they've found themselves in.

"It's like something from a magazine," Grace says, her eyes like saucers, and Alice feels a rush of fondness toward her—she looks like a child somehow. She wonders how long it's been since Grace went abroad—she never used to go much when they were growing up. Alice has always thought of her as being the most sheltered of them all. The most vulnerable, too.

Or at least, that's what they all thought.

"I have *got* to show Chris," Hannah says, pulling out her phone and taking a photo, though Alice wonders if really she wants it to prove to Instagram that she too can live a caption-worthy lifestyle. She has seen some of the pictures Hannah posts on there—none of herself, a few of the baby looking sweet, some of artfully arranged flowers and the odd nicely jacketed book. This is going to take it to a whole new level.

"God, look in here," Grace is saying, and when Alice looks around she's disappeared from beside her. She follows Grace into the next room, and can't stop her mouth from dropping open. One wall is entirely made of glass, facing out onto a huge veranda that stretches around the side of the lodge and must look out over the plains, although it's too dark to see at the moment. Alice can just about make out a wooden handrail, and outdoor furniture—six chairs, and another table, plus what looks like the shape of a barbecue. And is that another pool? The room itself is fairly empty, as though it's made for dancing, and Alice wonders if that's exactly what Felicity has planned, whether she's cleared the furniture to one side to make room for them all to enjoy her birthday. Alice used to love dancing, when she was in her early twenties. But Tom once told her it made her look stupid, so she sort of stopped and has avoided it since. The thought of this room awash with music and people and drinks though fills her with excitement—now that they're here, she can so see how amazing this party is really going to be. She can almost taste the champagne on her tongue.

Ten out of ten, Flick, Alice thinks to herself. Talk about a reunion. She isn't one to do things by halves.

Speaking of which—where is she?

"Do you think we're the only people staying here?" Hannah asks, and Alice shrugs, feeling a bit confused too.

"Well, we must be, I suppose." She glances at her watch, and adds the one-hour time difference; she hasn't changed it since they left England. It feels as though it should be more, given they've just come off an eleven-hour flight. "It's late now—I can't imagine any more guests will be arriving tonight, can you? They must all be staying close by, or maybe flying in in the morning? Maybe Felicity booked this place for us, and another place for her fancy New York friends? Though"—Alice grins—"I can't really imagine what theirs would be like if this is the downgraded version."

"Shall we phone her again?" Grace asks, and then a look of relief washes over her face as, simultaneously, all three of their phones beep, the contrasting sounds loud and jarring in the quiet of the lodge. "Oh! She's texted us all."

Alice reads out the message: "*I'm so sorry! Think I've got a tummy bug so having to stay in bed in Zebra Lodge but will see you tomorrow. Hope you like your rooms! Hannah, you're in Gazelle Lodge, Alice, you're in Cheetah Lodge, and Grace, you're in Lion. There are signs on the doors and you get a pool each too! Make yourselves at home—remember, what's mine is yours . . . x.*"

"So we're not staying in the main lodge?" Hannah says, and Alice shrugs again.

"Well, she must be saving it for the party. Everyone's probably descending tomorrow. It's nice to have our own private lodges—I'm not complaining."

"I'm not complaining either," she retorts, but Alice knows Hannah and she was, just a little bit.

"Poor Flick," Grace says. "Do you think we ought to just pop and see her?"

"No," Alice says quickly, "not tonight. I don't fancy catching some horrible Botswana bug the night before the party, do you? We can all go have showers then reconvene for something to eat tonight, then we'll see her in the morning."

They both look relieved that at least one of the group is being decisive. It is a little bit weird, being in this huge lodge on their own, probably because it all looks so untouched. It doesn't seem as though Felicity has been here for a few days already, but perhaps the cleaner came this afternoon. All her stuff must be in Zebra Lodge.

"Right," Alice says, "I've got to go shower, I feel disgusting after the plane journey. Shall we all go find our rooms? We can explore the rest of this place afterward."

The three of them head back outside, into the hot air, and Alice is relieved when Cheetah Lodge is the one closest to them, just down the walkway to the right. On the wooden door is a plaque with an intricate symbol of a cheetah carved onto it, mouth open, incisors poised, and the words *Cheetah Lodge* in dark curly script.

"Very nice, very on brand," she says to the girls. "You must be that way, look." She points toward the other two lodges—Zebra Lodge is the one on the other side of the main house, according to the signs attached to the walkway. The gas lamps flicker in the darkness, welcoming them all, inviting them inside.

"Meet back in the main lodge in forty-five minutes?" Hannah suggests, and Alice nods, smiles at them, eager for them to disappear for a little while and give her a chance to freshen up.

Inside Cheetah Lodge, it's just as beautiful and luxurious as the main one. Alice gives a little wriggle of delight when she sees the majestic four-poster bed, complete with pure white sheets and full, fluffy pillows that make her want to dive right into them and never come out.

The floorboards are wooden again, and there's a thick striped rug in the center; Alice steps on it and feels her toes dig into the fur. God, if only she could afford to hire something like this. She thinks of their flat back in Hackney, the peeling walls and the tiny bedroom that have cost them all of their savings, literally every single penny she has ever, ever earned. She thinks of herself and Tom arguing, their voices loud, naive in the small space, the words they can never take back. And then she thinks of the type of people that can come and stay here, and she feels a twinge of resentment in her gut that she quickly quashes. It's pointless to compare lives. At least she is here now, enjoying it.

There's a window on the far side of the room, framed by thick cream curtains patterned with tiny, stitched yellow cheetah heads. Alice smiles, touches one with the tip of her index finger. It's certainly a theme.

Leading off from the bedroom is the en-suite bathroom, and this is where Alice really starts to enjoy herself. The bath is gleaming white and curved, with clawed feet (of course) and a huge silver showerhead hanging above it. Lined up on a ledge next to the bath is a row of products—shower gel, shampoo, conditioner, body scrub, a loofah—expensive stuff. She picks up a bottle and sniffs it; it smells gorgeous, of honey and some sort of spice.

On the towel rail are four fluffy white towels, each embossed with gold-threaded initials: CL. She is momentarily confused and then she realizes: Cheetah Lodge. There's a sink, ceramic white set into a wooden dresser, and on the side is a clean water glass, a bottle of lemon-scented hand cream, and a square bar of soap, nestling neatly in a pretty, oval-shaped dish. A small wicker basket houses a white hand towel, folded neatly into a peak, and above the sink is an ornate gold mirror, shined to within an inch of its life. Alice stares back at her reflection, and she can see the glee in her eyes—almost like she's sharing a secret with herself. *I can't believe we're here!*

She can't decide whether to have a bath or a shower, but given it's not long before she needs to meet the others she decides on the latter, so that she can have a bit of time to relax afterward. Hopefully she can have a nice long bath in the morning, or on Sunday after the party, when she's hungover—that's always soothing. Alice used to have baths all the time at college, but she doesn't really now—Tom always moans about her using all the hot water. But she doesn't have to worry about that here, because he can't see her and this is someone else's house. Or should she say someone else's safari lodge.

Stripping naked, Alice turns on the shower and steps into the bathtub, directing the spray toward her body. The water is hot and hard on her shoulders and feels amazing after the horribly long journey and the heat of the day. As she washes her hair, massaging the expensive shampoo into her scalp, digging her nails in, she thinks about the girls, about how strange and yet natural it feels to be together after all this time. As though no time has passed at all, yet it's also as though it's been decades. Honey-scented foam froths under her fingers, and she rubs the top of her left arm out of habit, kneads her fingers into the skin, remembering. The bruises have long since healed, but the memory remains intact.

There is so much about her life that the others don't know.

Stepping out of the shower, Alice dries herself off, loving the feel of the soft white material against her skin. Her arms and legs feel sinewy today, thinner than usual—stress, perhaps, from the school and from Tom. She's glad; she needed to lose weight. She pads back out to the bedroom, goes over to where she's left her suitcase on the bed. When she looks more closely, Alice sees that there's a little note on the duvet, that she must have missed, surrounded by rose petals. It looks like something from a hotel, and she does a little victory whoop, just because she's feeling so excited. Tucking her towel around her, she picks up the note, and reads it quickly:

Dear Alice, welcome to Botswana! I hope you enjoy your stay in Cheetah Lodge. I put you in here because we both know it's a good namesake for you, don't we? Have fun! Flick. X

Alice stares at it, her eyes flickering back over the words, reading them twice, three times. A good namesake for her? A cheetah—does she mean a *cheater*? She studies the note more closely, though her hands, still damp from the shower, are beginning to shake ever so slightly. What does she mean? It's definitely Felicity's handwriting, from what she remembers. Have the other two gotten a note like this as well?

A sudden, hot burst of shame hits her and before Alice can stop herself, she crumples up the note in her hand and squeezes her fist tightly around it, blurring the ink into nothing. If Felicity wants to play games with her, she isn't interested. Alice has been through enough of that to last her a lifetime, and she wouldn't have come here if she knew this was what was in store.

Part of her is tempted to go to Zebra Lodge, sickness or no sickness, and ask Felicity straight. Perhaps there is a completely reasonable explanation—perhaps she's referring to something else, to a joke, a board game Alice once lost or something. She racks her brains, trying to think of what else it could mean, but every time, her thoughts come back to settle on the same conclusion. In her mind's eye, she sees the flash of a camera, the cold thud in her stomach when she realized what had happened, that somebody had seen.

If she is right, Alice doesn't want anybody else to know. Some secrets are supposed to stay hidden, and just because they're all here, back together again, doesn't mean that that has to change. If Felicity wants to expose her, now is not the time.

She'll make sure of it.

Chapter Eight

Hannah

Grace insists on Hannah walking with her to her lodge—she says she feels uneasy being so close to the river.

"I don't think there's anything to be afraid of," Hannah tells her, but she looks worried, and eventually Hannah links Grace's arm into hers and escorts her down the right walkway, trying to avert her eyes from the water below them, as actually, she's a bit frightened of seeing pairs of eyes in there too. Don't they have crocodiles in Southern Africa? Hannah can't help but feel that it's a bit selfish of Felicity not to even come out to greet them, no matter how sick she is tonight. They've basically been left to fend for themselves, with zero information about what to watch out for. *Though it being Felicity, I don't know why I'm still surprised*, she thinks, then immediately chastises herself. They're here as friends, after all. There's no point in Hannah hanging on to grudges from the past.

"Thanks, Hannah," Grace says when they get to her door, and she looks at her so gratefully that Hannah feels bad.

"It's no problem," she says. "I'll see you in forty-five minutes or so. Okay? And look, I'm going to be just over there." She points to Gazelle Lodge, smiles at Grace reassuringly like she would to Max.

"Okay."

She nods, and Hannah turns to leave her. When she swivels back, Grace looks so small and alone, framed in the doorway, her silhouette cut out against the lights of her room. In the darkness, Hannah hears a high, haunting sound—the far-off call of an animal, it must be. It's distant, but there, and she sees Grace's figure jerk slightly in fear. Poor Grace. Always so frightened of the world.

Perhaps out here, she has reason to be.

Finding a bar of signal, Hannah tries FaceTiming Chris from her bedroom in Gazelle Lodge, but he doesn't pick up. Disappointed, she sighs and lies back on the bed—which, it has to be said, is pretty amazing and a damn sight better than the one she and Chris share at home. They've had the same bed since they first got together, and it's safe to say the mattress is past its peak. Not that she spends much time in their bed these days; most of the time she is sitting up in baby Max's room, trying to stay awake and praying he does the opposite.

It's so warm outside but the air in here is cooler, and everything feels so crisp and new. Hannah pushes her body back into the bed and revels in the fact that she's got it to herself and that there isn't a screaming child waiting for her on the other side of the wall. Instead, there are her three oldest friends.

She turns her head and hears something rustle on the pillow. Sitting up, she finds a handwritten note, written on a piece of card, a bit like the card the invitations came on. God, it feels a million years ago, sitting in Maxy's room with the mail, but in reality it's only a few weeks. There are dark red petals surrounding it, that she must have missed when she flopped down onto the mattress.

Dear Hannah, welcome to Gazelle Lodge. I put you here because you've always been good at running from things. We all know how fast you can be. Flick. X

Hannah blinks. Rereads it, twice more. *You've always been good at running from things.* A coldness settles in her stomach, heavy as a stone. What does she mean?

You know what she means, the little voice in her head says, and not wanting to listen to it, she quickly gets up and heads for the bathroom. Standing under the shower, she forces herself not to panic, to focus on the actions of lathering up, watching the dirt of the day drain down the plughole. Planes always make her feel horrible, and her skin feels grimy to the touch. Hannah squeezes out some sort of scented soap and rubs it all over herself, trying to wash away the anxiety that is threatening to crawl all over her, but she's interrupted by the sound of her phone ringing, the chirping sound filling the lodge. Hoping it's Chris, she switches off the shower and steps out, grabs one of the big white towels from the rack and wraps it around her then skids into the bedroom, trying not to slip in her haste. She catches sight of her unpainted toenails as she does so—she should have done them, she bets the others have done theirs. That sort of thing tends to fall by the wayside when you're a full-time mum.

"Hello?" Hannah is slightly out of breath, and her hand is wet around the phone. Water droplets drip from her body down onto the wooden floor, and she quickly steps onto the leopard-skin rug so that at least she doesn't make a puddle on the floor.

"Darling?"

"Chris," she says, and suddenly, despite all the newfound freedom she's been enjoying, she feels a pang of homesickness for them both—the smell of Maxy's hair, the heavy warm weight of Chris's body next to her. The comforting normality of their little home, lumpy mattress and all.

"Are you all right? Sorry I missed your call. Long day this end," her husband says. "How's Botswana? How was the flight? How are the girls?"

"It's amazing."

She turns the FaceTime onto video mode and shows him the incredible room; he whistles in all the right places and Hannah can see the envy on his face. He wasn't sure about her coming, especially not with the girls, but she'd told him how much she desperately needed a break, how much good she thought it'd do her, and eventually he relented. She ignores his question about the flight, thinking guiltily of Adam, and tells him instead how hot it is here, how beautiful the lodges are.

"I miss you both, though," Hannah says quickly. "How is he, how's Max?"

"We're all okay, we're good," Chris says, sounding a tiny bit distracted, and he walks her into the baby's room, shows Hannah her son lying peacefully in his cot. She tenses up, worried the light of the phone will wake him, but he doesn't seem to stir. He never looks so peaceful when he's around her, she thinks sourly but doesn't say. She stares at his little form, the tiny limbs, the way his small fists clench above his head, his arms splayed out on the pillow as though he's celebrating.

"He went down all right?" She realizes she is hushing her voice, worried the sound of it will rouse their son.

"He was fine," Chris says. He's moved back into the kitchen and Hannah can see a few pots and pans out on the work surfaces behind him, an empty wineglass stood next to the fridge, a spill of red pasta sauce near the sink.

"Mucky pup," she says, nodding at the mess, and he glances around, then turns back to face her. Something odd flickers across his expression, and he quickly crosses the open-plan room so that he's sitting on the sofa, and she can no longer see the kitchen behind him.

"Yeah, well, it all falls apart without you, Han." He smiles, reaching up his free hand to loosen his tie then running it through his hair. His wedding ring glints in the lights, and automatically Hannah reaches for her own, fiddles with it, spins it around and around her finger. "Listen, Han, there's actually something I wanted to tell you. It's nothing to worry about, but when you get back—"

But as he's speaking, the signal begins to cut out; his voice crackles and blurs and Hannah can no longer make out what he is saying.

"Chris?" she says. "Chris!" There is a series of beeps and the screen goes black, the words *trying to reconnect* . . . flashing up over and over. It's no use—he's gone.

Sorry, internet issues. What were you going to tell me? she messages him, but the message doesn't go through. It seems the signal problem is on her end, not his. Oh well; she supposes they are in a remote area, after all. Hannah wonders what he was going to say. "Nothing to worry about." *Is Maxy OK?* she messages again, and the three little dots come up to show that her husband is typing but no response comes through. She tells herself not to be silly, that if there was something wrong with their son he would have told her; he wouldn't have told her not to worry if there was anything serious to say. Hannah knows all this, deep down, but it doesn't stop the butterflies starting to swirl in her stomach.

She is still damp from her abruptly finished shower, but it's almost time to reconvene with the others and so she quickly towels herself off and decides to let her hair dry on its own—God knows it's hot enough outside. Pulling open her suitcase, she tries to decide what to put on—she knows it's only Alice and Grace but she's so desperate for them to see her as she wants to be, not as a humdrum mother who spends most of her life with sick on her blouse. In the very early days, Hannah always washed it off or got changed, not wanting Chris to see her like that, but after a while she stopped bothering. She couldn't really see the point. The earrings she bought Felicity are tucked into a side pocket of her case—little emerald drops that make Hannah feel guilty every time she looks at them. In her heart, she knows they are a peace offering; a plea disguised as a birthday gift.

In the end, she goes for a long maxi-dress with the back cut out, printed with red-and-white flowers. The outfit feels loud, larger than life; she is faking confidence. It feels like something Alice might wear; even Felicity, perhaps. Slipping her feet into heeled wedges, Hannah opens the door of the lodge and steps out onto the wooden decking. Her personal plunge pool glistens in front of her, endlessly inviting, the water clean and fresh in comparison to the muddy river below them. The whole place really is utterly gorgeous.

Looking out to the west, Hannah stares into the darkness, listening to the lapping of the water, gazing into the wide plains of Southern Africa. She can't believe she's really here. As she breathes in the night air, something keeps nagging at her, tugging on the corners of her consciousness, but she can't quite put her finger on what it is. Something about the phone call. Hannah thinks of Chris saying he has something to tell her, of him loosening his tie, running a hand through his short, dark hair, the edges of it speckled with gray. The mess on the countertop; the spilled tomato sauce. His ring winking at her through the screen.

And then it hits her, and she sees it clearly. On the counter behind him, along with the pots and pans, there were two used wineglasses by the fridge, not one. The more Hannah pictures it, the more sure she feels, and she thinks about the expression on his face as he looked behind him and realized what she could see. The way he crossed the room so quickly. Two glasses, not one. Remnants of red wine in the bottom of them both—and yet he never mentioned having anybody around.

Suddenly the night air seems claustrophobic, the darkness threatening rather than beautiful. Something stirs in Hannah's stomach, a spool of unease. Who has been around to her house with her husband and her baby, while she is thousands of miles away in the wilderness?

Grace

There are definitely crocodiles in Botswana; I read about it on my phone while we were in the car on the way here. I hadn't realized the whole place was going to be on the water. Even if it is just man-made streams for aesthetics, they still must connect to the river. I've never liked water, not really. I didn't learn to swim until I was seventeen—people thought I was a bit of a freak but whenever Mum tried to make me as a child I just screamed my head off, and I think eventually she decided it simply wasn't worth the hassle. Someone once asked me if I had traumatic memories of water—I remember the phrase because I thought it was over-dramatic. *No*, I'd said, *not at all*. But later that week I'd asked my mother over the phone, wondering if something had happened when I was little, too far back for me to remember. There was a brief silence before she spoke.

No, Grace, she said, *you're letting your imagination run away with you. Nothing happened to you. You're lucky.*

That was back when I trusted my mother to be on my side. I don't anymore.

All the same, I've never been able to shake the unease I feel around water, the immovable feeling that it could consume me, reach liquid fingers out and wrap them around my throat.

Still, I try to reason with myself as I get ready for dinner, surely Felicity wouldn't have booked somewhere that was actually dangerous. This place is probably always ready for tourists; there must be all sorts of health and safety regulations. It's just a shame Felicity isn't up to talk us through it all, put our minds at ease.

I dress in a silky top and wide, billowing trousers, hoping they will keep me nice and cool, stop me from sweating as much as I did earlier. For some reason I feel a keen need to impress them both, so I stick big hoop earrings through my ears and paint on some bright red lipstick, trying to conjure up a vitality that I don't quite feel. Although I wanted to see Felicity, and feel bad for her being cooped up on her own, a huge part of me is glad that Nathaniel is nowhere to be found, and that our suspicions about their breakup are confirmed.

I take a photo of the room, planning on sending it to Rosie (admittedly only to make her jealous in the hope she'll show awful Ben), but the signal has completely gone from my iPhone so I can't send it through. Annoying—but there must be WiFi in the main lodge, and hopefully it stretches all the way out here if I can log on later.

I unpack my belongings, hanging up my dresses in the gorgeous wooden wardrobe. The handles are shaped like lion heads and I wrap my hands around the wood, feeling how soft and smooth it is under my palms, more like silk than wood. This is beyond doubt the nicest place I've ever stayed: the lap of luxury. I feel somehow that I do not deserve it.

I tuck my pajamas underneath my pillow, a habit I've had since childhood, and as I do so I see the note.

Welcome to Lion Lodge, Grace! I gave you this room because you've always been the bravest of us all. I'm so glad you could come. Flick. X

I smile at first, because she obviously means it nicely, doesn't she, but actually, it's a bit of a weird thing to say. The bravest of them all? Am I? I guess it's a compliment, though. And I do like this room—I wonder if the others are as nice.

But something in my mind can't settle, and I find myself rereading the note again. *The bravest of us all.* Suddenly, my own words come back to me from that night: *I'm trying to be brave here, Felicity!*—and my stomach gives a sickening lurch. Does she remember that? Is she trying to taunt me somehow? I remember with horrible clarity exactly what she said back: *There's nothing brave about telling lies, Grace.* I felt as though she'd slapped me, her words leaving a sharp print on me like the back of a hand. In fact, I'd rather she *had* hit me; the damage wouldn't have been anywhere near as bad.

Carefully, I fold the note in half and slip it into my suitcase; out of sight, out of mind. Perhaps I'm reading far too much into it, and I'm not going to let my paranoia get the better of me. This holiday is about me being strong. I know what the other girls think of me—they think I'm scaredy-cat Grace, timid Grace who never leaves Peckham and wouldn't say boo to a goose. Well, perhaps they don't know me as well as they think they do.

Perhaps they don't know what I'm capable of.

I walk back along the walkway, trying to push the note from my mind. I zipped up my suitcase, smoothed down the pillow so that it all looked good as new. I've come this far, haven't I? I've come on an adventure, broken out of my rut, and I'm not letting one tiny thing ruin this for me.

"Grace?" The sound makes me jump but it's just Alice, hurrying toward me down the wooden walkway. Her face is shining—she must have just showered.

"God," she says, "how amazing are the rooms? Mine is gorgeous—is yours?"

"Yes," I say, "it's beautiful. I've never been anywhere like it."

"Me neither," she admits. "I feel like we've really lucked out here. Although I'm not sure what we're going to do for food—I've texted Felicity to ask if there's anything in the house, but she hasn't replied and I don't want to ring in case she's asleep. I don't know if they have Deliveroo out here, what do you think?"

She laughs—a loud cackle that takes me back to nights out in London, her with a wineglass in her hand, throwing her head back and laughing at something one of us said. She always had a wicked laugh, did Alice. It's on the tip of my tongue to ask her about the note, whether she had one too, but something stops me. Being honest has never gotten me anywhere in the past; perhaps on this trip I should learn to keep things to myself.

"Let's go investigate," I say brightly. "Felicity must have left us something—she's probably already ordered in all the food for the party, so I'm sure we won't starve."

"Have you seen Hannah yet?" she says, following me toward the house, and I shake my head, glance in the direction of Gazelle Lodge.

"Not yet. She might already be inside."

"Hey," Alice says, "have you got a key for your lodge? I couldn't find one, and it was open when we arrived."

"No, actually," I say, "that's a good point. I guess it's only us here tonight, but when everyone arrives tomorrow I would prefer to lock it. Not that I've got anything particularly valuable." I give a little laugh. "But still, you know. I don't want some drunkard rooting through my things. Or an animal getting in!"

"God, d'you remember when Felicity's old flatmate went mental at us for sleeping in her bed that time?" Alice says, chuckling at the memory. "She was so unreasonable, though."

I did remember—it had been years ago, back when we all

lived in West London. Felicity had told us her flatmate wouldn't mind us crashing in her room one night after we'd had a bit too much wine, but the girl—I forget her name—came home at four in the morning and woke us up screaming. We were forced to all sleep in Felicity's room. We thought it was funny at the time, but looking back, it wasn't really. It was horrible. I was exhausted for all of the next day. Felicity didn't stay in that flat long after that, I don't think. Mind you, she never stayed anywhere for that long—New York is, so far, a record.

"God, yes," I say, with feeling, and for a second Alice and I lock eyes. I feel a rush of warmth toward her, for the friendship we once had, for all the years and years of memories we have built together. She smiles back at me, and my heart momentarily lifts.

"Hannah?" I call, pushing open the door to the main lodge, and to my surprise she calls out from a room to the left, in the opposite direction to the way we walked before. This place is so big, I think we've only seen a quarter of it.

"In here!"

We follow the sound of her voice and both of us stop dead in the doorway.

We're in a dining room, even bigger than the rooms we saw before. In the center of the room is a long wooden table—it looks like it could easily seat twelve but there are only three place settings, complete with folded white linen napkins and shining silver cutlery. By each place sits a tall, sparkling glass of champagne, full to the brim. Hannah is standing awkwardly to the side, hovering.

In the center of the table sits a feast—there is no other word for it. There is a bowl full of fresh fruit—guava, pawpaw, flat yellow peaches, inky purple grapes—and two large blue patterned plates laden with meats and cheeses. A couple of bottles of red wine sit neatly beside them, and globe-like wineglasses are ready and waiting. A loaf of bread stands on a wooden board, a serrated knife next to it, and a dish of butter glistens beside it, not melted even in the heat. Water jugs stand at each side of the wine, ice cubes and thin slivers of lemon jostling inside, and three candles are burning brightly, wax collecting rapidly on the rims of their tall silver candlesticks, gathering speed as we stare. Elsewhere in the room, someone has lit a joss stick on the mantelpiece, and the scent of jasmine drifts slowly around us, heady and aromatic. The fireplace is empty, but for a beautiful statue of a lion on its haunches, cut from gold, with dark marble eyes that seem to be watching us as we gape at the spread.

"Wow," Alice says. "God, who did all this? Did you lay this out, Han?"

She shakes her head.

"I wish! My domestic skills aren't quite up to it, I'm afraid—you should see what poor Chris has to put up with! Fish fingers, mostly. No, I got here just a minute before you and it was like this. It must be the staff—I guess Felicity left them instructions. It all looks as though it's just been done. Look—the butter's not even melted, and the candles are freshly lit."

There is a pause while we all listen, but there is no other sound in the lodge apart from the three of us breathing, and the soft lap of the water outside.

"Maybe there's a separate staff lodge," I say at last. "There must be. Felicity probably gave them instructions to make themselves invisible—a bit like the driver. Some people do that sort of thing, don't they?"

I'm talking rubbish, really—it's not like I've ever stayed anywhere with *staff*, and I've no idea how rich people behave, whether this is normal or not. I think of my own arrangements back home—a scrubbed pine table stained with Rosie's nail varnish, dotted with faded wine rings. A world away from where we are now.

"Look, we've got place names," Hannah says, pointing, and we all step forward to the chairs, which are high-backed and imposing. There are twelve all in all, but three are pulled back slightly, as if showing us where to sit. To be honest, they don't look as comfortable as the Ikea ones Rosie and I have, but they're impressive, giving the room an almost regal air.

Little white cards are propped up next to our champagne glasses, and I see our names embossed on them in the same curly script as the invitations. I am on one side of the table; Hannah and Alice are on the other. It enters my mind that this is the third time I've been put alone, separated out, but I know I am being ridiculous so I push the thought from my head and stretch my red lips into a big smile, determined not to show the others that actually, this has made me feel a little freaked out. As I do so, my stomach growls, and I realize how hungry I actually am—I haven't eaten since before we got on the plane, seeing as I slept the whole way so unexpectedly.

"Well, it all looks pretty amazing," I say. "Nobody's veggie, are they?"

None of us used to be, but we don't know each other as well anymore. The sharpness of this fact raises its head, stark in the glossy surroundings. I force myself to stay upbeat, cling to the moment of warmth I felt with Alice out on the deck. We can get to know each other again, can't we? There is nothing stopping us.

"Not me, carnivore till I die," Alice says, and she pulls out her chair and sits down, reaching almost simultaneously for her glass of champagne.

"Nor me," Hannah echoes, and she does the same, taking a long gulp of her drink before raising the glass in the air.

"Well, here's to the staff, whoever they are. Everything looks delicious, and I'm gasping for this drink."

The three of us clink glasses, and I tuck my chair in underneath the table, feeling the wooden back hard against my spine. The champagne is deliciously cold, and the bubbles fizz happily on my tongue. Hannah and Alice are both smiling, and as I drink more, I start to feel the uneasy feelings drift away, as my body loosens and relaxes into the sumptuous surroundings of Deception Valley Lodge. Honestly, I don't know what we were worried about—being served a mouthwatering meal and free champagne is hardly something to be concerned by, is it? I've got to unwind a bit, to stop taking everything so seriously.

Felicity's note on my bed flashes before my eyes, and I momentarily feel my breath catch in my throat, but I rationalize that there must be a simple explanation, that it must just be a joke—harmless, meaningless. I'm just being silly, taking it to heart—silly Grace, over-sensitive as always.

Though as I look at my friends, I can't stop myself from wondering if they got a note too, and if so, what did theirs say?

"Wine, anyone? We seem to have finished our fizz," Alice says, grinning, and I watch as she effortlessly uncorks the first bottle of red, pours it into our bulbous glasses. The dark red liquid reminds me of blood, and I think about the wilderness outside, about the wild animals that surely cannot be too far away. I don't like the photographs in the hall—upon inspection, the lion close-up had blood on its teeth, and the zebra looked like it was being chased by a predator, as though the end was near. I think of what the next shot would be, a shutter clicking to capture the zebra's body, mauled on the ground, purple insides spilling out onto parched earth. There is something vaguely aggressive about them all.

"This is good wine," Hannah says. "God, it's been forever since I had a guilt-free drink." She gestures to her breasts. "Max is still breastfeeding, so I have to be careful."

"I thought that was a myth," Alice says, and Hannah frowns, but I can see she's sort of smiling underneath.

"Well, no, it's not a myth," she says. "If I drink booze, it can go through to him via the milk, so I just have to watch it, that's all. Though"—she grins—"there *are* times when I'm tempted to sedate him with a drop or two of whiskey."

I take a sip of wine, it is nice, she's right, though I mainly drink the Co-op's finest so I don't have much to compare it to.

"How is it, having kids?" Alice asks suddenly, and Hannah sighs, reaches for the platter of meat and cheese and begins loading her plate. I watch her, trying to work out whether she's taken aback by the bluntness of Alice's question, but her body language is impossible to read. I break off a piece of bread and slather it in sunshine-yellow butter, my mouth watering. The champagne has made me even more hungry, but really, there's no need to stand on ceremony, is there? Especially as it's only the three of us here. I add some cheese to the bread; it's a soft, gooey kind that my knife sinks straight through.

"I'd rather we didn't talk about it too much in front of Felicity," Hannah says, looking at us meaningfully; we nod dutifully and she looks relieved, as though she's gotten something awkward out of the way that she hadn't wanted to say. "Well, okay, so we've only got the one," she continues, chewing thoughtfully, and her eyes look a bit wistful. "For the most part, it's brilliant, you know, it's what we both wanted, Chris and I, but it is—it is full-on." She looks a little stricken even at this, as though she's admitted something terrible. But of course she hasn't—anyone looking at her could tell that she finds it full-on. It's funny, I think to myself, the way we all imagine our secrets to be hidden, when in fact, so often they're in plain view.

"Max is still so little, really," Hannah continues, "and Chris is out at work all day so that leaves me alone, most of the time. It's why I decided to come here in the end—I just wanted to be around adults for a while, even if it's only for a few days." She laughs, but the sound isn't genuine. "I get a bit sick of talking to Peppa Pig, that's all."

"It must be hard," I say, and to my horror, I see that her eyes are beginning to fill with tears, glittering in the light of the lamps and threatening to overflow.

"Han, oh no, are you okay?" Alice asks, setting down her wineglass, and putting a hand on her arm, her red-painted nails shining.

"Sorry," she says. "God, how embarrassing. I'm fine, I'm fine. It's just—it's a relief to talk to you guys, I suppose. Nobody ever asks how it's going, really."

Her words fill me with sadness, thinking about all the conversations we have missed in these last two years—about Hannah's wedding, her firstborn, huge life milestones that we all imagined we'd be part of. We used to talk to each other about everything and anything, our lives full of each other's words, but now there are just gaping holes, blank with everything we've missed out on.

"Not even Chris?" I say, passing her my napkin and watching as she dabs her eyes. She looks pretty in the candlelight, even though her skin's going a bit blotchy now that she's upset.

She sniffs, the sound watery. The room seems to shimmer a little; a drop of wax disengages itself from the candle, falls to the table, and begins spreading into a plump, rounded stain. We used to light candles up in Felicity's attic as kids; I picture them still there, the wax stiff and cold, forgotten. Holding on to old secrets.

"Chris is a lawyer," Hannah says, though we both know this—he was a lawyer when they first met six years ago. "He works such long hours, and although I know he loves Max—and I know he loves me—his job is always the thing that comes first. A few weeks ago we had his colleagues around for supper. I think he thought it would cheer me up—God, it was the absolute *last* thing I needed. But for him, it's all about keeping in with people." She pauses, gazes at her wineglass as if it will give her the answers. "I think he is—or he tries to be—a good father. But sometimes I think he doesn't really know what makes me happy at all." Her expression is wistful, as though her mind is far away from us, wandering over an uncharted territory that neither of us can approach.

"I think that about Tom," says Alice, pulling off a couple of grapes from the bowl in the middle of the table and popping them quickly into her mouth, one after the other as though they're sweets. "We've bought this house together—well, it's a flat actually—and when I look back, the whole thing was what he wanted, not what I wanted. I just went along with it. I didn't know what else to do."

She swigs her wine, smiles ruefully. "Still, at least I'm doing something I want this weekend. And, Han, I bet Chris is a better father than most. Better than Felicity's, at least."

Her words seem to turn the air around us cold. All at once, the image of Felicity's father, Michael, comes to me—his slightly stooped back, the sound of him clanking around downstairs as we huddled up in the attic. He spent most of Felicity's childhood ignoring her, until her mother died. And then he took matters into his own hands in that dreadful, dreadful way.

"Remember Michael?" I say suddenly, and their expressions change; Alice gives a little shiver, rubs her hands up and down her arms, and Hannah pulls a face.

"God, of course. Poor Flick."

"He wanted to control her, didn't he?" Alice says, and she looks around the room, her eyes darting into the corners, as if Felicity's father might stalk out of the darkness at any time.

"He used to scare me," Hannah says, taking a sip of her drink. "The way he looked at you. I don't know how she stood it. And then of course, when she was older, and he did what he did—" She breaks off. "You know, I sometimes think we should have talked to—"

"I can't bear thinking about it," Alice says, interrupting Hannah and pushing a strand of black hair behind her ear. Her big earrings jangle. "Let's talk about something else. I prefer moaning about men our own age."

The pair of them look at me, their eyes swinging toward mine almost in unison. I'm reminded suddenly of one of the photos on the wall—a still of a pack of hyenas identifying their prey. I know they're waiting for me to contribute, to talk about the man in my life, but of course, there isn't one. There hasn't been for a long time now, but neither of them knows why.

"I fancy some more champers, actually," I say, abruptly—the red wine is making me feel lethargic and sad, but the bubbles will lift me up. "Shall I go see if there's a wine fridge anywhere?"

I stand up, feeling the blood rush to my head as I do so. The floorboards creak slightly as I cross the room and exit through the double doors, leaving them sitting there. My heart is pounding—I don't really want to venture into this huge, dark lodge on my own but I can't stand the thought of them pitying me, of recognizing that look on their faces. It's the kind of look Rosie and Ben give me, and I've flown thousands of miles to avoid it. *Poor, single Grace. Always on her own.* I can almost see the thought bubbles rising sadly above their heads.

The next room I come to is cooler, and almost smells dusty, in contrast to the rest of the place, as though nobody has been in here for a while. I feel for a light switch with my right hand, running my fingers across the bumpy clay wall, feeling the rough ridges of the thick paint beneath my skin. The darkness is intimidating—the talk of Michael Denbigh has freaked me out and I feel my heart rate accelerate again. I left my phone at the dinner table, so I don't have a light, and I'm just contemplating going back when I find the switch and flick it on, illuminating the room.

It's a little library—two soft, squashy armchairs are sat

facing each other on top of a sheepskin rug, and on the wall behind them are rows and rows of bookshelves—the pages must have gathered a bit of dust. On the low table between the chairs sits a board game, chess, with the pieces laid out in perfect symmetry. It's a nice set, high-end, and I pick up one of the pieces, the carved black Queen. The wood is smooth in my hand, and without thinking I pocket it in my wide-legged trousers, feel the weight of it thud against my thigh. The most important piece in the game, I think: underestimate her at your peril.

Moving to the bookcase, I run my hands over the spines of the books, dirtying my fingers with gray flakes of dust. There are some guidebooks, possibly left by tourists, and a collection of classics—Shakespeare, Jane Austen, Rudyard Kipling. I pull out a battered copy of *The Jungle Book*—it was always my favorite, as a child, and to my surprise, something flutters out of it, falls to the floor and lands softly on the sheepskin rug. Stooping to pick it up, I see that it's a piece of paper, folded into an origami square, the corners tucked in like the games we all used to play in the school playground and up in Felicity's attic as children. We called them fortune-tellers. You used to have to pick an option to unlock the next layer, before you got to the answer in the middle. There is nobody to play it with me, so I unfold the corners myself.

The first four corners say: zebra, cheetah, lion, gazelle. Heart thudding, I open lion, the name of my lodge. Underneath that are four more options: truth, lie, truth, lie. I pull back one of the truths, and when I read the words underneath, the paper in my hands begins to shake.

The birthday party isn't the only reason you're here.

Alice

Now that Grace has said it, Alice would like some champagne too, but Grace being Grace she is taking bloody ages about it. Alice drains her red wine in the meantime and opens the second bottle—Hannah places her hand over her own glass, saying that she's had too much already, but Alice laughs and shifts her fingers to one side, and Hannah stops protesting as Alice knew she would when she fills her friend's glass to the brim.

"Are you nervous about seeing Flick?" Alice says to Hannah, watching as she chews a piece of meat. There's a breadcrumb to the side of her mouth, and she reaches up to brush it off, frowning at Alice. There's a pause before she answers; she's wondering how much Alice knows.

"Nervous? No."

So that's how she's going to play it. Well, fair enough.

"I just wondered," Alice says, running her fingers around the edge of her wineglass, "because of what happened last time, that's all."

Her face changes, but only slightly. Nothing an outsider would notice. But Alice isn't an outsider, is she? She's her best friend.

Hannah and Alice were always a little bit closer than the rest of them. They had more shared experiences, Alice supposes; their houses used to be only a street away when they were growing up in Richmond, until her parents moved, that is. She always felt as though they had a bond that outweighed the others', somehow—as if when it came to it, if the four of them were stuck in a burning building, she and Hannah would choose each other. Felicity would choose Alice, she thinks, or perhaps just save herself—and Grace? Who would save Grace? Hannah would try, but if she'd already saved Alice, she might not be able to go back. But her mind's wandering—they're not in a burning building, are they, they're in a luxurious lodge in Botswana having a wonderful time.

"No," Hannah says again, more clearly this time, more confidently. "I'm looking forward to seeing her. It's just a shame she's not well tonight."

Another pause.

"I wonder what happened between her and Nathaniel," Alice says. She looks down at her plate. "I can't imagine going through a big breakup now, at this age. It would be hard, I think. There's so much pressure, isn't there? Although sometimes, with Tom . . ." She trails off, leaves the sentence unfinished. When they were teenagers they'd spend forever dissecting the text messages from whichever boy was in favor that month, analyzing whether a single kiss meant more than a double, stalking the boys in their year on Facebook, giggling helplessly all the while. But things are different now. That closeness is no longer appropriate. And besides, Tom isn't some teenager.

"With Tom?" Hannah says, prompting her, but Alice shakes her head. The candles in front of them have begun to burn down low; Alice reaches out, begins picking at the molten wax, soft and yielding beneath her fingers. She feels as though the two of them are edging toward truths, skating around secrets like dancers on thin ice. Alice doesn't want to get too close—not yet.

"Where's Grace got to?" she says, tutting, and Hannah shrugs. She pulls out her phone and begins fiddling with it, looking anxious.

"Everything okay?" Alice asks her, concerned, and Hannah sighs, lays the phone on the table. Alice glances at the screen, sees the words *no service* in the corner.

"I'm worried about Chris."

"Worried? Why?"

"He—no, it's stupid, honestly. It doesn't matter."

Alice places her hand on hers; Hannah feels clammy, hot.

"You can tell me anything, Han. You know that, don't you?"

She nods, squeezing Alice's fingers. "I know—thank you. It really is good to see you, Allie."

Allie—she hasn't called her that in years. Tom calls her Allie, sometimes, when he's bored of using *babe*, but it's never sounded quite right coming from his mouth, somehow. It's always what Hannah used to say.

"It's good to see you too," Alice says slowly. "So why are you worried about Chris?"

But she's shaking her head, the moment clearly gone. Alice feels a flash of disappointment, but squashes it down. It's unkind of her to want to see the cracks in Hannah's relationship, to want to hold a mirror up to Hannah and Chris and peer into the darkness. Not everybody's relationship has sharp edges. She should want her friends to be happy. Sometimes looking in a mirror simply shows you what you already know.

"Do you remember the last time we were all together?" Hannah says instead of answering, more quietly now. "Do you think Grace does?"

Alice snorts into her wineglass.

"Grace was drunk, though granted not as drunk as you." She pauses. "And I thought you didn't want to talk about last time."

Hannah nods. "I know, but . . ."

There is a sudden, loud crash from the next room, and a high-pitched squeal. Both of them leap to their feet.

"Grace?" Hannah shouts, and throwing Alice a worried look, she races from the room, leaving Alice hurrying after her.

"Grace?" Alice calls, the word coming out slightly slurred. She must've drunk more than she'd thought. *You always drink more than you think*, Tom's voice says in her head, *funny that, Allie.*

"It's okay, it's okay." Grace is standing in front of them, in a smaller, colder room that houses two large fridges and a freezer. On the floor at her feet is a smashed bottle of champagne; shards of dark green glass have flown everywhere, and the liquid is forming a golden puddle on the dark wooden floor. The expression on her face is frozen; a bit of an overreaction, Alice thinks.

"My hand slipped," she says. "I'm so sorry. Do you think Felicity will mind?"

Hannah pats her on the arm. "Well, not if we don't tell her," she says. "Now, there must be a dustpan and brush somewhere in this place. Alice, do you want to fetch another bottle out of the fridge?"

Alice obliges, stepping neatly over the mess, careful not to let her sandaled feet come into contact with any of the sharp pieces of glass. Trust Grace to make a mess in this beautiful place—she always was a bit clumsy. Alice remembers when they were back at school, they'd both gotten waitressing jobs in the pub down the road, the one by the river, and Grace ended up losing her job because she broke so many plates. They gave the job to a new boy instead, and Alice remembers being quite pleased because she'd fancied him—until she'd found out he'd already kissed Hannah, that is. Even now, the rejection stings—it's funny how old wounds last for so long.

You never know when they might resurface.

As Alice makes her way back to the dining table, clutching the icy bottle of champagne, she realizes why that room was so much colder than the rest. She pictures it, the white curtain flapping slightly in the breeze from outside. Yes, she's almost sure that when she went into the room the window was wide open. As if someone, or something, had just been inside.

Chapter Nine

Hannah

Poor Grace, she looked as though she'd seen a ghost when they'd walked in to find her with the smashed champagne bottle. Hannah clears it up as best she can, and they head back to finish their meal, even though truth be told Hannah has drunk enough and is starting to feel really tired. But Alice seems determined to polish off the lot—until, that is, Felicity's second text comes through.

Hannah leaps for her phone, thinking it's Chris, hoping for some sort of explanation about the double wineglasses— perhaps he'll text her goodnight and mention the fact that a colleague popped in earlier. But the girls' phones go off too:

Sleep well, ladies! I've booked a treat for you in the morning, to say sorry for not seeing you tonight. That's right . . . We're all going on safari! The Land Rovers will pick us up at 7 a.m. sharp, from out the front of the lodges. Just my little way of thanking you for coming all this way to celebrate with me. I'll see you by the gates in the morning, then, and when we get back—it's party time! Hope you've got your outfits ready . . . remember, it's dress to impress! Night night. Flick X

The message is followed by a string of heart emojis; a rainbow of colors. Grace gives a little squeal of excitement, her weird reaction to champagne-gate gone, and looks up at the two of them, like a child who's just been told they're off to Disneyland. Hannah feels excited too—she was hoping they'd get the opportunity to see the animals, and this gives her the perfect excuse to turn in early—she can't handle drinking any more if they're starting at seven.

"Seven a.m. start!" groans Alice, but Hannah tells her that actually, seven is practically a lie-in when you've got a breast-feeding baby. It comes out more snappily than she intended, and she smiles at Alice afterward, to show she doesn't mean it, but Alice doesn't meet her eye.

"God, what d'you think we'll see?" Grace says, sounding a tiny bit nervous now, and Hannah remembers what she'd read in the guidebook on the plane.

"Well, the plains out here definitely have elephants, over by the river bend, and there are supposed to be gazelles and antelopes, that sort of thing. Jackals, maybe? I hope we see giraffes, too. And we ought to see lions and cheetahs. You're meant to try to spot the big five, I think, at least that's what the guidebook said. So"—Hannah ticks them off on her fingers—"the lion, the leopard, the elephant, the rhino and . . . shit, what's the last one?"

"The buffalo," Alice supplies, and Hannah feels a flicker of satisfaction. She must've been looking over her shoulder at the guidebook a bit after all.

"In that case," she says, "I think we ought to get some sleep, don't you? I can't be dealing with the buffalos with a raging hangover!"

Alice laughs, tips the rest of her drink down her throat, and rolls her eyes at Hannah.

"Spoken like a true mother."

The words sting, but Hannah's too tired to mind. The wine has hit her all at once, and suddenly, all she wants to do is sink down into the gorgeous white bed in her lodge and pass out—put aside all thoughts of wineglasses and empty lodges and the odd expression on Grace's face when she walked in on her in the next room.

"Do you think we need to clear all this up?" Grace asks, and Hannah frowns.

Alice jumps in. "Nah, I don't think so. If the staff put it all out, surely they'll clear it up. Besides, we don't know where any of it goes."

Hannah feels a bit bad leaving it all in such a mess, but her eyelids are beginning to droop and she can't face stacking up all these plates tonight. Anyway, Alice must be right—clearly, Felicity is paying for a catering service as part of the deal and so they may as well make use of it.

It's as they're walking back out to the lodges that Hannah notices there isn't another lodge nearby, not that she can see, anyway, though the darkness feels even more intense now, as though if one of them turned too quickly, they'd be swallowed up into it.

"I don't understand where the staff actually *are*," she says to the others, but Alice just shrugs and Grace is too busy glancing anxiously at the swirling dark water beneath the walkways to be paying proper attention to what Hannah is saying. Her eyes skate over the muddy banks, the dank, slippery sides. Hannah leaves them both at the corner of the walkway and makes her way back to Gazelle Lodge, excited at the prospect of washing the makeup off her face, drinking a tall glass of water, and sinking into the sheets. She shouldn't have drunk so much—it's way more than she's used to. She'll try phoning Chris again before she goes to sleep; the alcohol has softened her, and suddenly she longs to hear his voice, imagines him tucked up in their bed at home, his arms flung above his head like they always are when he goes to sleep. She hopes he's kissed Maxy goodnight, that he'll hear their son if he starts to cry.

As Hannah turns the handle of her lodge, she catches sight of something tucked inside the door frame, a flash of white against the wood. Frowning, she reaches for it, thinking that perhaps it's a note from one of the cleaners, like you might get in a hotel.

She wiggles it out carefully, opens the door to read it in the light of her room. The words make her sober up immediately, and shock pounds through her, fast and unpleasant. *I know what you did.*

Chapter Ten

Grace

I wake up at 6 a.m., heart pounding in my chest, mouth dry. For a second, I can't remember where I am, and a splash of fear hits me before I remember that of course—I'm in the lodge, I'm on holiday with the girls. Relieved, I lean back against the fluffy white pillows, reach for the cloudy glass of water on my bedside table. Thank God I had the foresight to put it there last night. My mouth feels as dry as the sands outside. As I grab the water, my hand connects with something else and I see the wooden Queen beside my bed; the chess piece, surveying the room from the bedside table. Nausea swirls in my stomach; the sour taste of champagne furs my tongue. How much did we drink?

With a thud, it comes back to me—eating the fruit and meats until my stomach was full and my hands were sticky with juice and fat, the fizz of the champagne and the clean, brutal smash as the bottle hit the floor, the chess game and the fortune-teller with the strange, cryptic words inside. I'd opened out the paper, but each of the other flaps were blank. Whoever wrote it knew I would be the one to find it, knew I'd choose "lion." But how? And what does it mean—*the birthday party isn't the only reason you're here*? We're here to see Felicity, to celebrate with her. There's no other reason, as far as I'm concerned. At least, not for anyone else.

I try to think—it could've been one of the unseen staff, I suppose, or it could have been Felicity herself. Or—I feel a shiver run down my spine even though the room is warm—it could have been Hannah or Alice. We all went our separate ways for almost an hour—one of them could easily have snuck back into the main lodge and put the fortune-teller in its place. We loved them when we were younger, after all.

Or maybe—the thought hits me with a rush of relief—maybe that note is nothing to do with us at all! Maybe it's been left here by another family, or another group of friends—this place must be rented out to wealthy tourists all the time, I expect it's often used for birthday parties. It's not like Felicity owns it, is it? We're probably the fourth or fifth group to arrive this year, for all I know—lots of people might have celebrated here; the whole place is perfect for big events. One of the families might've had kids, and it's just someone playing a prank on a sibling. Yes. Of course. That room didn't look like anyone had been in there for a while, what with all those dusty books, so it makes perfect sense. I almost laugh to myself—how ridiculous I'd been last night, worrying about it so much. I'd been so jumpy that I'd dropped the champagne, caused all that mess. The other two probably thought I'd just drunk too much—I saw the disapproving looks on their faces when they came into the room.

Buoyed by this explanation, I hop out of bed, luxuriating in the feel of my toes in the soft rug beneath. I glance at my watch—there's time for a quick shower, though I wish I could get a coffee. It's always been part of my morning ritual, wherever I am—the soft, dark smell of the granules, that first bitter taste like oxygen to a tired brain, followed by the fizz of artificial energy working its way through my veins. I scan the room quickly, and see a fold-down panel in the wardrobe that I hadn't spotted before. Perhaps there's a machine in there?

I pull it open and crow with delight when I see it—a gleaming Lavazza machine complete with coffee pods and a bone china cup. The milk comes in powdered sachets, but I can live with that, and as I plug the machine in and wait for the water to heat up I pull open a few other drawers that I hadn't opened yesterday, wondering what else is available. I find a mini hair dryer, a shower cap, even a sewing kit, though I'm not likely to do any of that while we're out here. I wonder what I need to take on safari—I tried to google it late last night but my phone doesn't have any signal out here and I forgot to look for the WiFi code when we were in the main lodge.

I think about going over to ask Hannah or Felicity, as presumably she will know and Hannah had the guidebook, but it's still quite early and I worry about waking them. Padding to the window, I draw back the heavy white curtains and am met with a dazzling blue sky. It is azure, cloudless, perfect. Now that it's light, everything on the complex looks much less mysterious, less spooky—it all just looks beautiful. Releasing the latch on the window, I open it and lean out, looking left to where the plains stretch out ahead of us, great swaths of dark sand and green scrub, hot flames of red desert flowers standing bright among the earth, clusters of shrubs crouched close to the ground. The sound of birds—kingfishers, maybe—and the hum of insects filters into my room and I take a long, deep breath, tilting my face to feel the sunshine on my skin. I bet it's raining in Peckham. I hope Rosie and Ben are getting wet.

Turning back to the room, I make myself a coffee—it's delicious, surprisingly, with a deep, earthy taste that feels different from the stuff I have at home. I've never been on safari before—a cousin of mine did once, said it was amazing, and although I know it's not the main reason why we've come, I'm really glad that Felicity has organized this for us. No matter what's happened between us in the past.

After showering, I rub sun cream on, the scent taking me back to London, to long muggy days reading in the park, shaded by the London plane trees, keeping out of Rosie and Ben's way. Pulling on a T-shirt and some leggings, I pack a bag with my mosquito spray and sun hat and then step outside onto the walkway, pulling the door to behind me. It is weird that there aren't any keys, and I make a mental note to ask Felicity this morning. I wonder what time the other guests are arriving. At the thought of the party, of being around strangers, men I don't know, my palms are instantly slick with sweat. I wipe my hands on my leggings, leaving greasy smears. The material is too hot against my skin—I should've packed more appropriately. All at once, I want to have another shower, scrub my skin under boiling hot water, but I resist the urge, thinking of what my therapist would say. Habits are easy to form; hard to break.

The other two are already waiting for me at the entrance to the main lodge. Hannah looks suitably kitted out for a morning in the wilds, of course, with khaki cargo pants and trainers, paired with a soft white T-shirt and a cap that shields her eyes from the glaring Botswana sun. Alice is wearing sunglasses, but when she lifts them to greet me I see that her eyes look a bit red, as though she might have been crying.

"Morning," I say uncertainly, and then, lowering my voice slightly to Alice, "You okay?"

She nods. "Just didn't sleep well, that's all. Thought I heard something in the night." She half laughs. "Convinced myself it was a lion roaming around or something. It's the wine, gives me bad dreams. Tom says I shouldn't drink as much."

She stops, as though she's said more than she meant to, and lowers her sunglasses back down over her eyes. The lenses are mirrored; I stare at my tiny reflection, shimmering back at me in the heat. I hate it when people wear mirrored glasses, it always feels as though they've got an advantage over you, as if they can see you but you can't see them. Still, I can hardly ask her to take them off—I'd sound completely mad.

"Where's Felicity?" I say, looking at my watch, and Hannah shrugs.

"I don't know, I thought she said she was coming."

It's just gone seven, and we decide to head out to the main gates to where Felicity has said the Land Rover will pick us up. Yawning, I press a discreet silver button on the wicker fencing on either side of the gates, but nothing happens. I try again, and feel my pulse quicken as the tall gates remain resolutely still.

"I can't get out," I say quickly, hating the way my voice is rising at the end but not being able to control it. For a moment, I feel a horrible sense of claustrophobia, as though we really are trapped here; despite all this luxury, all this wealth, the sensation of not being able to get out is as panic-inducing as it would be if we were in a prison cell.

"Let me try," Alice says, sighing impatiently, and to my annoyance when she presses the button the gates swing open first time, cutting smoothly through the dust and releasing us from the complex.

"Sorry," I mutter, and Hannah gives me a kind look before we head through the gates, back onto the main road where the driver dropped us the day before. It is deserted.

The three of us look up and down the road, expecting to see our lift rounding the corner at any minute, but nothing materializes and it somehow feels as though nobody has been down this way for a long time—the tarmac sits silently, burning in the heat; the gum trees don't even sway. Everything is still, silent. Waiting. The same sense of foreboding that I had when we first reached the lodges comes over me as I stare down the track, stronger this time, and I shiver as if someone's walked over my grave. We should have waited inside the gates, not out here. It doesn't feel safe.

"Give Flick a call, would you, Grace?" Alice asks and I oblige, pulling out my phone before I even think to wonder why she can't do it herself, why she feels the need to give me orders. I am so used to playing my part that it has become second nature now.

"Ugh, my head," Alice says, putting a hand to her forehead and pulling a face at Hannah. "This is way too early the morning after champagne. Why did we agree to this again?"

"Come on, it'll be so much fun," Hannah protests. "I've been reading up on it—apparently you have to stay well back from the elephants when they're with their young, they get very over-protective. Everyone always thinks they're all tame and innocent but really, they're not."

"They've got a dark side?" Alice says, laughing, and there's something in her voice when she says it that makes me feel uneasy, a chill washing over me despite the heat of the day.

"There are snakes out here," Hannah says, glancing down at our feet as though one might appear on cue. Alarm reverberates through me; I hadn't even thought about snakes.

"It's all right," Hannah says, "we just have to be careful to always wear shoes. Pretty deadly, some of them, it said in the guidebook. When we get out there I was thinking we could carry sticks, too, you know, to beat the snakes with if they get too close."

Alice groans, her hangover clearly not up for dealing with this new and unwelcome piece of information.

"They're late," Hannah says, checking her watch again. I press my phone against my ear, listen to the ringing, but Felicity doesn't pick up. My eyes are still on the ground, terrified now of a flicker in the grass, the snap of a tail or a flash of color. I imagine the tiny dart of pain, the poison making its way into my veins, and give a little shudder.

"She did say she was coming, right?" says Alice, and I nod.

"Definitely. Perhaps she's still sick, though? She might have changed her mind. Or perhaps she moved the pickup time and forgot to tell us?"

"Let's give it five minutes," Hannah says, sensibly. "They might turn up any minute and we don't want to miss them."

"Shall we wait back inside the gates?" I say, trying to keep the nerves from my voice.

"Oh, Grace, we're fine out here," Alice says, and I retreat back into myself.

We lapse into a silence, broken only by the sound of Alice popping two acetaminophen from a packet in her bag and swallowing them quickly. I stifle a yawn—it still feels really early, and if the safari guides are a no-show I'd rather go back to bed, get another hour or so of sleep so that I'm not completely exhausted by the party tonight. The coffee doesn't seem to have done the trick.

"Maybe we ought to go check on her?" Alice ventures eventually. "We could just go to Zebra Lodge, make sure she's okay? Check that she's happy for us to go without her if needs be?"

We hesitate a few moments longer, but there is no sign of anyone coming on the horizon, and at least Felicity will be able to call them on our behalf.

"Maybe she's still asleep," Hannah muses, "although you'd think she'd have set an alarm, or at least popped out to tell us what was going on. To be honest, I actually think it's quite rude of her not to have come and said hi last night." She sniffs disapprovingly. There's a sharpness to her tone, a tinge of bitterness that I might be imagining.

"Let's go back," I say. "I want to make sure she's all right."

As we head back inside the gates, Hannah taking one final look over her shoulder to make sure we haven't missed anyone arriving, my phone beeps and I see a message from Rosie come through. *Your mum rang the flat. Wants you to call her back.*

I put my phone away. There's no time for my mother right now. We need to find Felicity.

Hannah

To be honest, she's really disappointed—yes, okay, she feels a little bit hungover and she wishes she hadn't let Alice top up her wine so many times last night but Hannah had really wanted to go on safari today, and now it looks like yet another one of Felicity's promises that don't quite come true. God knows there have been enough over the years that they've known her.

There was the time when they were fifteen, when Felicity promised Hannah she'd get her an invite to Danny Loughnane's party, that she'd make her case and get her on the list—which, of course, was reserved for the popular girls of which Felicity was, ostensibly, one and Hannah was not. There was the time a few years ago, when she said she'd help Chris and Hannah get on the property ladder, that she had a friend of a friend who was an estate agent and might give them a discount. There was the time she swore blind to Hannah that she'd come to her birthday dinner—then turned up four hours late and missed everything.

But why is Hannah dredging this all up now, when they are staying here in the lap of luxury, completely at Felicity's expense? Why must she be such a vulture?

The note wedged into her door frame is stuffed into the side of her suitcase, hidden from view. She'd passed out last night without phoning Chris, her mind circling the message over and over. *I know what you did*. She keeps sneaking glances at Alice and Grace, trying to work out whether one of them could have written it. But it's such a horrible thing to do, and she can't shake the feeling that it seems like a threat. If someone is testing her, trying to make her feel guilty, they have another think coming. Hannah dreamed last night of wineglasses stained with red, of Chris holding their son, of Felicity laughing, of bare feet and a dark night sky.

"You okay, Han?" Alice says, linking her arm through Hannah's, and Hannah squeezes her arm without thinking, the warmth of her reassuring. Alice wouldn't have left her a message like that, surely? Grace is up ahead, her back to them. She looks like she's going on a run, not on safari—she must be sweltering in Lycra leggings in this heat.

Hannah feels a stab of self-loathing as they troop back through the gates onto the walkway, heading for Zebra Lodge. Nothing ever contents her, does it—she's always got to pick holes in people. She thinks of Chris and Max back home, bobbling along contentedly with their lives, and wonders if they are missing her. Or whether they have barely noticed that she's gone. She texted Chris when she woke up, asking what he'd wanted to talk about last night, but he still hasn't replied and the signal is so patchy that Hannah can't call. He'd tell her not to worry, that perhaps the note is just a joke, or a mistake. She'll have to pluck up the courage to ask the girls about it, though, or else it'll drive her mad.

"This way," Grace says, and Alice and Hannah follow her down to the right, to the only remaining lodge that none of them has been into. As they walk, Hannah's heart begins to beat just a little bit faster; her chest tightens like a drum. Though it is hot, a slight breeze winds its way through the air, disturbing the long grasses that surround them. There is something eerie about the way their fronds move, like fingers brushing against each other, or reaching out toward the girls. Hannah watches as Alice lifts a hand, pulls a few leaves off as she walks, crushing them in her palm absentmindedly, and makes a mental note to warn her about the poisonous plants out here: Hannah has read about them in the guidebook. Some of them will cause a rash; some of them are lethal.

Abruptly and with no warning, Grace freezes in front of them and yelps, but it is only a lizard, darting across the walkway, its small body quick and afraid. It skitters away, down the brown bank toward the water. Hannah sees the glint of green beetles in the mud, their shiny backs winking at her, as if they're guarding a secret.

The curtains to Zebra Lodge are pulled tight.

"Nathaniel can't be in with her, can he?" Grace says, her voice sounding unnaturally high-pitched. "He can't have been cooped up in there all this time, without us knowing?"

"Firstly, I don't think he's here, but secondly even if he was, he could easily have gone out," Alice says, snapping slightly. "He might have gone into the nearest village or something." She pauses. "It's not like any of us have ever really been that close to him. And there must be *some* signs of civilization around here."

"Ssh," Hannah says, as they approach the door to the lodge. "He might hear us, if he is in there with her."

Grace hesitates, like she always does, outside the door. Alice pushes past her.

"I've had enough of this, it's ridiculous."

She lifts a hand and bangs on the door, loudly, causing the little wooden sign on the front to bounce slightly against the boards.

"Alice, she's sick!" Grace says, but Alice simply rolls her eyes and, to be honest, Hannah's on her side here. They were meant to be going on safari, and they've been here for hours now—for Felicity to not come out feels rude and strange. No matter how sick she is.

"Felicity," Alice calls, "it's us! Wanting to see how you are. Let us in, can you?"

A pause. The three of them are frozen still on the walkway.

Above them, a bird calls shrilly, the sound desperate, like a plea, mirroring their own frustration.

"Flick!" Hannah says, trying to make her voice softer. She pauses, tries again. "Felicity! Are you in there? Is anyone with you? It's Hannah."

Alice glares at her, obviously thinking that she can do better, but still there is no reply and Grace begins to look frightened. Her breathing is quickening, and panicky blotches of red stain her cheeks.

"What's going on?" she says. "Where is she?"

"Let's try to get inside," Alice replies, and she bangs on the door again, much harder this time. There is a cracking sound and the door gives, the small metal lock swinging forward, clearly broken. Darkness spills out of the lodge; the lamps are all off and there is a strange, musty smell emanating from inside, at odds with the scent of pine that permeates everything outside.

"Flick?" Hannah says again, but quietly this time. Alice, braver than the other two, pushes the door farther back and steps inside, and with some trepidation, Hannah follows her.

Both of them look toward the bed, anxious to see her shape under the covers, the familiar slightness of her figure, the dash of her golden blond hair on the pillow.

But that's not what they see at all.

Chapter Eleven

Alice

Felicity isn't there. The lodge is completely untouched—as though it has never been used. Alice flicks on the lights, and the room is illuminated—the bed is pristine, neatly made, the curtains are drawn but tidy, and there is no sign of any belongings—no suitcases, no handbag, no clothes strewn about—nothing.

Behind her, Grace gives a little scream and Alice follows her gaze to see the flat, glassy eyes of a zebra head on the floor, attached to a black-and-white striped rug. The effect in here is somehow not luxurious; it's macabre.

"Well," Alice says, trying not to show how unnerved she's feeling inside, "she must be feeling better. Must have gone out."

"Don't be ridiculous," Hannah says, snappily, which is unlike her. "It's obvious she's not here but she can't have left without telling us. She wouldn't."

Alice goes into the bathroom, which is set up exactly like her own, and touches the marble sink—it is completely dry. The towels hang pristinely on the rack, and the shampoo bottles are full—there is none of Felicity's trademark messiness, the trail of life a person would leave. There are no signs of anyone being unwell—no scattered tissues on the side, no medicine bottles or half-empty packets of acetaminophen. There is just silence, and a growing sense of unease in Alice's stomach.

"I'm trying Nathaniel on Instagram, just in case he knows anything," Hannah calls from the bedroom. She taps away at her phone, relieved to find a bar of signal, and navigates to his page—"it's NateinLdn," Grace says—but then frowns, confusion creeping across her face.

"It says *user not found*," she says uncertainly. "He must have deleted it."

"Try Facebook," Grace says, and Hannah opens the app, types in his name. All three of the girls stare at the anonymous gray circle that confronts them.

"It looks like he's blocked you or something," Alice says. "Let me try." She does so, but is met with the same results. She can't help but feel a flicker of annoyance—*Really, Nate?*

"I'm calling Flick again," Grace says, and she does, but this time they all hear the sound of Felicity's chirpy voicemail, instructing them to leave a message.

Where are you??? Alice messages her, but the WhatsApp message gives her only a single tick—a sign that it hasn't yet delivered to her phone.

"She must be out of signal, it's so up and down here," Alice says, but Grace is already whining.

"Something's wrong," she says, "I know it is."

She shivers slightly in the cool air of the lodge and Alice switches off the light, opening the door to let the natural sunlight flood in. Dust motes glow in the air as they go back outside.

The air feels even hotter now, and Alice has a sudden urge to duck back inside the lodge, away from her friends, and burrow down into the cool white pillows of Felicity's empty bed. Well, it's not as though she's making use of it.

The three of them look at each other. A vein stands out in Grace's forehead, thin but prominent, and Hannah's hair is frizzing at the ends, frying slowly in the baking heat. Sweat coats Alice's upper lip and the underside of her arms, prickling her skin.

"Don't be silly, Grace," says Hannah at last. "Nothing is wrong, I promise."

But Grace is right—the whole complex is beginning to feel very eerie, and as Alice looks around at the flat African plains and the elusive water running below them, she realizes how isolated they are. By all accounts, they are alone behind these gates; apart from the wild animals that surround them in the bush. They don't even have a car.

"I vote we double-check the main lodge," Hannah says decisively, and in that instant Alice is glad that she is here—mother hen Hannah, the sensible one, the one you can always count on. *The boring one*, she hears Felicity's voice mutter in her ear, and suddenly Alice hears it, the sound of her cackle, loud and slightly drunken, knowing she's saying something she shouldn't. Alice's head whips around but of course, Felicity isn't here—she is imagining it, recalling a memory, as if the thought of Felicity might conjure her up in front of them, get the holiday back on track.

"Okay," Alice says, shaking her head slightly to dislodge the disloyal thoughts; that is the past, after all, and they are where they are. Hannah is good to have around—better than Grace, at any rate, who is trying Felicity's mobile repeatedly, resolutely ignoring the fact that it is obviously switched off.

"Will you stop that, Grace?" Alice snaps, irritation at the tinny sound of Felicity's voicemail pushing her over the edge, and she instantly looks cowed, hurt spreading over her features like melted butter onto bread.

"Sorry," she says quietly, but Alice can tell she thinks she's being unreasonable. She knows she ought to feel bad, but right now she doesn't have the capacity to care—she's on edge, and Grace's over-sensitivity and constant anxiety is really the last thing they need in this admittedly strange situation.

"Come on," Hannah says, ever the peacemaker, and she puts a hand on Grace's arm, gently steering her in the direction of the main lodge.

Inside, they agree to split up—Alice is to take the west side, from the dining room onward, Hannah is checking the outside decking that surrounds the lodges, and Grace is to look in the bedrooms. Alice wanders through the luxurious rooms, her sunglasses on her head, wondering what to do—it's not as if she'll find Felicity lurking underneath a cushion or inside a chest, though she does pull open the doors of the cupboards in the kitchen and the living room, peering into darkness and finding nothing out of the ordinary each time. As she searches, Alice thinks of the games they played in Felicity's house, of cowering inside the wardrobe while the others hunted for her, her palms sweating, her tongue sticky with alcohol, terrified that Felicity's father would come home and discover her hiding place before Felicity herself could. For some reason, the thought of being in a confined space with him made her feel sick with nerves, but it never happened. *Hide and seek!*—the girls used to call, *ready or not, I'm coming!*

As Alice paces around, she feels an odd sensation, as though somebody or something is watching her. The statues at the sides of the room cast shadows onto the floor, as the heat of the morning sun pulses through the windows, and she feels as though the eyes of the painted animals can see her fruitlessly hunting for their friend. She finds the room with the fridges, where Grace spilled the champagne, and runs her fingers over the window ledge, feeling the catch beneath her thumb. It's closed now, shut tight, but she could have sworn it was open yesterday evening. Alice squeezes her eyes closed, trying to think, to remember the moment when the bottle smashed and she and Hannah had walked into the room. The air was definitely colder, wasn't it? She can't work out if she's misremembering—her mind feels slow and sluggish, the hangover making her brain foggier than usual. There is a patch of something sticky on the sill, and Alice sees a couple of ants, trailing a line from the window to the substance, feasting on the spill. Soon, she thinks, they will become a writhing mass of black.

There is a scream from somewhere else in the lodge and Alice's heart jerks instantly, adrenaline flooding her from head to toe.

"Grace?" she shouts, because it sounds like her, and she turns on her heel, racing toward the bedrooms. She finds Grace shaking slightly, her hand clapped across her mouth.

She shakes her head at Alice, color flooding her cheeks.

"Sorry," she says, "it's fine, I'm fine. It's just a spider, that's all." Alice follows her finger to where an admittedly huge black spider is sitting in a delicate cobweb inside the large wooden trunk at the foot of the bed. Seems Alice is not the only one looking in hiding places.

"You're fine, Grace," she says impatiently. "No sign of anything, I presume?"

"No," she says, "you?"

"No." Alice pauses. "There's no need to scream like that for no reason, Grace. You scared me, you know."

They look at each other, and something almost unmissable scrolls across Grace's features—just a flash of it, that if Alice didn't know her so well she would say was imagined.

Anger.

Grace

Something really weird is going on, and it's obvious neither of the other two is prepared to listen to me. As I search the bedrooms, I am terrified—and I know it's because I am dreading what I might see.

You've watched too many horror films, I tell myself as I pull back curtains and push open doors, but I can't shake the image of Felicity's body on the floor in front of me, the imagined sight of a pale, bloodless arm poking out from behind a bed. Strands of her hair caught in the sheets. Spots of blood on the shiny wooden floorboards. I can't bear the thought of it—I've been angry with Felicity in the past, but the thought of her being hurt makes me feel physically sick. Of course, I can't tell the others what I'm thinking—they will think I am mad. Despair flares briefly inside me at the endless catch-22; if I tell the truth, people don't believe me. If I lie, nobody seems to care.

"Grace!" Alice says, and I realize I am staring into space,

unsettled by the spider (I've never liked spiders—do they have poisonous spiders in Africa?) and the fact that she is irritated by me. Again.

"Sorry," I say, although I'm not really, and she gives me a weird look, like she can see right inside my head to everything I'm thinking, all the little thoughts spiraling away in my mind.

But she can't. Nobody can.

Hannah

It's boiling hot out on the decking. Sweat is dripping down the back of Hannah's neck, pooling at the base of her spine; she feels like she needs another shower already. The wooden slats surround the house and Hannah makes sure she's walked around twice before giving up and accepting that Felicity isn't here. Sighing, she leans her arms against the wooden railing that separates them from the Botswana plains. Tall, spindly trees dot the landscape, and in the far distance she can see movement—yellow shapes that dance under the heat. Her body tenses; are they lions? Cheetahs? She squints, but her eyes aren't good enough—Chris is forever on at her to go get new glasses but what with baby Max and everything else, it's slipped right to the bottom of her to-do list. Hannah watches the horizon, hoping to see more and yet not wanting to at the same time, and for the first time since being out here she begins to feel prickles of fear. The succulents out on the plains stare blankly at her, surrounding the lodges, hemming them in. *Don't come any nearer*, they seem to say. *Don't look too closely, Hannah.*

How safe is it out here, really? What is to stop the wild

animals from approaching the lodge? There's the water, but it's not deep, and besides, most of the animals out here can wade or swim through, she's sure of it. Hannah wishes desperately that she'd read up more on this environment before she came out here, that she'd concentrated on the guidebook properly on the plane rather than flirting with that sandy-haired man, Adam, and pretending to be a single, carefree woman. She feels embarrassment curdle inside her—what on earth was she thinking? Felicity, if she was here, would be laughing at her.

There's a sound from inside and Hannah spins around, for some reason imagining that an animal will confront her, but of course it's just the girls. Alice looks annoyed and Grace looks a bit shaken. She hopes they haven't argued.

"Look," Alice says, "there's nobody here, obviously. I think we ought to get a taxi into the nearest village, or town or whatever—it can't be far. We can get something to eat and perhaps find someone who might be able to help us—shed some light on where Felicity might be. At the very least, they'll be able to tell us how to get back to the airport—without Felicity we haven't even got a way of contacting the driver who dropped us off."

"Okay," Hannah says, "that's a good idea." If she's honest, she's a bit annoyed she didn't think of it first, but then again she can't be expected to think of everything, always be the one in the group who will sort things out. Sensible Hannah. Responsible Hannah. Everyone else do what they like because it's okay, Hannah is here to sort out the boring bits.

I know what you did. She pushes the image of the note from her mind.

"Do we actually know where we are, though?" Grace pipes up, and the two of them stare at her. God, she's right. They don't have a proper address with a postcode or house number, just the name of the complex, and the area.

Hannah scrolls back through their messages with Felicity—the excited photos, her constant exclamation marks, her euphoria about them all coming out here. All that and then this. It doesn't make sense, it doesn't add up that she isn't here with them. Hannah can't shake the growing sense that something bad has happened.

"She just said the driver would get us from the airport, she never gave more details, no postcode or anything. It's just Deception Valley Lodges," Alice says slowly, and Hannah feels something sink slightly in her gut because she's right. They fall silent, all of them remembering that strange, quiet car ride, the moment the man dropped them off outside the lodge complex, leaving them alone in the unknown, in the heat and the darkness.

Hannah imagines Chris back at home, scolding her for not taking more precautions, for not taking her safety more seriously—but then again, she thinks with a flicker of annoyance, it's not like he asked her for an address of where she was going. He was preoccupied on the morning she'd left, in a rush on his way to work. There was a piece of slightly burned peanut-butter toast poking out of his mouth as he said goodbye, leaving Hannah to take Max to his mother's house for the day until Chris returned from the office. He told her to have a good time, but he didn't ask her for any details of where she would be staying. He called goodbye quickly, the door slamming behind him. Maybe he was a bit annoyed that she was going at all, Hannah thinks—possibly even jealous that she was daring to leave him with his own son. Perhaps if he had shown more of an interest, they wouldn't be in this situation—but no, she thinks, it's not fair to blame him. He's the one at home looking after their baby, after all, while she is stuck in the African wilderness with no bloody idea where they are. Hannah thinks of the two wineglasses. *One problem at a time, Hannah.*

"Let's look on Google Maps," she says at last. "We should be able to pinpoint our location that way. We know the name of the complex, it must be a popular tourist spot, surely."

The three of them gather around Hannah's phone and watch as the app loads, slowly—the signal is poor out here on the decking and she edges closer to the lodge in an attempt to speed it up. They all stare as the colors fill the screen—a vast expanse of green surrounded by a river of bright blue. No detail, no clarity—just wide, anonymous terrain. There are no names, no identifying marks, nothing that could be used to show anyone where they are.

"It'll work if you zoom in," Grace says, and Hannah tries but all that happens is more green, more blank space with their tiny red dot flailing desperately in the middle. For a second, the three of them stare at it in silence, the reality of the situation sinking in. Hannah's mouth feels dry; she is desperate for a drink.

"Let's try inside the house," Alice says, and she pulls out her phone.

"I don't think you'll have any more luck than me, I'm not doing it wrong," Hannah says snappily. She can feel herself becoming defensive, like she always does when things aren't going her way. It's far too hot out here and she's so thirsty— she'd pictured them having the time of their lives this morning, taking some amazing photos of the animals to show Max and Chris back at home, feeling stimulated by a brand-new experience that wasn't feeding a baby or listening to mindless cartoons that she prays will keep her son calm. But no—thanks to Felicity, instead they're stuck out here in the middle of nowhere and she has to put up with Alice thinking she's better than her—like she always has, despite their closeness, despite their past professions to be best friends forever and ever.

As they troop back inside, Hannah feels tears begin to prick her eyes. Her breasts hurt, and she has a sudden desire to be back at home, safe with her family. Something strange is going on here, and despite trying to keep calm and stay levelheaded, be sensible Hannah who the others can rely on, she feels panic beginning to creep into her, blur the edges of her vision.

"Surely the party prep needs to start soon," Grace is saying as they head into the living room of the main lodge, which feels even darker in contrast to the bright heat of outside. Neither of them bothers to reply. It doesn't feel like there's a party starting in eight hours—it doesn't feel like that at all. It doesn't feel as though more guests will be arriving, as if the champagne will start flowing and music will play—it feels as though they're stuck here, the three of them, alone. The sunshine feels incongruous—the opposite of how they're all feeling. Hannah feels stupid, frustrated tears prick at her eyes. This morning was supposed to be exciting—she'd looked forward to the rush of adrenaline that would come with seeing one of the Big Five game animals, she'd longed for the sensation of being alive, of doing something other than breastfeeding in a quiet baby's room. But no. Felicity has taken that chance away from her too.

Is this Felicity's way of punishing her?

"Mine isn't working either," Alice says, shaking her phone in frustration. "Maybe there's something written down in the lodge itself, an address book or a brochure or something? Something with more details on, the name of the nearest town? Or a taxi number even?"

"Let's look in the hallway," Hannah says. "That's the obvious place."

Her arm is itching and she scratches it, finding a hardening red lump under her nails. She'd doused herself in mosquito spray before leaving her lodge this morning, but clearly it wasn't enough. She imagines the poison seeping inside her, entering her bloodstream, the skin frantically trying to resist it, forming the bump. Too late, too late. The damage, such as it is, is done.

To get to the hallway they have to head back through the dining room. Alice enters first and Hannah hears her give a little gasp of horror that prompts Grace to run after her, barreling into her as she stands in the doorway, one hand clamped over her mouth.

"Someone's laid out a meal," Grace says, and her voice is wobbly now, beginning to shake in that way she has when she's frightened. Hannah pushes forward, peers into the room. She is right.

The table is once again laden—four champagne glasses are full to the brim, ready and waiting, and there are four sets of cutlery and plates laid out for lunch, the silver glinting in the sunlight that is pouring through the huge windows. A huge bouquet of flowers sits in the center of the table; blue irises, their open mouths mocking them all, their green leaves pointing straight upward into the air like sharp blades of knives.

"Did you do this?" Hannah says, finding her voice and

turning to the others. Both of them are gazing at the table, as though transfixed.

"No," Grace says, shaking her head vehemently, "of course not!"

Alice glares at her. "I didn't either. Obviously."

Hannah can't help it: she doesn't believe them.

"Why are there four settings now?" Grace asks, a tremor in her voice, and Hannah shrugs, trying to think.

"Felicity could have come back and done it?" Alice says hesitantly.

The atmosphere in the room feels different, charged. A coldness has settled between them, and as Hannah looks at the two of them, her oldest friends, she starts to really wonder. Are they telling the truth? Does one of them know more than she does about why they are here? Did one of them leave her that horrible note?

She thinks of Alice, first in the door to the living room. Her gasp, her throwing a hand up to cover her mouth. Genuine surprise—or an act? She always was good at performing; they used to say that about her at school. She used to star in every play—Sandy in *Grease*, Maria in *West Side Story*, while Hannah sat in the audience and, afterward, told Alice she was proud. And Grace, cowed in the corner, always submissive to Alice—to all of them. Does it ever get on her nerves? Would she have a reason for playing a trick like this?

"It must be a trick," Alice says, breaking the silence. "You know how Felicity liked to play games sometimes. The real Felicity. You must both remember."

And then Hannah thinks of another day, an evening, of Alice's bare white shoulder exposed, her red top halfway down her arm, her mouth open wide, laughing. The scent of wine and cigarette smoke in the air. She thinks of Felicity's eyes flashing, of Grace crying small, animal-like sobs. She remembers the cold sensation of the ground on her bare feet, the feel of Nathaniel's arms around her. That was the night they stopped trusting one another, but if she's honest, the cracks were formed long before. Perhaps they had always been there, ready to splinter, just waiting for the right moment, the point at which all four of them saw each other for what they were.

"Felicity!" Grace shouts suddenly, her voice whiny but loud, echoing back at them as if the walls too are playing a trick, amplifying the sound yet never letting it leave the room. The mirror seems to bounce the cry back at them, and Hannah stares at their reflections, the three of them standing stock-still, their eyes on each other.

She doesn't think any of them trusts the others now, not really.

Alice steps closer to the dining table, runs a hand across the high ornate wooden back of a chair, her long, manicured fingers casting dust motes into the air.

"She must be here somewhere," Grace says, and her voice is desperate now. "I'm going to go look for her. It's part of the birthday thing, it's some sort of surprise."

She sounds like she might be going to cry, and Hannah feels frustration brim inside her. The last thing they need now is Grace's hysterics—unless she is putting them on? Hannah has always thought of Grace as someone who would be incapable of deception, but she knows Felicity didn't always agree. As Hannah looks at Grace, she is reminded of the trapped zebra in the photos in the hallway that she knows they all spotted—of prey, waiting to be caught. But by whom? Who is here in the lodge with them? Or is the table setting a deliberate trap, to make them think a fourth person will be coming, when in reality they're here alone? Botswana is one of the most sparsely populated areas of Africa—there could be nobody else around for miles.

"Let's all look one more time," Hannah says eventually, and the three of them disperse, going their separate ways into the huge building. Hannah hangs back slightly, wanting to see where each of them goes. If one of them is in on this—on whatever weird joke is being played—she wants to know which one. She sees Alice's hair flick behind the doorway of the living room, hears Grace's tread as she pads over to the bedrooms.

"Felicity!" Hannah yells, as loudly as she can, but her throat feels hoarse and scratchy because of the heat. The insect bite on her arm itches and she scratches it impatiently, not noticing until afterward that she has made it bleed. Dots of bright red blood stand out on her arm; when she puts her fingers to her mouth, she tastes iron on her tongue.

They reconvene ten minutes later in the hallway.

"She isn't here. It's pointless," Alice says. She looks angry, flustered, her bangs sticking up at odd angles from her sweaty forehead.

"Did one of you set this table to freak us out?" she says then, looking directly at the other two, making eye contact with first Grace and then Hannah. They mutely shake their heads. Hannah resents her now for having the bravery to ask what she herself could not—she bets Alice wouldn't be keeping quiet if she'd had a note pushed into her door.

"Alice," she says, "it's not helpful to make accusations. Why would we want to freak each other out?"

Alice raises her eyebrows without saying anything, and Hannah feels a surge of frustration. Is this how she is with Tom, refusing to answer questions, playing little mind games? If so, perhaps it's no wonder that they don't seem like love's young dream.

"Let's go outside, out to the front," Grace says. "I want to get out of this place. It's stifling. We can walk to another village perhaps, or flag down a passing car."

None of them says what they're thinking: how unlikely it is that there will be any cars passing at all, given how quiet it was the night they were dropped off, how remote and isolated this entire place feels. None of them is ready to voice their fears.

Chapter Twelve

Grace

I put my hand on the door handle, go to wrench it open—I really have had enough of this, of Alice going around madly accusing people, of the suffocating feeling inside this lodge—the dust in the air, the weird, still dinner table like something from the *Mary Celeste* ship. The door handle doesn't budge and I try again, harder this time, thinking it must be jammed.

"What are you doing?" Alice asks impatiently, barging me out of the way, her shoulder knocking into mine—quite hard, actually, it might even leave a bruise—and she tries the door too. But there is no doubt about it now—it's locked.

"Is it locked?" Hannah asks, and Alice nods, confusion written across her features.

"This isn't funny," I say, trying not to sound like a two-year-old. "Did one of you lock it? It was open earlier when we came in."

"Of course we didn't lock it, Grace," Hannah says, giving it a go herself, banging the flat of her palm against the wooden door to no avail.

"Where's the key?" Alice says. "There must be a key."

We look at each other and it strikes me how utterly stupid we have been. None of us bothered to ask for a proper address or contact details of the owner of the complex, none of us asked for the basic safekeeping one normally would—keys, being an obvious one—but then it's because we didn't need to, isn't it? We thought Felicity would be here, our friend and our host. We thought she'd tell us everything in person, that she'd be by our side right now, laughing and drinking and discussing what to wear for the party tonight. I feel a stupid stab of disappointment, thinking of myself earlier, wondering about what I might wear and who I might meet. Thinking that this might actually be a chance for me to break out of my rut, to shake things up and move on, to have stories to tell Ben and Rosie when I get back home. Well, this is a story all right. But it's not a good one.

There's a sound, light at first as though I'm imagining it, but then louder and louder. It's rain—drumming on the roof of the lodge; hot, thick rain beating down on us, trapping us inside. I've read about the rainfall in Africa—the way it appears suddenly during this season, out of nowhere, drenching everything in drama. So different from the British showers.

"We can try the windows," Alice says, and we follow her through to the next room, where the huge glass panes are slimy with water, dirty green droplets running down like tears that are growing more and more hysterical. We look out onto the rest of the complex; the plunge pools are beginning, already, to overflow, water splashing out onto the decking. The sound feels like it's building, reaching for a crescendo. Reminding us that we're trapped, powerless against the circumstances.

"They have monsoons here," Hannah says, but her voice is small and quiet. "I don't think it'll last long—it's just really intense rain for a short period of time. It'll stop soon. It said so in the guidebook."

The bloody guidebook; anyone would think it was the Bible.

"Does the window open?" I ask, and Alice tries the white-painted handle. It too is locked, and I feel claustrophobia rising up inside me, threatening to take over. Suddenly, all I want is to be back in Peckham, in my stuffy, drab little flat, wearing my stained dressing gown, drinking hot tea and listening to a Nineties playlist on Spotify. I don't want to be here, trapped in this luxury lodge with two friends who walk all over me and treat me as badly as Ben does. Why do I let myself be treated like this? What is it about me that makes the others dismiss me? Is it the same thing that made me a victim, all those years ago, some sort of weakness that is visible to all, a tattoo on my forehead that only I can't see? Because they do dismiss me, they do. They discount my ideas and push me out of the way and laugh at me behind my back. I shouldn't have come here. I should have known better, after all this time and all these years.

This entire trip was a mistake.

"I want to get out," I say, quietly and then louder, until I'm almost shouting it. "I want to get out of here!"

"Jesus, Grace, will you calm down?" Alice says, and there it is again, the disdain in her voice, the casual way she speaks to me, as though there is never any doubt about which of us has status in this friendship group and which of us most definitely does not. Why do we pretend to be on an equal footing, I wonder, when the lines between us are so obvious?

Hannah is kinder, as she always is. She puts her arm around me, and actually it feels nice—soft and comforting. Motherly. The anxiety inside me begins to dissipate, just a tiny bit.

"It's okay, Grace, it's okay. We will get out, don't worry. We'll get out and find someone that can take us to a town, somewhere we can find out what's going on. We won't be trapped in here, and hey, look, even if we are, I can think of worse places, right?"

She smiles at me and I know she's just trying to be nice, make a joke, make light of things. I probably am overreacting, I think, as her thumb strokes my shoulder, nothing terrible has happened, we just don't know where Felicity is and we don't know where we are. But they don't know about the note in the library, the note that only I found.

Perhaps now is the time to tell them.

Alice

She can't believe they're bloody trapped in here. Furious, Alice stomps away from the hallway, back into the dining room, thinking that at least if they're stuck inside while it rains like mad and while the door is locked, she may as well have a glass of champagne to take the edge off and maybe ease her hangover. Hair of the dog, and all that.

Grace is driving her absolutely mad, and Hannah isn't much better, obsessed with the guidebook even though it's patently obvious something fucking strange is going on. What was she thinking, coming here? She should have listened to Tom, let bygones be bygones, left the past in the past.

Tom hasn't even bothered to reply to her last message, and the thought makes Alice feel sick. It's Saturday—he will have been at football all morning but he'll definitely be finished by now.

She pictures him in the pub, making jokes with his ridiculous "lad" friends, downing pint after pint as they make jokes about "his mistress" being away. Perhaps he doesn't even miss her. Perhaps he's glad she's gone.

Alice can't tell the girls how things are between her and Tom—she doesn't want to admit it. She wants them to think she is perfect, as good as Felicity, no, better. She doesn't want them to know about their constant sniping, their snide remarks over money (or lack of), the cruel way he sometimes looks at her, even when they're in bed, their bodies tangled together. The tiny hints at violence. She wants to push all of these things down deep inside her where nobody can see them; her messy insides.

In the dining room, Alice pulls out a chair and sits down heavily, her hair falling over her face. The rain on the roof is incessant and annoying—she pictures the river outside bursting its banks, overflowing and sweeping them and the entire lodge away. At least it'd get them out of here.

The champagne is warm on her tongue—it's been sitting out for too long but that doesn't stop Alice from necking the glass. She wants the buzz of the alcohol in her bloodstream, she wants it to relax her and help her figure out what to do. Fucking Felicity.

She tries calling her again but it's fruitless. Voicemail clicks in and Alice hangs up without leaving a message.

"What if something's happened to her?"

Grace has come up behind her without Alice hearing. She always was light on her feet. Alice used to be jealous of how thin she was, how a size 10 on her would be baggy, loose. She's gotten even thinner in the last few years; she's like a rake. All skin and bones, as opposed to Alice's curves that are undoubtedly still there, no matter how sinewy she felt yesterday.

"Who?" Alice asks flatly, not bothering to turn around, reaching for a second glass of champagne from in front of the empty seat beside her.

Grace appears, sliding into the chair opposite and looking disapproving as Alice takes another gulp of her drink.

"Felicity."

Alice pauses mid-sip.

"Why would something have happened to her?"

"Well"—Grace spreads her hands flat on the table—"we don't know where she is. She's not picking up her phone. She hasn't been online. If we were back home we'd be worried. We'd think she was missing."

Honestly, she's so dramatic.

"Missing? No, we wouldn't, Grace, don't be ridiculous. We'd think she'd swanned off with her boyfriend or something and left us in the lurch—it's not like it'd be the first time, is it? Felicity is tough. She can look out for herself."

"What if she went on a walk or something though?" Grace persists, her voice grating on Alice. How has Alice never noticed how nasal she sounds before? She wonders now how she ever put up with seeing so much of her. Alice glances away from her, focuses on the fruit bowl on the other side of the room; the soft flat peaches, beginning to rot in the heat. Soon, she thinks, they'll attract flies. She feels like she is rotting too, disintegrating with every second that goes by in this place, time becoming thick and soupy.

"What if she did?" Alice says, playing devil's advocate just for the sake of it, because really, she knows what Grace is getting at.

"Well, she could have been . . ." Grace trails off and her eyes travel to the huge statue of the marble-eyed lion standing proudly by the fireplace. The grate is empty; Alice pictures flames, more heat, the room filling with smoke, the lion springing to life and leaping for the door, away from the fire.

"I don't think she's been eaten, Grace," she says with a snort and Grace flushes red, blotches appearing on her cheeks and her neck, a telltale sign that Alice has rattled her.

"I wasn't suggesting *eaten*, Alice," she snaps back. "I just meant she might've been . . . attacked. We're surrounded by wild animals, it's not out of the question. There are hyenas out here. You don't need to sound so—so scathing."

Alice sighs, puts her head in her hands. She feels mean now, just a little bit—Grace is staring at her with puppy-dog eyes and she knows she's being too harsh to her. Her heart is racing—whether it's the champagne or what Grace is saying, she's not sure.

"She might have been attacked." Hannah comes into the room. Her face is pale, with a strange, waxen-looking sheen to it.

"Are you okay?" Alice asks, and she nods, comes to sit down.

"I've texted Chris," she says. "I managed to get signal out on the deck at the back. I want someone to know what's going on. Just in case, you know. I want a record of it."

Alice sees Grace look down at the table and wonders if she's thinking about who she'd text—who she'd call on. She surprises herself by stretching out a hand across the table to Grace, grasping the other woman's fingers. She's bitten her nails—Alice feels one of them catch unpleasantly beneath her touch.

"Sorry for being scathing," Alice says, forcing a smile, trying to get her to smile back. "I didn't mean to snap. I'm just a bit stressed."

"We all are," Hannah clarifies, and Grace finally looks up, meets Alice's gaze.

"It's okay," she says, squeezing Alice's hand, "I know you didn't mean it."

She forgives easily; it's a good trait, Alice supposes. Felicity could learn a thing or two from Grace in that department.

"What's that?" Grace says suddenly, and she holds out a little white card from the table, one Alice hadn't noticed. Flipping it open, she reads the contents aloud, and Alice watches as the blood slowly drains from her face. She shows them, ashen. There is a single line, written in the same curly script as the original invitation. *Don't ignore me. One of you knows why you're here. And one of you will pay.*

Hannah

"Give me that!" Hannah says, a little bit more harshly than she was intending, but she can feel her frustration beginning to bubble over. Grace hands her the card and Hannah stares at it, her mind racing. She can feel her two friends watching her, their eyes burning into her forehead. She counts to three before looking up, *one, two, three.*

She's had enough of this.

"Right," Hannah says, taking charge, looking them both square in the face. She used to think she was good at reading people; when they first met, Chris said he thought she had a real knack for it.

"You're like a mind reader!" he'd laughed at her on one of their first dates—Hannah can see his smile now, grinning across the table at her. They'd been in a French restaurant, talking about past relationships. Even early on, she'd known it was serious between them; that insatiable need to know everything and anything about the other person you were considering giving your heart to. Chris didn't have surprises, but Hannah liked that about him. She liked how dependable he was, some might say staid. That's why the sight of two wineglasses has gotten to her. She can't bear to think of him having skeletons in the closet.

"Is there anything anyone wants to share?" she asks, feeling like a teacher in front of a naughty classroom, and she can feel Alice bristle. Well, let her. Something strange is going on around here, and one of the two of them clearly has something to do with it.

Grace reaches for a champagne glass, takes a quick sip, something desperate in her movement. Hannah can see her cheeks flushing, wine-red stains creeping up from her neck, peeping out of her T-shirt collar.

"Of course not," she says. "This is nothing to do with me. But look, now that we're discussing it, I've been feeling the same. I found another note, last night. It was in a fortune-teller, you know, like the ones we used to make as kids."

The others stare at her, and Hannah remembers them all, crammed into Felicity's attic, staring at the square folded paper in Felicity's hands, a bottle of wine between them in the center of their circle.

"Pick a color," she recalls Felicity saying, her face flickering in the candlelight, and then, "Truth or dare? Come on, Hannah, pick one."

She had, and Felicity had crisscrossed her fingers, unfolded Hannah's fate. Dare. It was always dare.

"What did it say?" Alice says, in a slightly strangled voice. Hannah watches her out of the corner of her eye. Either she genuinely doesn't know, or she's doing a very good job at pretending.

"It said that there was another reason for us being here—that we're not only here for a birthday party. It felt—sinister." Grace pauses; the word hangs in the air like an ax waiting to fall. "And now this," she says, "saying one of us knows why we're here. Whatever that means, it's not me. It's one of you."

Hannah glares at her. "You found that last night and didn't think it worth mentioning?"

Grace looks abashed, then annoyed. "I thought it must be left over from another group—maybe the people who rented this place out before we did. It's a holiday complex, after all. I just didn't think it could be anything to do with us. I trusted you guys. But now . . ." Her voice tails off.

Alice looks rattled, her usually smug face (Hannah can admit it now, she does think Alice has always had a touch of smugness about her, of superiority) looks shaken. Hannah can see by the look in her eyes that she's going to turn on Grace.

"Really, Grace, if we're going to talk about trust, do you think you're the best person to judge?" she says snippily, and Hannah sees Grace's features fall. "You haven't trusted anyone in years, Grace. You've successfully built a perfect little wall around yourself, haven't you? You wouldn't know the first thing about trust."

"Allie," Hannah says, "come on, there's no need for that.

All I was asking was whether you two know more about why Felicity invited us out here than I do—I feel very in the dark about this whole thing."

"That's what you'd like us to think, isn't it, Hannah?" Grace hits out at her, and Hannah is taken aback by the amount of venom in her voice. She's usually softly spoken, and yes, okay, she's been fairly whiny so far on this trip, but she never normally talks to either of them like that.

Hannah sighs, wishing she hadn't started this. "Look, I don't think turning on each other is the answer, do you?" she tries, hoping to regain a sense of control, but Alice has pushed back her chair and is on her feet, pacing up and down the dining room like a caged animal. It's on the tip of Hannah's tongue to tell them about the note she found last night, but something stops her. Something tells her she needs to put herself first now, keep her cards close to her chest. Give nothing away.

"This is bullshit," Alice says angrily. "I hardly ever get any time off work and the one chance I get to do something different, to do something fun, has to be with the pair of you. We all know it was a mistake to come here—Felicity's obviously come to the same conclusion. She might have left already—her stuff isn't even here."

She's breathing fast, her long dark hair whipping back and forth across her face as she moves.

"Alice," Hannah says, but Alice holds up a hand, silencing her. Hannah bristles. She'd never do that to someone. She'd never be so bloody rude.

"No, Hannah," Alice says. "I think I'm allowed to be honest. We may as well admit that there are things in this friendship group that need talking about. We've kept our distance for a long time, now, and maybe we ought to have stayed that way. But if you're going to come in here and accuse me of knowing more than I let on, then I think it's only fair I defend myself. Don't you? I'd rather get it out in the open than put up with these little missives, too—I suppose you thought me being in Cheetah Lodge was the perfect fit, didn't you? The little note on my pillow implied as much. Perhaps you and Felicity conjured that one up together! You've had plenty of time to yourself out here, and it wouldn't be the first time you'd pulled a disappearing act, would it? All this time you say you've been looking for Felicity, you could easily have been writing these little messages!"

"I don't know what you're talking about, and no one's accusing you of anything," Hannah says, getting up too, trying to put a hand on Alice's arm. Alice flinches, pushes her away, and Hannah stumbles backward slightly into the dining table. There's a little squeal from Grace, and Hannah watches in horror as the champagne glass she was clutching tilts from her hand and smashes onto the table, splintering into three large pieces. Liquid runs across the wooden surface, soaking into the crevices of the table, leaving its mark. For a beat, nobody speaks, and then Grace looks up at them, her face eerily calm. Her voice, when she speaks, is quiet. Too quiet.

"Let's talk about *why* we kept our distance for so long, shall we?"

Grace

"Who remembers that night properly?" I ask the two of them, keeping my voice measured, not letting them see behind my eyes. I watch as their faces change, and I know they are all picturing a smoky courtyard, the smell of alcohol in the air, the cold February night. Felicity had been wearing a fur coat ("Oh for goodness' sake, Grace, it's not real," she told me), and Alice was smoking a cigarette, the long gray plumes of smoke spiraling into the air like thin little ghosts. I remember her face, the sight of Tom standing over her in his hoodie, the darkness obscuring his eyes.

Both of them fall silent—for all Alice's hot air, I know she doesn't like being confronted like this. She doesn't like remembering the night we all fell apart.

I place my hands on the table, careful to avoid the shards of glass, and stand up, keeping my eyes trained on Alice.

"I know you don't like remembering," I say, "but perhaps it's best that we do."

Hannah's voice shocks me.

"GRACE! For God's sake, will you stop it! You're being dramatic, and unhelpful. If you're so keen to dredge up the past, perhaps it's you who's been writing these notes!"

I gasp. "Of course it isn't! I'm not the one with something to hide! I know you both have secrets about that night. If anything, *I'm* the victim here. I always have been." My voice catches on the word *victim*; it hits too close to home.

"I've had enough of this." Hannah pulls out her phone. I notice her hand is shaking slightly, little tremors of anger pulsing through her body. Or is it fear? "I'm going to find a signal, and then I'm going to get us out of here. I've a baby at home who needs me."

This seems to ignite something in Alice, bring her back to life.

"Oh, and I suppose that makes all the difference, doesn't

it, Hannah? You've got a baby so you're the most important one. No wonder Felicity got fed up of that attitude. We've all got people to get back for, we've all got lives that don't involve this bloody lodge!"

I don't say anything. I'm not sure I do.

"That isn't what I meant," Hannah says, but Alice is rolling her eyes and shaking her head, clearly glad to have found something to latch onto, somewhere to channel her anger. She always did like a good rant.

"It is what you meant. You've always been like this. First it was with Chris—you and your relationship had to come first, you were the serious couple, the proper adults, the important ones. Now it's your baby—you're always trying to find ways of proving yourself, of showing the rest of us how far behind you we are. How much we are failing."

Hannah looks hurt. "That isn't true at all!" she says hotly, and I raise my eyebrows, because to be honest, much as I hate to admit it, I do think Alice has got a point. Hannah has always been a bit like that—sanctimonious, traditional. She wants everyone to be like her and looks down on those that aren't.

"Well, it is a bit true," I say, and Alice starts laughing, a high-pitched, unnatural sound that sets my teeth on edge. The sound is eerie, and her eyes are flashing, wild.

"D'you know what, Hannah, Grace? Fuck off."

There's a second where we stare at each other—we never spoke to each other like that, not even back then, and then she is gone, her body moving so quickly that it blurs in front of my eyes. She vanishes from the room, and both of us hear her footsteps slapping against the tiled floor. She's heading in the direction of the door.

"It's locked," I murmur, but to my surprise there is the unmistakable sound of the main door swinging open.

Hannah and I exchange glances, then quickly follow Alice. Sure enough, the door is wide open and we find Alice standing in the entrance, staring out at the pouring rain. I can't see whether she has the keys, whether she's the one who locked us in. If not her, who?

She's facing away from us, looking out over the plains, but when I say her name she turns around, looks us dead in the eye. Tears are glistening on her cheeks and immediately I feel a splash of guilt.

Hannah clearly feels the same.

"We shouldn't argue," she says softly, stepping forward and putting an arm on Alice's shoulder, and Alice nods mutely, before giving in to Hannah's embrace. I feel a stab of something in my guts. Even after all that, they are united, and once again, I am on the outside. Alice could behave as badly as she liked and Hannah would always forgive her—that's how it works, isn't it? There are people in the world who get away with everything and anything—they will always be forgiven. I should know that by now, at least.

"I think we should search the surroundings," Hannah says matter-of-factly, clearly deciding that ignoring the fact that we've all just argued is the best way forward. "There must be someone else here and if we can't find them, we'll head out to the main road and walk until we find a car. There's no point us three accusing each other of anything when there's still the possibility that there's someone else here, playing a trick on us. A fourth person. Or even more than that."

"Who would do this, though?" Alice asks, her voice sounding resigned. Hannah looks at her, and I see something pass between them, almost like a warning look.

"That's what we're going to find out," Hannah says firmly. "Come on, let's go."

"What about the animals? If we leave the complex on foot it could be dangerous," I squeak, hating the way my voice sounds, but Hannah just sighs.

"Let's search the grounds first, when it stops raining."

It's growing darker now, we have spent almost the whole afternoon arguing, and the heavy, threatening rain clouds make everything feel gloomier. A wave of exhaustion hits me—we've been up since 7 a.m., and the day feels like it's run away from us. The idea of a party this evening feels like a distant, far-off dream.

"We should get torches," Alice mutters, and after a rummage, we find some in the cupboard in the hallway. Alice switches hers on, the light illuminating her face. It is blotchy with tears, but when I try to meet her eye, she looks away.

"I want to be on my own for a bit," she says, her voice thick. "I'll go alone. You guys look together."

"Are you sure that's a good idea?" Hannah says, but I keep quiet. Maybe letting Alice have time to cool off and calm down is for the best. I don't need her swearing at us again, do I? *Fuck off, Grace.* The words sting; I've always hated swearing. My mother used to swear at me, harsh, guttural syllables reminding me of her disappointment, her failure to have produced a child who could make her happy and fulfilled. She swore when I told her what had happened to me, too, quietly and firmly, stopping my story in its tracks. Leaving me to deal with it alone. *Stop it.* I push the thoughts away.

"I think the rain is easing off," I say instead, and the three of us pause in the hallway, torches in hands. Sure enough, there is a quietness to the air now, and the heavy drumming of water on the roof has slowed to almost nothing.

"Great," Hannah says, attempting a smile, and I feel a sudden, strange rush of love for her—her positivity, her ability, for the most part, to keep it together. I'm glad she's coming with me—I don't want to be on my own out there with the running water and the insects—and God knows what else.

Outside, the air feels wet—thick and cloying, as though it might suffocate us. The visibility is low—when I look out to the plains I can barely see the gum trees, although I know they are there. Waiting for us. Watching. How many others have they seen come and go from this place, I wonder as we set off down the wooden walkway. How many people have walked in our footsteps? There is something comforting about the thought—of course we will get out of here. We will find Felicity, or whoever is leaving the notes, and we will get an explanation. God, even the thought that it could be me behind all this—it's ridiculous. Is that really what they think of me?

When we reach the place where the pathways split, the two of us look at Alice.

"Come, on, Allie, let's all just stay together," Hannah says gently. "It's the sensible thing to do. We don't know what's out there." I see her eyes flicker nervously to the streams below us, the place where they connect to the main river. Fear twists inside my stomach, thinking of the guidebook. I imagine a crocodile's jaws rising out of the water, snapping toward us, and the glare of a hippo's hooded eyes.

"I'll be fine," Alice says, and her voice is firmer now, the ice creeping back in. "I'm sorry for losing my temper, really I am. I'll be fine on my own."

She turns, and I watch as her slim figure disappears toward Zebra Lodge. A breeze follows her, ruffling my hair and causing the leaves in the reeds around us to waver, as though they too are uncertain of what we're doing.

"Come on," Hannah says, after a pause, "we need to search wider than just the complex." We look at each other, and I know she's thinking that perhaps we ought to run after Alice, that we shouldn't let her go off on her own.

I take her arm, decisive all at once. "Alice will be all right."

The two of us make our way toward the end of the walkway. There is a short drop down to the ground, and I hold the torch as Hannah crouches down, throws one leg over the side of the decking and then the other. Her mouth is set in a firm, straight line.

"Careful, Han," I say, fighting to keep the nerves from my voice, and she nods before pushing herself off the wooden ledge. She lands safely, her shoes making a soft squelching noise in the wet ground, then looks up at me, holds out a hand.

"Come on. Careful."

Down on the ground, away from the safety of the raised platform, everything feels darker. There are no outdoor lights, and Hannah reaches out to hold my arm as we move forward, away from the complex and into the surrounding bushland that encircles the lodges. Puddles stand on the earth, and swallows dip and dive in the gloom, fluttering closer to us than they do back at home. Out here, they remind me of bats—quick and unpredictable. I swing the torch around, scanning the scene for movement, half expecting to see Felicity laughing, her blond hair catching the torchlight, as though this has been one long, bizarre game of hide and seek.

"Let's go this way, we can move in a circle. We'll probably bump into Alice," Hannah says, and wordlessly I do as she suggests. We continue to walk in silence, although the air between us feels charged. My eyes are flitting around, unsure of what I might see.

"I think we're getting close to the river," Hannah says at last. "Pass me the torch?"

I hand it to her, and the beam of it swings forward, highlighting the rush of water that is flowing parallel to the walkways behind us. As she does so, two glowing pairs of eyes are illuminated in the gloom, and I can't help it, a whimper escapes me. I clap a hand to my mouth and Hannah gasps.

We step backward, holding hands, and I can feel the rub of Hannah's wedding ring underneath my fingers. Tears are pricking my eyes—what are we doing, out here in the middle of nowhere, surrounded by the water and God knows what else? I wish we'd never come.

"So do I," Hannah says, and I start. I hadn't realized I'd said the words aloud.

"Do you really think there's someone else out here?" she asks me, and I shiver in the darkness, imagine it—a faceless, nameless presence following us as we walk, their shadow darting out of the way of our torchlight. Or worse—someone who isn't faceless at all. Someone I know all too well.

"Do you think Felicity was ever here?" Hannah says, her torch beam dipping in front of us, bouncing off the ground.

"I don't know," I say eventually. "I don't know what to think."

There is none of the ease there was between us earlier in the day, and as we walk I wonder—does Hannah honestly suspect me, too?

"D'you think Felicity planned this?" I ask her, when we've scrambled back far enough away from the water that my heart rate has slowed down a bit.

Hannah stops, looks at me.

"Grace," she says, and the expression on her face scares me, "look, I think we need to—"

She's interrupted by the sound of a high, shrill scream, cutting through the darkness like a knife.

Hannah

Grace is about as useful in this situation as a chocolate teapot, as Hannah's mother would say. God, has she become her already?

The thought of her mother reminds Hannah of Max and she feels a terrible pang of guilt—what with the argument and Alice's outburst she hasn't texted Chris to check how her son is; her message to him didn't even mention Max. What kind of mother is she? An incredibly smug one, according to Alice. Her words still sting. Are they true?

"We need to get back!" Grace is saying, and she's right, of course she's right.

"Alice!" Hannah yells, as loudly as she can. It must have been her screaming, but it sounded strange. Different. Unless—

"Felicity!" she shouts, but the only sound is Grace whimpering next to her and the constant burr of the insects, even though it's late now. Something stabs into her arm, a little sting, and Hannah slaps a hand to her wrist, feels the tiny crunch of wings beneath her touch, of legs snapping into dust.

They scramble back together; Grace has the torch now and she moves faster than Hannah. She is heavier than she used to be before she had Max, she knows she is. A stupid thing to be worrying about, Hannah chides herself, but as Grace runs ahead she hates the way her thighs rub together and her breathing labors as she tries to catch her up.

They're by the main gates, now, and Hannah feels disoriented. She'd thought they were around to the east of the main lodge. The complex itself feels as if it is tricking them, an endless maze designed to trip them up.

Grace runs onto the walkway, and Hannah feels a spurt of annoyance—Grace hasn't even turned back to see if she's all right. There's a funny taste in her mouth which might be panic. She forces herself to calm down, to think of Maxy and Chris, her little family back at home. She needs to stay calm, for them.

"Alice, Alice!" Grace is calling, but there's no response, and she turns a corner, disappears out of Hannah's sight. The darkness looms in front of her, as though it could swallow her up, and she forces herself to run faster, even though her lungs are burning and her legs are tight with strain.

When Hannah reaches the wooden decking, the boards are slippery under her feet and warm puddles spoil the way forward—the rain has made everything more dangerous. She pulls out her phone, but there is only one bar of signal. In spite of this she calls Alice, but the phone just rings out. She strains her ears, trying to listen for the sound of it ringing.

She's worried Alice has fallen on the wet decking and hurt herself. That's the logical explanation—that must be why she screamed.

Rounding the corner, Hannah sees Grace, doubled over and panting.

"Try the main lodge," she says breathlessly to her, glad she has finally had the decency to stop and wait. There's no point in them all getting separated.

Hannah skids slightly as they reach the main doors, still slightly ajar as they left them. A trail of water directly inside the front door makes Hannah think Alice must be inside, and she feels a wave of relief, but there's no sign of her and the water marks fade away partway down the entrance hall.

"Her shoes aren't here," Grace says, voicing exactly what Hannah was thinking. She looks at her, and Hannah can see how frightened she is. No matter what's happened between them all, Alice is their friend. Hannah thinks of the snakes, sliding through the undergrowth, looking for bare feet; the thought makes her shudder.

"Where is she, Hannah?" Grace asks, and Hannah stares at her. Grace is looking at her oddly, almost as though she's suspicious. As though she thinks Hannah knows the truth.

"I don't know," Hannah says slowly, "I just need to think, Grace. Hang on."

"I'm going to check her lodge," she says. "You try calling her again. Text her too. Anything that might get through." Before Hannah can stop her, she's out of the door, heading toward Cheetah Lodge. Hannah waits for a moment, watches her go. There's something she needs to do first.

Grace

I almost fall over as I make my way to Cheetah Lodge. The sky is clearing now, but water still drips from the leaves, landing on my shoulders and the top of my head. I realize how long it's been since I've eaten anything, and my stomach growls with inappropriate hunger.

Maybe I imagined the scream, I think to myself, trying to keep calm, but no, Hannah heard it too, didn't she? It's not just me being paranoid. It's not.

I keep my eyes trained on the Cheetah Lodge doorway, focus on the cheetah head knocker on the door. I count my breaths—in for three, out for two, trying to force myself not to panic even though everything feels so strange.

"Alice!" I call, pushing the door open, but still there is no reply. My gaze adjusts to the dimness inside, and horror fills my chest.

The lodge looks as though it's been ransacked. Alice is always so neat—she likes to be put together, she's not messy at all—but there are clothes all over the floor, and when I go into the bathroom the bottles of shampoo are scattered everywhere, one of them open and leaking onto the floorboards, a thick, viscous white liquid that is gradually spreading into a wider puddle. Her makeup is all over the sink, a smear of red lipstick slashes across the white porcelain like a wound, and I raise my eyes to the mirror, see my own scared reflection staring back.

Keep going, Grace, I whisper to myself, *you can do this.*

By Alice's bed, I notice a pool of water, and reaching down I find the jacket she was wearing earlier, soaked through. So she's been back here, then. But why leave the place in such a mess?

Unless she didn't do this at all, of course. My eyes fall on her suitcase, half-open, with sandals spilling from the insides. Someone was looking for something in here. The question is, what?

Quickly, my hands fumbling, I take a photo of the room with my phone, somehow wanting proof to show Hannah. For some reason I feel as though the moment I step outside the room, everything will rearrange itself, go back to normal, like some sort of twisted version of *Alice in Wonderland*. I save the photo, then with one last look around the room, I go back outside.

I look around for Hannah, but then, over by Lion Lodge, my lodge, something catches my eye. There is something in the plunge pool, something big, the shape of it moving slightly in the bright blue of the water. Terror grips my chest.

I am running as fast as I can, my feet skimming over the wet boards, my eyes focused solely on the dark shape in the water. I know what it is.

"Hannah!" I call. "Hannah!" I need her to help me. As I run, my left foot collides with something and I trip—my hands coming out automatically, hitting the wooden decking hard but saving my face. Scrambling to get up, my palms throbbing, I see what tripped me up: one of Alice's shoes is lying abandoned on the decking, the strap torn, the gold fray of it glinting. A half sob escapes me; I get up, continue to run, though my legs feel like they might give way.

In the water, Alice's dark hair is inky black. There is a bloom of red drifting into the water around her head, the particles of it separating and rejoining, colliding and disconnecting in dark spirals as the water swirls.

I kneel down, my breath coming in hot, ragged pants. She is facedown. Pushing aside my fears, I plunge my hands into the water, grip onto her shoulder, trying to turn her around, but she is heavy, so heavy, and I'm not strong enough. My tears are falling fast now, joining the water below, pointless weeping that won't help anyone and certainly won't save our friend. Footsteps sound behind me and I can hear Hannah's horrified scream, and then she is next to me, reaching for Alice's other arm.

"It's not working," I say, and I take a deep breath, then jump feetfirst into the pool. One of us needs to be behind her, to push her upward. The pool is much deeper than it looks; my feet flail before finding the bottom, and water splashes up my nose and into my eyes, making them sting. The old fears clamber up my throat; the water feels all-encompassing, as though it will drag me down too, claim both of us if I don't fight to survive.

My arms encircle Alice's waist, and Hannah grunts as together we heave our friend's body from the water, both of us wincing at the dull thud of her landing on the decking. There is no sound from her—no coughing, no spluttering. Her feet are bare, the soles dirty.

"My God," Hannah says, and I can't speak, I am just staring at Alice's face. She is deathly-white, aside from the makeup that is smeared across her cheeks—black mascara, red lipstick, orange smears of foundation that have run in the pool.

I bend down, put my mouth to hers, my hands on her sodden chest the way they taught us in school, but it's been years since I learned any kind of first aid and I can't remember what to do, I can't remember. My mind is desperately trying to calculate how long it has been since we first heard her scream, how long she has been submerged in the pool, alone. I imagine her lungs filling up like balloons, the terror she must have felt as she gasped for breath, the heavy, insistent pull of the water as it dragged her body under, her eyes, her head. Did she think of Tom? Did she think of us?

Blood is steadily forming in a dark, sticky patch around Alice's head, like spilled oil, and even as I cry I can hear Hannah's voice, telling me that we are too late, telling me what I already know, that Alice, our friend, is dead: she is gone. My fingers find her neck, the slick white skin of it, clawing for a pulse. There is nothing.

"Grace," Hannah is saying. "Grace."

I realize I have been holding my own breath, and release it in a moan, clutching Alice's T-shirt, sodden wet, in between my fingers, thinking of how only an hour ago she was shouting at us both, telling us to fuck off, severing any last ties of our friendship with her cruel tongue and sharp memory. But of course it cannot be severed, can it? Friendships like these can't be put to bed, no matter what happens. Not really. Not ever.

All of us know that, deep down. Don't we?

Memories crowd my vision, threatening to overtake me. I picture Tom back in London, oblivious, waiting for her to come home, perhaps enjoying the freedom for now, playing on the Xbox uninterrupted. I think of Alice's parents, Linda and Dave, at home in their suburban bubble down in Cornwall, maybe out in the garden, carrying on their day with no idea that their daughter is currently lying lifeless in my arms. Her face is so pale, stark against the darkness of the decking. Her jaw is slack, her voice forever stilled. I've often wanted Alice to stop talking. I've wished she'd be quiet, let someone else speak, I've resented the way she talks over me and quietens me, stamps me down as though I am an irritating mosquito. But I didn't want this.

Did I? Guilt pulls at me, fast and deep.

There's a hand on my shoulder: Hannah. She tugs at me, urgently.

"We're not safe here," she says. "We have to get help, call for the police." Her eyes, usually so calm and placatory, are wide with fright and I can see her deliberately avoiding looking at Alice, her eyes flitting almost anywhere except at our friend's cold, still features.

I let her pull me up to my feet, and she puts an arm around me, her cold wet skin snaking its way around my waist. My teeth are chattering, my jaw beginning to ache. I know I am at risk of going into shock, force myself to breathe in through my nose, out through my mouth.

"Grace, come on!" Hannah says, her voice high and desperate.

"We can't just leave her here!" I say, horrified, and Hannah looks at me.

"What else are we going to do, Grace? I can't lift her. Neither of us can." She sniffs. Droplets of water are running from the ends of her hair, dampening her T-shirt. "It's not like she'll know, is it?"

I stare at her, shocked by the tone of her voice. It seems at once cold, uncaring, as though a switch has flicked inside her.

"Hannah," I say slowly, "this is our friend. I'm not leaving her out here in the middle of Botswana on her own. What if something—gets to her?"

She looks at me, and her eyes look slightly strange. Different.

"Fine," she says, "have it your way."

She lets go of me and turns back to Alice's body, bends down and grabs one of her sodden arms. Grimacing, she begins pulling Alice away from the plunge pool, but to my horror it looks as though she's trying to roll her off the decking, down into the river water below. Something isn't right about this—she's behaving strangely.

"Stop it!" I shout. "Stop it!"

Hannah is panting, out of breath; her face is flushed and her eyes are wild. She's not coping, I realize, she must have gone into shock. She isn't thinking straight because this isn't like Hannah, it isn't like Hannah at all.

"We can't have the animals trying to get her, you said!" Hannah shouts, her voice too loud, spittle forming in the corners of her mouth. She is almost sobbing, her breath coming in short, sharp pants.

"We need to bring her to safety," I say, trying to keep my voice calm and gentle, ignoring the way my heart rate is accelerating as I watch Hannah drag our friend's body across the decking as though it's a sack of rubbish. Nausea swirls in my stomach. I take a deep breath, trying to think, changing my mind several times in the space of a few seconds.

"Come on, Han, let's go inside now," I say. "We can come back for Alice. I think you need to sit down for a bit."

I am cold, despite the fact that the air is still warm; my clothes are soaking and I feel chilled, as though the very bones of me are cold and will never be warm again. The darkness feels like it is closing in on us, our horrible tableau—three friends, one dead, and one who seems to be losing her mind. But despite the horror of the situation, I know I have to think clearly—what happened to Alice may not have been an accident. I have to make sure Hannah and I are safe. And I can't rely on Hannah anymore.

I can only trust myself.

Hannah lets go of Alice's left arm, and it falls back onto the decking, landing with a sickening thud. I take hold of Hannah, who is crying now, fat tears falling down her cheeks, and begin to guide her back toward her own lodge, murmuring to her the whole while: "Ssh, it's okay, it's going to be okay." It is as though our roles have reversed; I feel odd, but a tiny part of me, the part I'd never admit to, the part I'd never tell anyone about, is relishing the idea of being in control. Hannah is listening to me now. I am no longer being ignored.

Chapter Thirteen

Hannah

Grace shepherds her back to her lodge as though Hannah is a child.

"Come on, there you go," she says as they reach the threshold. Hannah can feel her hand on the small of her back, hot and damp against her shirt. She pushes open the door to the lodge and Hannah stumbles inside. Everything is exactly as it was before—the luxurious bed, the ornate lamps—but somehow it feels different. Tainted. Darker.

She can't stop picturing Alice's body—the swirl of her blood, dark red in the water. Did she slip into the pool? Or was she pushed? Hannah imagines hands on the top of her head, forcing her down; Alice pushing up against them, desperately trying to get air. Why would she have gone that close to the plunge pool in the first place, just after a rainstorm? It doesn't make any sense.

She thinks of Grace's figure disappearing before her, the flash of her hair as she turned the corner, out of her sight as she ran to keep up. Alice screamed before that, but did Grace have time to get to her before Hannah did? Did she push her, then run back to Hannah? *Could* she have? Hannah thinks of the look on her face when Alice swore at them—*fuck off, Grace.*

Alice's little cruelties, stacking up over the years. She wasn't always nice to Grace. There is no getting around that fact.

"Why don't you call Chris?" Grace tells Hannah rather than asks her, guiding her into the room and over to the bed. Hannah sits down, shakily, not quite trusting her legs to carry her any farther. Alice's eyes stare up at her from her consciousness, dead and unseeing. Guilt claws at her, gripping her by the throat. *I know what you did.* No. *No!* What happened two years ago has nothing to do with tonight. It's unrelated; it must be.

"Hannah, Hannah!" Grace has hold of Hannah's shoulders, is shaking her almost roughly. It's only then that she realizes she has been saying it aloud.

"No! No!"

"It's okay, Hannah, it's okay," Grace is saying, but her eyes are worried and she looks almost frightened. Of her! Ridiculous. But Hannah knows she's not thinking straight; her thoughts are becoming tangled, the past is confusing itself with the present, and all she can see is her friend's body, the dark, unholy mass of it.

"I need you to stay in here for a bit, Hannah," Grace is saying, but it's as if her words are coming through a mist, or a fog—taking too long to reach Hannah. Things feel slurred, as though she is drunk, but Hannah knows it is shock, anxiety, a form of panic. It has happened to her before, once, in those endless, lonely days after she gave birth to Max, where the world tilted and tipped around her and she felt inebriated with exhaustion. She never thought it would happen again. She told herself that it wouldn't.

"Where's your phone, Hannah?" Grace is asking her, her eyebrows raised. She lifts her hands and to Hannah's horror, she sees that one of them is stained with red, with Alice's blood. Vomit rises in her stomach. She can't do this anymore.

But Grace is pointing at the pocket of Hannah's shorts, to where her iPhone is nestled, oblivious, and numbly Hannah pulls it out, hands it to her. She is careful not to let Grace see what else is in her pocket; her fingers brush against it, a small spike of reassurance.

"No," Grace says, "you keep it. Call Chris, tell him what's happened. Keep the door shut, stay inside. I'm going to go find help, Hannah, okay, I'm going to go find help but I'll be back. I promise."

"Can't . . . lock . . ." Hannah says, thinking about how weird it is that they have no keys, that none of these lodges is really secure, that whoever is out there could be coming for her next. If someone got to Alice, there's nothing to stop them getting to her too.

But Grace isn't listening to her, she's leaving, turning her back and closing the door behind her. Hannah sits, sobbing, on the beautiful white bed that is now stained with blood from the smears on her hands.

The door slams, jolted by the wind. After a little while, Hannah stops crying and picks up her phone. Her thumb hovers over her contacts—Chris's photograph smiles out at her. In it, he's holding Max, just a few days old at the point the picture was taken. Max's face is just a scrunched-up little ball of pink, Hannah can barely make it out at all, but Chris's smile is wide, it fills the screen. His eyes stare out at her, willing her to call him. To do the right thing.

Instead, she swipes her finger across the screen to call someone else—the one person who listened to her that night, the person who she thinks might be able to help. She lied when she said she didn't have his number, wanting to see which of the others would offer it up, confirm her suspicions. Hannah tried to call him earlier, and now she tries again. She knows he will help her—he has helped her once before, and promised he would again.

But Nathaniel doesn't answer the phone.

Grace

It's so dark as I try to drag the heavy, wet weight of Alice's body toward my lodge. I know I need to get some rest—we haven't eaten all day and exhaustion has seeped into my bones, my muscles already straining and my throat dry from the horror and the heat. I do my best to move her gently, but it's impossible—I'm not strong enough and so I am forced to screw my eyes shut when her head bumps against the slats in the wooden decking, leaving behind it a viscous trail of blood; to think about something else as her T-shirt tears, the sound ripping through me.

My breathing is loud and ragged, and despite the tiredness, my body is on high alert—as though it is waiting for whoever did this to Alice to come for me too. A hand on my shoulder, a blow to my head. An arm closing its way around my neck. I force myself to stop moving for a moment, to take some deep breaths. My throat feels as though it's closing up, but I know that it's just panic, the anxiety making itself known as it so often does. I think desperately of my therapist back in London, the one I started seeing after what happened. Her calm, clear voice fills my head and I force myself to listen to it, to focus on staying in control. My clothes are soaked too; water drips off me, forms puddles in my wake.

With Hannah safely in her lodge, there is no sign of anyone else. The darkness is all-encompassing, and I think longingly of home, of London, of the bright green lights of the off-license on my road, the glare of the car headlights that light up my dingy bedroom window when I am trying to sleep, the golden rectangles of bright pub windows. What I wouldn't give to see any of that now, to have the feeling of normality wrap itself around me like a comforting cloak. I want my small life back. At least it was safe.

I am holding Alice's wet sleeve, but as we reach my lodge the material slips slightly, and suddenly, her cold, lifeless hand is in mine. I shudder, and the urge to drop it is strong, but I force myself not to. This is Alice. My friend.

Instead, I look down at her hand, feel the bones of it in mine. How many times have I held this hand? Thousands. Too many to count. I remember us as teenagers, giddy on vodka and youth, hands linked as we walked up the stairs of a shitty, sticky nightclub; as twenty-somethings, me holding her hand on the duvet as she sobbed about her horrible ex-boyfriend. The three of us, hands linked together at Felicity's mother's wake—we'd all known Diane, we'd all gone to support her. Michael, at the front of the church, his arm around Felicity, her body pressed tightly into his side.

I know Alice found me irritating, and that I found her rude. But we shared so much together. That has to count for something. I didn't confide in her when I should have, though. I didn't let her in.

Her nails are painted red, but the polish has chipped, and her skin is wrinkled, prune-like from the plunge pool. She wears a silver ring on her forefinger, the metal twisted around her bone. It is icy to the touch. I wonder if Tom gave it to her.

Tom.

I know I will have to make the calls, find help. Hannah seems in no state to do so. But I can't bear the thought of having to break news like this—life-altering news, news nobody can ever come back from. I'm not cut out for it, I realize, then inwardly chastise myself for being so selfish at a time like this. I'm letting myself get sentimental. Alice found me annoying at the end, I know she did. An irritant. But still, we loved one another, underneath it all. Didn't we? We all accepted this invitation, welcomed each other back into our lives.

I feel as though I don't know anything anymore.

As carefully as I can, I shift Alice's body over the ridge of my doorway, move her inside so that at least she is in the warm and dry, safe from whatever is out there. For a second, I close my eyes and picture it: the heavy paw of a lion dragging its claws across her chest, the sight of red flesh, dripping blood, spilled organs. A mass of ants crawling over her body, beetles feasting on her eye sockets. No. I can't let that happen. I'm doing the right thing.

I move her to the side of the room. She's lying facing upward, gazing up at the ceiling. One eyelid is half-closed, but the other is wide open and I can't bear it—I run into the bathroom and grab a white towel, the towels I'd practically salivated over the other day, unable to believe my luck that I was really here, in such a luxurious place, ready for a party, ready to meet Felicity's glamorous friends. It feels like a lifetime ago—in reality, it's been only twenty-four hours.

Careful not to meet the dead, awful stare of her eyes, I lay the towel over her body, covering up the lumps and bumps of it, everything that made Alice who she is. Who she *was*. Only once this is done do I realize I've been holding my breath, and I let it out, a gush of air filling my lungs. Tears rise up my throat, threatening to choke me as I pull out my phone. I'll call the police. I have to. But when I look at the screen, I'm horrified to find that it's blank. Black. Water has filtered into the holes at the bottom; I hadn't thought to take it out before jumping into the pool. Frantically, I press the on button, shake the phone, rub it dry as best I can, but nothing happens. I need to try to bring it back to life. Scrambling in my haste, I go to my bedside table, where I'd left my charger plugged in since last night, but it isn't there. The only thing there is the chess piece, the Queen, her blank face giving nothing away. Fear thuds through me but I force myself to keep calm. Perhaps I didn't plug it in after all—perhaps it's still in my suitcase.

With trembling hands, I pull open the case, rifle through my things—already, they seem as though they belong to another life. A red one-piece and my wraparound, the long maxi-dress that I was going to wear to the party that never was, my high-heeled wedges that I thought might impress the girls. All of it seems foolish; ridiculous now. My hand catches on a wire and hope fires up in my chest, but it's my headphones, used briefly on the plane before I fell asleep, and then promptly forgotten about. A moan escapes me as I shake everything out onto the floor—there is no doubt about it, my phone charger is nowhere to be seen.

I know I charged the phone last night—it won't last more than a day, so that only leaves one option—someone has taken it. I feel terror ripple through me as I picture somebody in here—hands pawing through my things, eyes gazing at my belongings, easy access to this inner world. Who is doing this to us? Can it be Felicity? Or someone else, someone who perhaps has her captive—I imagine her tied up, straining at the ropes around her wrists, mouth gagged. My mind is racing—what if Felicity had gotten on the wrong side of someone out here, fallen into the wrong hands. What's happening out here feels personal, but what if it's not? What if all of us are simply in the wrong place, at the wrong time? I think of the airport, of the sandy-haired man who watched us all depart, his eyes never leaving Hannah.

Then I think of Felicity's text messages, the syrupy sweet tone, luring us in. They could have been written by anyone. Was she ever really here at all? I feel as though she is a ghost; a presence that flits around the complex without us catching sight of her, as though if only I can think hard enough, figure out the answer to all this, she will appear, grinning wickedly, blond hair flowing down her back. I think of those awful words she said to me, the last time I saw her: *There's nothing brave about telling lies, Grace*, and all at once, I am glad she isn't here. If I told her what had happened, she wouldn't believe me anyway, would she? She has a history of not believing a word I say.

I sink down to the floor, near to where Alice's body lies, shrouded by the towel. I know I should go to Alice's lodge, try to find her charger, or go to Hannah's—but something inside me is reticent. Hannah's behavior was so strange today, so off-kilter. I think about the way she babbled, out by the pool, the wild, staring look in her eyes. What was she thinking, when she spoke like that about Alice? I always thought she and Alice were the closest of us all. To tell the truth, it's always made me jealous.

I take deep breaths, trying to think clearly—or as clearly as I can when there's a dead body lying next to me. A horrible thought hits me—how soon will it be before Alice's body begins to smell? I've seen the TV shows; I've read crime novels. I know she won't look like Alice for very much longer. The water will be disfiguring her insides, and it won't be long before it transforms her outer appearance, too, stiffens her limbs and changes the color of her skin.

I don't have a phone—I've no way of phoning for help. Alice is dead. Hannah is in her lodge. Felicity is—I have no idea where she is. And what about Nathaniel, the lurking ghost of him, the mystery of what happened between them? A memory comes to me, of that night, and I force myself to push it away. There is no point thinking about that now, it won't help. I need to be constructive, rationalize my thoughts.

The best-case—and I feel awful for using the word best to describe her death—the best-case scenario is that Alice really did have an accident. Perhaps she slipped on the wet decking, lost her balance, hit her head as she slid into the water, screaming once as she went down. I picture her underneath—the water filling her mouth, her nose, her body sinking deeper, deeper than she thought. Did she try to scream again, the sound coming out silent? Did she call for us, for Hannah maybe? Did she try to stay afloat? I look sideways at the white towel, think of the blood on her head. She'd have had to have hit it hard to become unconscious, incapable of pulling herself out. I imagine hands scrabbling at the sides of the pool, grasping nothing. Vomit rises in my throat and before I can stop it, it's spilled out of me, splashing onto the floor of the gorgeous lodge and dripping slightly onto my shirt. Saliva fills my mouth as a drop splashes onto the towel, and I retch, hating myself for being so weak. Alice wouldn't be like this. If our roles were reversed, she'd take control of the situation. Even now, she taunts me from beyond the grave.

Slowly, every muscle in my body aching, I get to my feet and stagger toward the en-suite bathroom. Running cold water over my hands, I splash it on my face, wipe my mouth, trying to avoid looking in the mirror. But my eyes catch on my haggard reflection—my skin is a ghastly pale color, and there are flecks of blood on my left cheek—I must have smeared it on there after touching Alice. Carefully, I wipe it off, taking deep breaths to avoid the sickness starting again. I feel shaky and weak now, my throat raw with that awful feeling you get after throwing up, but I can't let my guard down—I have to find a way to get help. I wonder whether Hannah has managed to get hold of Chris. I wonder whether she tried at all.

As I stare at my own reflection, I'm forced to confront reality. It's not just the unknown out there that I'm scared of. It's Hannah, too. *One of you knows why you're here. One of you will pay.* Is that person Alice? Have we paid the price already?

I can't trust Hannah anymore, I decide—I can't trust anyone apart from myself. But the lodge doesn't have a lock—perhaps I could barricade the door, wait until the morning and then go out onto the road, try to flag down a car, or walk to the next village. Do they have phone boxes here? I try to remember seeing a landline inside the main lodge, but the thought of going back out there into the darkness fills me with fear.

I drag my eyes away from the mirror, checking to see that all of the blood has gone, and that's when I see it—the little golden lock on the bathroom door. It's not much, just a slim bolt, but it's something. I can stay in here. Just while I think.

Relieved, I pull it across quickly, my hands still slightly shaking from the shock of everything that has happened tonight. I'll stay in here for a little while at least, until I can figure out a proper plan, work out what to do. I can feel tiredness over-taking me, making even my small movements sluggish, slow.

With the door bolted, I feel a sense of control begin to return, but can't stop myself sinking to the floor, allowing my head to rest gently against the wood. Around me, the bathroom glimmers—the expensive toiletries, so decadent only a day ago, seem ridiculous, absurd. The gold taps wink at me. The silver showerhead hangs above, like a poised knife, waiting to fall. I know something more is coming. The only question is, when?

When I wake up, I don't know where I am. My mouth feels stale, dry, and my eyes are sticky—I've been asleep in my contact lenses. For just a few seconds, I forget what has happened, imagine myself back home in Peckham, the day stretching out before me—but then with a thud of dread reality kicks in. Horrified that I've allowed myself to fall asleep, I glance at my watch to find that it's edging toward six o'clock in the morning. I've slept for hours.

My neck, when I move it, is horribly stiff from being upright all night, and when I put a hand to my cheek I find a smear of dried saliva, crusted onto my skin. As I stand up, the bathroom sways around me and I put out a hand to the sink to steady myself—the dizziness will be because I haven't eaten in so long.

When the world rights itself, I stand completely still, listening. The lodge is deathly silent; I can't even hear birdsong, as if the landscape knows what has happened, knows that death has enveloped us in its cloak. Sliding back the bolt on the bathroom door, I step out into the bedroom and am immediately hit by the weird, creeping atmosphere—the hint of a sickly, rotten smell that curls up my nostrils. Gagging, I realize that I can't stay in here a minute longer, not with Alice's body. I have to go get help.

My phone, still dead, is in the pocket of my leggings, and, without thinking too much about it, I also grab my passport from where it—thankfully—sits in my handbag, untouched since the day we arrived. Picking up my jacket off the end of the bed, I slide it on and pull back the main door to the lodge. So early in the morning, the light is only just beginning to rise, and even in spite of everything I can't stop myself from noticing the strange beauty in it—the orange burn of the sun beginning to creep across the horizon, sneaking through the thorn trees, illuminating our complex and shining off the water underneath. Looking at the scene from above, you wouldn't know that anything had happened, wouldn't be able to tell what horrors the complex has seen.

Treading carefully, I make my way along the walkway. I feel calmer than I did last night; able to think more clearly. My instincts are telling me to go straight to the house, try to find a phone, but I know I have to check on Hannah. Despite what I thought last night, and the weird way she behaved, I have to look out for her. I have to make sure she is safe. *And that I'm safe from her.*

Outside Gazelle Lodge, I hesitate. It's still so early, but surely

Hannah won't mind being woken up. She can't want to stay here. Not with our friend lying dead; not with what we saw.

Raising my hand, I knock on the door, my breath caught tight in my chest. What mood will Hannah be in this morning? But there is no answer, not even when I try again. I think of Alice's scream echoing across the grasses last night and feel fear wrap its ice-like hand around my heart—what if something's happened to Hannah too?

Unable to wait any longer, I push back the unlocked door, my heart hammering in my chest. But the lodge is empty—the bed is made, and save for a small pile of what look like her pajamas curled up in a ball on her pillow, there is no sign of her.

I exhale—though I don't like to admit it, part of me, a large part, is relieved. I *don't* trust Hannah anymore, and if I go alone to get help, she can't blame me. Then a thought strikes me—has she gone already? Have we both had the same idea? The thought of her suspecting me is absurd—but perhaps I am wrong. Perhaps in this situation, none of us is safe from each other at all.

I look over her things, unsure even what I'm searching for. Her suitcase is half-open, and her makeup bag is on the side— the place is untidy, even though Hannah is usually so ordered, so neat. She's the type to hang up all her clothes, make herself at home, even if we're only here for a few nights. I step to the wardrobe, and sure enough, three dresses are hanging there, still but slightly rumpled, as though Hannah has just stepped out of them. As I turn my head, I get a whiff of her perfume; the ghost of her lingers in the air. The hairs on the back of my neck stand up, as though someone has run an icy finger across my skin.

Leaving the door on the latch, I go back outside, where at last the first birds are beginning to sing. A white butterfly zings past me, incongruous and strange, its wings beating fast and urgently, as though it is warning me of what lies ahead. Other than that, it is eerily quiet; there is no Alice, sashaying along the walkway, her words biting into me, and there is no Hannah, speaking to me as if I am a child. And there is no Felicity, her golden hair swinging in the breeze, her mouth open, laughing. I am the only one, now.

There is, of course, the possibility that Hannah is in the main lodge; if not, I decide I will leave her a note—so that she knows I've gone to get help. It's the right thing to do—I know it is. It would look strange not to. Guilt gnaws at me—already, I am picturing how this will look to other people. There will be an investigation, I know there will—a woman is dead. There is no going back from that. There will be questions, and inquiries, and they will want to know what each of us did and when. I have to do the right thing, for when the time comes.

It is odd walking down to the lodge on my own—I feel so alone, as if I might be the only person left on Earth.

The air in the lodge feels stale, trapped, and in spite of myself I hold my breath, almost expecting to see Felicity sweeping through the rooms, her long hair trailing behind her, her arms outstretched to me. It strikes me how much I would love someone to put their arms around me, the feel of another person's body around mine. I want to call my grandmother, to be with people who know me, really know me, to be in a place I feel truly safe. But, Felicity doesn't come. Nobody does.

In the hallway, I look around for a landline, but the dead-eyed photos of the animals stare back at me from the walls, giving nothing away. I go through to the dining room—and stop dead in my tracks. I'm not alone, after all.

Hannah is sitting upright at the table, facing away from me. Her blond hair is tied up, hanging neatly down her back, and her shoulders are still, almost rigid. There is something odd, though, about the angle of her neck, and I let out a little cry, the sound strangling in my throat.

"Hannah?"

There is no reply. She doesn't move.

I circle around her, terrified that there is someone in the room with us, my eyes darting from corner to corner, and then I see it—the wound in the center of my friend's chest. Dark and deep. Recent. It looks like she's been stabbed. Blood spreads down her front, sticky and wet, and when I look down I see that it has dripped onto the floor, is beginning to pool at the base of her high wooden chair.

I do rush forward then, I run to her and I press two shaking fingers against her neck, desperately feeling for a pulse even though I know it is fruitless, I can tell by the strange stillness in the room and the way her neck is tilted and the waxy pallor of her skin. On the table in front of her is a cup of coffee—I reach out, touch the china, feel the cold. How long has she been up? Who did this to her?

A sob escapes me, rising up through my chest and bursting out into the room, too loud, too loud. I have to get out of here—I have to go. There is no sign of a weapon near Hannah, which means whoever did this must have taken it with them—and the farther away from the lodges I can get, the safer I will be. A thought hits me—Hannah's phone. Sure enough, I see the shape of it nestled in the front pocket of her shirt, the same one she was wearing yesterday, back when we thought we really were going to go out on safari. Carefully, I ease my fingers into the pocket, wincing as they brush against the blood. My hand catches on something else, and I gasp as the sharp edge slices my finger—Hannah has a long, thin shard of glass in her pocket. I remember the champagne flute breaking, the splinters on the table. She must have gone back, picked one up, hid it here, a secret weapon, without telling me. Drops of blood bloom from the cut on my finger as I slide it into my own pocket, heart thudding, then turn to Hannah's phone. The screen lights up, asking for a passcode or a thumbprint, and before I can think about it for too long, I pick up my friend's hand, press her thumb onto the roundel, watch as the phone whirs to life. Tears roll down my face as the picture of Chris and Max appears, their faces pressed together, beaming out at me, oblivious. I cannot stay here any longer.

As quietly as I can, I leave Hannah, let myself out of the lodge, and begin to run. Even though I haven't eaten for hours and still feel exhausted from a night spent sleeping sitting up, once I begin to move the adrenaline hits me, and the fight or flight instinct kicks in. Whoever did this to my friends is still out there. I clench my fists together, feel the wetness in my palm—my finger is still bleeding; a thick splash of blood falls to the ground and I put the cut quickly to my mouth, trying to stem the flow.

I feel awful for suspecting Hannah last night—that I didn't comfort her properly after what happened, didn't suggest we stay together and wait the long night out. I should never have left her in an unlocked lodge while I barricaded myself in the safety of the bathroom. Selfish Grace. Again.

I'm running so fast that I haven't looked where I'm going—I've ducked down off the walkways, into the long grasses below that lead out onto the plains. Glancing behind me, I see the lodges retreating farther into the distance and know I should have gone out toward the main gates, back the way we came, but perhaps that's what someone would expect me to do. Maybe this way, I'm safer.

The sun is up now, and despite the fact that it's still so early in the morning the warmth of the day is coming already— oppressive and thick as icing in my mouth. I have no water, nothing to eat. I try to run faster, but the grasses are whipping against my bare lower legs, stinging my calves like tiny knives. My chest is beginning to burn—I'm no runner, that was always my flatmate Rosie's complaint about me—she'd look at me disapprovingly as I sat on the sofa, used to tell me to come out with her for a jog. *You'll feel better, Grace!* I wish I'd joined her now—wish I was better equipped. Sweat is beginning to pour down my back, pooling at the base of my spine and the nape of my neck. As I reach the edge of the plain, I stop, gasping for breath, bent over. What am I thinking, running out here into the wild? My muscles tense beneath my leggings; I keep expecting the roar of an animal, the soft tread of a predator, and wonder whether I have simply swapped one danger for another. I have to keep going.

I look to my left and see the swell of the river—surely, if I follow it for long enough I will come to a main road, to something or someone that can help me. I check Hannah's phone—13 percent battery. There's a new message, too, and at first I avert my eyes, wanting to respect her privacy even now, but it's on the screen and I can't help myself from reading. It's from Chris: *Got your message. Have you talked to them yet? Call me, Hannah, please. I'm worried.*

I stare at the words, confused. What was she going to talk to us about? *Them* can surely only mean us—Alice and me. Did Hannah know something more about why we're here than she let on? I think of the fortune-teller, the strange little notes. *One of you knows why you're here.* But none of us gave up our secrets. And now two of us are dead.

PART TWO

Chapter Fourteen

Felicity

I'll always regret the night I introduced Nathaniel to the girls, because it was the night that our friendship imploded.

Letting them meet him was my first big mistake.

It was February, and London was cold. At night, I pushed my feet up against Nate's, loving the way our toes nestled together like kindling in a fire. We'd only been together for two months, well, nine weeks, really, but already, I was in at the deep end. Sinking fast.

He made me laugh, is what it was—he was clever and witty and when he looked at me it was as though he could see right through to my soul. *You're so dramatic, Felicity*, my mother used to say before she died. I wonder what she'd have made of Nate—in my dreams, she loves him just as much as I do.

It helped that he was beautiful—dark hair that curled around his ears, bright blue eyes that made me feel as though I was falling whenever I looked into them. Like staring at the sun; almost unbearably painful after a while. He was tall, classically handsome—like everyone I dated, I suppose you could say, but

Nathaniel was different from the very beginning. He saw me, in a way that nobody had since my mother. Certainly not my father, who after my operation seemed to shrink further away from me, as if looking at me only served to amplify the gravity of what he had done. I longed for the days when he looked at me properly, when he pulled me close to him, told me I was special. But they were fading, and Nathaniel became the only one who could really see me for who I was.

Or at least, that's what I thought. *We all see what we want to see, Felicity*, I was told afterward, but I didn't find the phrase especially comforting.

He had strong hands—he was a doctor, and I used to imagine how reassuring it must be for his patients to see him approaching, to feel one of those hands pressed against a hot, feverish forehead. I was almost jealous of them when he told me about his day. I found myself wishing he'd do that to me, which sounds ridiculous, I know. I hate illness, have been terrified of it since it took my mother, so to wish it upon myself simply to be close to Nate was undoubtedly insane.

The night we first met, just before Christmas, I knew I stood no chance—I'd found my version of perfection, and everyone else's, if they were honest with themselves. Think about it—who *doesn't* want a handsome, clever, funny doctor for a boyfriend? Anyone who says they don't is lying, and believe me, I know a liar when I see one. Christmas is, I suppose, always a particularly funny time for me, because it's when my mother died, so on the evening I met him you could say that I was almost looking for something to happen—something to distract me from memories. I know some people would use the word *vulnerable*, but that's not the term I would choose.

I didn't introduce Nate to anyone for another week after we passed our two-month anniversary. The girls were getting desperate, clamoring to meet him, moaning how weird it was of me to keep him secret for so long when I usually introduced men to them after about an hour. I had to. They were my board of directors, my litmus test. If they didn't like him, there was something wrong and he was out before he could protest—that was usually how it went. Grace, Alice, and Hannah were my closest friends, the only people I trusted—and I relied on them to tell me when my judgment was off. Which, let's be honest, it often was. I didn't have a mother to warn me anymore, to try to stop me from making the same mistakes as she did, and so I relied on the three of them more than ever, I suppose. I trusted them.

That's the second mistake I made.

So, I guess what I'm saying is, I *did* know why I was waiting to introduce them to Nathaniel—I simply couldn't bear the idea of them finding fault with him. I'd never felt like this before, was scared by the depth of my feelings. Without anyone to pull me back, I absorbed myself in his world—his friends, his views, his way of life, and I knew that by the time he finally met my friends, it would be too late. I wouldn't hear a word against him. Mistake number three.

That final mistake: that was the one that broke us.

Chapter Fifteen

February, two years before Botswana

Grace

I'm applying lipstick in the mirror of the toilets in the Red Lion, peering at my reflection through the cracked screen. This place is becoming a bit of a dive, we all know it is, and yet we continue to come here, seeking out the ghosts of our youth in the sticky tables, the familiar bar staff, and the memories. It's where we always reconvene for moments that feel significant—where we huddled together, the four of us, before we went off to university, our last night of innocence before the madness of freshers' week and the influx of new people, none of whom managed to dilute our friendship. It's where Hannah had her first kiss, with Toby Davies back when we were fourteen, and where Alice smoked her first cigarette—one of many, as it turned out. It's where we first got drunk, because it was the only place that would serve us, a Richmond institution that didn't care too much about fake ID or school uniforms—the Red Lion only cared about money. And so we came, and kept coming, and now we come again, as twenty-eight-year-old women who really should know better.

"Grace? What are you doing in there? Flick will be here

any second!" Alice bursts into the Ladies, trailing a cloud of perfume in her wake, the strong, memorable scent she always wears. She's been drinking white wine, and her movements are loose, sloppy as she puts an arm around me, presses her face close to mine. Her cheeks are cold—we're sitting outside, and the outdoor heaters are temperamental, to say the least. But Alice insists on it so that she can smoke, and none of us argues with her. Besides, it's quieter out there—we can hear each other speak, which is what Hannah said she wanted.

"Han okay? Is Tom here yet?" I ask, pressing my lips together carefully, hating the way the dry flakes of skin make me look old, older than the girl I feel inside. I tend not to wear lipstick that often anymore—I don't like drawing attention to myself, but tonight I forced myself to be brave.

"She's fine, in a bit of a grump," Alice says, waving a hand airily, but I frown, not quite believing her. There is something strange about Hannah tonight; she's barely drinking, and seems incredibly subdued given this is the night we've all been waiting for—the night we meet Felicity's new man. Alice ignores the question about Tom, her boyfriend, as if I haven't mentioned him at all.

"Okay," I say, "sorry, I'm ready. Let's go back outside. You shouldn't have just left Han on her own!"

"I need a wee!" Alice says tipsily, and she goes into a cubicle, leaving me standing there. I laugh at the sound of her unbuttoning her jeans ("God, I'm too fat for these!"—she isn't, she's never been overweight) and tell her I'll see her back outside in the pub garden.

I say garden; it's more of a courtyard, really—stone flags with a little cobbled section which hints at the history of the pub, the age of it. Built in the 1700s, the pub's courtyard is an enclosed space, backing out onto the more modern car park, hardly glamorous but just around the corner from where we grew up and from where Hannah and Felicity still live. My parents have since moved away, over to Surrey, and I live farther east now, in Peckham, while Alice and Tom live over in Hackney. It's a trek to get across to Richmond, but Hannah has promised the three of us—me, Alice, and Tom if he turns up—can stay with her and Chris, sleep on the sofa and a double airbed. Already, she seems more grown up than the rest of us; always has, probably always will. I picture her and Chris in their cozy, adult life, with silver-framed pictures on the wall, and I cannot imagine myself ever getting to that stage. It's taken me long enough to move on from what happened to me last year; fortnightly therapy on the NHS, sessions in which I try to feel whole again. I've never told my friends what happened, not after the way my parents reacted, and I've never so much as smiled at a guy since. Dating hasn't exactly been top of my radar, so God alone knows how I'd be able to progress toward something more, something deeper.

I find Hannah where we left her, sitting alone outside under the orange glow of one of the heaters, a red tartan blanket wrapped around her knees. That's another good thing about coming to the Red Lion; they give you free blankets when it's the wintertime, and they do unlimited Aperol Spritzes in the summer, heavy on the Aperol, less so on the spritz. It's a nice place to be—it feels like coming home, without the presence of my parents. Nostalgia settles in my throat at the sight of Han, huddled up on her own, her bum probably growing cold and numb on the wooden seat, like mine always used to when we were teenagers.

"No sign of Flick yet?" I plonk myself down next to Hannah, reach for the gin and tonic I was drinking before I went to the bathroom—disappointingly, there's not as much left as I thought. There's no answer from Hannah and I nudge her gently with my elbow.

"Han? You okay?"

"Hmm?"

She looks up at me, as though only just noticing that I've come back from the toilets, and I feel a flicker of alarm. There's something off about her gaze, as though she's not really with it, she's lost in a world of her own.

"Sorry, sorry," she says, "yeah, I'm fine, are you? Where's Alice?"

"She's just in the loo," I say, picking up the edge of her blanket and pulling it gently my way so that it covers me too. It's a chilly night out here, but there's still something nice about the air—the freshness of the cold, and the gin is doing a good job of warming up my insides. I take another sip, the feel of it tangy on my tongue. They do all different flavors here—blackberry, lemon, even rhubarb. *What will they think of next?* I hear my mother say in my ear.

"Right, right," Hannah says, and then, impatiently, "come on, Flick, where are you?"

"She'll be here any minute," I say, smiling at her. "What's up with you tonight? Why don't you have a drink?"

"All right, then, I'll get one," she says suddenly, as though making a split decision. "Watch my bag, will you? Back in a minute." She stands up, the blanket falling abruptly off her knees. I look up at her when she says, "D'you want anything?" but it's almost like an afterthought.

"Another gin, please," I say, "just regular flavor. No need to push the boat out." I grin at her, trying to make her laugh, but it doesn't work; she just spins on her heel and disappears through the back door of the pub. There's definitely something up with her tonight—I resolve to ask her when she comes back out.

I look around the courtyard, my breath misting the air as I exhale. I wonder what Felicity's new boyfriend will be like— we've been waiting weeks to meet him. I'm happy for her—she sounded so excited on the phone earlier, giggling like she was twenty again. I haven't heard her so happy in ages, not since her mum died. My own mother always says that Felicity needs someone to look after her, to take her under their wing—*poor little motherless mite*. I bite my tongue when she says that.

Sometimes, no mother is better than a bad one. A mother like mine, who doesn't believe her own daughter, is a mother not worth having.

"Grace!" And just like that, she is here, bursting through the doors of the pub and out into the courtyard, spilling light from inside along with her. Felicity's hair is loose, flowing golden down her shoulders, and she's wearing a white fur coat flecked with light brown. Briefly, she reminds me of an ice princess, or something out of Narnia. I half expect to see snow fall in her wake, for her to reach out and offer me dusty Turkish Delight.

There's a figure behind her, someone I can't make out, and at first I think it's Alice, finally back from the bathroom, but then Felicity turns and reaches out a hand, grabs the person behind her and thrusts him forward, into the light of the heaters where I'm sitting. I stand up, hastily putting my almost-empty glass of gin down.

"This is Nathaniel," she tells me, beaming at me, her lips pink and glossy, her hand now on the small of her new boyfriend's back. I feel a jolt at the name, but ignore it—it's a common name, I'm just being silly.

"Nathaniel," she says, "this is Grace, one of my best and oldest friends. I'm so happy you guys can finally meet!"

His face is cast into the light; the bright blue eyes, the inky black of his hair, the sharp jut of his cheekbones, and I almost stumble backward in shock. My breath catches in my throat and I feel dizzy, sick at the sight of his face after all this time in which I've tried my hardest to forget. Blood beats in my ears; my whole body feels like it's pulsing.

Not such a common name, after all.

"What's the matter, Grace? God, you look like you've seen a ghost," Felicity says, immediately concerned, but I can't answer her; I sink back down onto the wooden pub bench, my legs shaking, and just for a second, I close my eyes. The small, smoky courtyard spins around me and I'm back there, with him, pain bursting through me, repeating a chant to myself: *hold on, hold on, hold on.*

"Grace? Grace?" Felicity is saying but I can't answer her, I can't speak, and I can't look up at him, see the face I have tried to block out of my nightmares.

This can't be happening.

Alice

Alice is smoking another cigarette as she comes out of the Ladies, making her way through the pack, furious with Tom for not showing his face yet. He promised he'd be here by eight, but, surprise surprise, she is bottom of his priority list once again. She's drunk too much already, she knows because she almost fell asleep on the toilet in there, but at least they're staying over at Hannah's tonight and she hasn't got to trek all the way back to bloody Hackney.

Were are you? she texts Tom, her fingers blurring stickily over the keypad, and she sends it before realizing she's spelled *where* wrong. Ugh. He'll know she's drunk now. Another reason to tell her off. Maybe she deserves it.

Outside, the cold air hits her and for a moment Alice thinks it's sobered her up. The courtyard seems to have gotten busier—a group of teenagers is clustered over in the corner, their laughter drifting toward her on the February night air— at least they're far enough west that they can't be anyone from the senior school—and a couple sit on one of the round tables, kissing intermittently, their fingers entwined. She feels a little pull in her stomach. Why can't she and Tom be like that?

"Alice!" She turns to see Felicity waving at her—ah good, she's here. Next to her is a tall guy, God, he's attractive, the thought registers with Alice almost without her meaning it to. Dark hair, broad shoulders, a big smile that he's currently beaming toward her. Trust Felicity to have found someone who looks like that. Alice pastes on her best smile and sashays over to them, ignoring the way her jeans are digging into her flesh, dropping her ciggie and grinding it out quickly with the heel of her boot. These little gray ones are new and already rubbing her heels—bloody things. When will she learn not to wear new shoes on a night out before trialing them around the house first?

"This is Nathaniel," Flick says, and he steps toward Alice, a hand outstretched.

"Very formal," she giggles, thrusting her own hand out to meet his, stumbling slightly on her stupid heeled boots.

"I'm Alice," she says, "Flick's oldest friend. It's so nice to meet you—we've heard a lot about you."

"All good things, I hope? And please, call me Nate," Nathaniel says, which is a fairly standard response to be fair, but he's got a lovely voice. His hand is warm and dry in hers, and Alice feels a flicker of disappointment when he lets go, which of course she quashes as quickly as it came. She's just a bit drunk, that's all. No big deal. She is used to herself by now.

We all have our foibles.

"All good things," Alice clarifies, smiling at Felicity who is hovering next to Nathaniel like an anxious bird. She's never normally anxious, or at least if she is, she doesn't let it show. She must really like him.

"Nice coat, Flick," Alice says, nodding at Felicity's furry new number, and she preens a bit, stroking it with her left hand while the other remains attached to Nathaniel—or should she say Nate.

"Where are the others?" Alice asks, peering behind them to the empty picnic bench, which contains Grace and Hannah's handbags but no sign of the girls.

"I think Hannah must be at the bar." Felicity shrugs. "And Grace went to the bathroom just now, said she wasn't feeling well all of a sudden."

"Oh," Alice says, wrong-footed; she doesn't want the night to end yet, Tom still hasn't made an appearance, and besides, it's only just gone eight fifteen. She's enjoying herself too much for everyone to have to bail early because of Grace.

"I'm sure they'll be back," Felicity says. "Shall we just sit down?" She gestures to the bench and Alice laughs; she seems nervous, somehow, not quite her usual confident self. She keeps darting little glances over at Nathaniel, who meets every one of them with a reassuring smile. Wow. She has got it bad.

They sit down; Alice budges the girls' handbags up a bit, moves an empty glass out of the way, and sits opposite the pair of them, fumbling for another cigarette, needing another nicotine hit already. Felicity and Nathaniel are both smiling at her, their eyes wide, their cheeks flushed with that giddy, strange look people get when they're in love. She wonders when the last time Tom looked at her like that was, and finds she cannot remember. The thought makes her feel unbearably sad.

"Nathaniel is a doctor," Felicity tells Alice, which she already knows, but she forces herself to smile at him, pull herself together. Tom will be here soon and then they'll straighten everything out, have a talk about it all, the Hackney flat, their relationship and the way it feels like it's floundering even though Alice cannot put her finger on why. Felicity is her friend, she's excited; Alice can't let anything get in the way of them meeting Nate when Flick is so clearly besotted.

"Do you specialize at all?" Alice asks him politely, and he nods, tells her that he's an A&E doctor, specializing in major trauma.

"God," she says, "that must be full-on." Felicity frowns slightly and Alice can almost sense her nerves radiating across the pub table; how badly she wants them to get along. Interesting that Felicity has picked a man with the same occupation as her father, she thinks. Michael is a doctor too, though he retired early after Diane died.

"Amazing, though," Alice says quickly, "doing a real job, you know, one that makes a difference."

Nathaniel smiles, and Alice can't help noticing the way his mouth crinkles at the sides, the way his eyes absorb her, as though he's genuinely really interested in what she is saying. It's the way she wishes Tom would look at her.

"Aren't you a teacher?" he asks, and she coughs slightly on her cigarette, lifts a hand to waft the smoke away from them. She ends up blowing it toward them by accident; Felicity coughs dramatically, but Nathaniel pretends not to even notice. He has manners, too, then.

"Well, yes," she says, "I am. Sorry about the smoke." Alice looks away, embarrassed.

"Nothing more worthwhile than education," he tells her, clasping his hands together on the table, nodding as though to emphasize how strongly he agrees with his own words, and Felicity beams. Alice can't quite work out whether it's her she's proud of, or him.

"Isn't Tom coming along tonight, Al?" Felicity asks, and Alice rolls her eyes at her.

"He's late, I guess."

The tip of her cigarette burns orange in the gloom.

There's a brief pause, and Nathaniel must catch the flicker of something in Alice's words, because he stands up, clears his throat, and offers to get them some drinks.

"That would be great," Alice says, "thank you." She fumbles for her debit card but he waves her away, insisting that these are on him. A good job too, seeing as, as usual, Alice is broke. They've just paid the rent and it always leaves her a little short, every single month. She slides the plastic back into her wallet, breathes a sigh of relief.

"Wouldn't be making a very good first impression on Felicity's friends if I didn't even buy them a drink, now would I?" he says, smiling down on them. And then he's gone, and both of them twist their heads to watch him walk away, into the pub. *Like puppets on strings*, Alice thinks.

Felicity is on her immediately and her enthusiasm makes Alice laugh, cracking her grumpy exterior at Tom's continued and persistent absence.

"So?" she says, her hair swinging down around her face as she leans in close to Alice, grabs her hands. "What do you think?"

Alice grins at her. "He's lovely, Flick, you know he is. Not to mention bloody gorgeous."

She smiles, self-satisfied, the cat that got the cream.

"I really like him, Alice," she says, and her voice sounds suddenly serious, surprisingly so.

"That's great!" Alice says, wanting to lighten the mood again, and Felicity nods, but her eyes are far away, as though she is lost in thought.

"I want it to be different this time, Al, I really do. I think this is it, you know."

Alice resists the urge to snort; Felicity has a habit of being dramatic, and this would not be the first time she's pronounced undying love to someone she's only known for a matter of weeks. Still, she's her friend, so Alice indulges her. What's the harm, really? She ignores the tiny voice in her head that says she ought to know how much harm the wrong relationship can cause.

"Well, maybe it is, maybe it isn't, Flick. He seems great, really, he does, but you know what you get like." She means it kindly. "Don't get—carried away."

Alice expects her friend to roll her eyes and laugh, groan that she knows Alice is right, that she does tend to throw herself headfirst into love affairs, but she doesn't. She frowns at her, and Alice feels her fingers stiffen slightly in her own.

"This is different, Alice, really it is. I'm in love. He loves me too, I know he does." There is a note of uncertainty in her voice; perhaps cruelly, Alice picks up on it. But she doesn't *mean* it cruelly—she is just attuned to Flick and her feelings; after all, they have known each other for so long. Alice doesn't want to see her get hurt. After what happened to her poor mum, she deserves to be happy.

"Has he said so?" Alice keeps her voice light so that she won't read anything in it; airy, judgment-free, but perhaps because of the wine she's already drunk she doesn't quite manage it, and it comes out sounding mistrusting, as though Alice doesn't quite believe her.

Felicity reddens, just a little, under the glow of the heater. And then it goes off, plunging them into a chill, and Alice has to remove a hand from underneath hers to reach out and press the button that turns it back on.

"Well, not in so many words, not exactly, but I know he does, Al. I've never felt anything like it before—this thing between us, it's electric. I feel like I'm fully awake for the very first time, you know, as if everything is heightened. The world is in Technicolor! You must know what I mean."

Alice doesn't tell her that she is merely spouting clichés, phrases her Year Six English class could dream up. She just squeezes Felicity's hands and tells her that it's wonderful, that she's so glad Flick has met someone so perfect. She tries not to sound sarcastic.

"He really is perfect, you know." Felicity moves away from Alice, runs a pale, elegant hand through her long hair, presses her lips together. She's wearing a ruby red–colored lipstick; one of the expensive Chanel ones, Alice bets. She looks utterly, inconceivably beautiful, and for a moment Alice feels it; the horrible smack of jealousy, the sickly worm of it writhing in her stomach. She's right, to all intents and purposes—Nate does seem perfect. He's here, isn't he? It's more than Tom's managed; Tom, her boyfriend of two and a half years, whose only duty is to be here with her, and he can't even manage that.

Speak of the devil. As if on cue, a shadow is thrown over them both, and Alice looks up to see Tom standing over them, wearing his hoodie and tracksuit bottoms. He'd promised her that he'd come here straight from work, but clearly there has been time to go home first. He knows she hates that hoodie—he looks like a sulky child, a fifteen-year-old compared to Nate's shirt and slightly loosened tie.

"Tom!" Felicity squeaks, and she stands up and throws her arms around him, obviously overcompensating for Alice's own stony silence and lack of greeting. She watches the way Felicity presses herself against him, her curves fitting his body perfectly before breaking away.

"How are you?" she says. "We thought you weren't coming!"

"Held up at work," he says, and he grins but it doesn't meet his eyes. "Hi, Alice."

Alice takes a deep breath, *be nice, be nice*. She wanted to make things right between them and here he is, he's right in front of her, but somehow all the rage she's been feeling over the last few weeks is just bubbling up inside of her. She knows it will make her say something she'll regret so she stands and gives him a quick kiss, just a peck on the lips, before telling them both that she's going to find Grace.

"Pint while you're at it?" Tom says, taking her seat and smiling broadly at Felicity. The two of them have always gotten on well, but let's be honest, what man doesn't like Flick? Something cold curdles in Alice's stomach and she turns away from them both, leaves them in the courtyard, the sound of their easy chatter ringing in her ears as she quietly disappears.

She's become quite good at that.

Hannah

Having almost made her way to the front of the throng of people at the bar, Hannah is surprised to see Grace by the door. She looks as though she's about to leave; her coat is on, and she's moving quickly, pushing her way through the throng of people—this pub has always been popular, especially on a Friday night when everyone's making up for the lost time that is dry January—and her mouth is set in a thin, determined line.

Hannah glances at the bar—she is so close to the front, and she's been waiting for almost ten minutes. The barman nodded at her a few seconds ago—an *I'm coming to you next* gesture. But Grace looks upset; she can't just leave her.

"Grace!" Hannah tries to shout across to her, but the Red Lion is too big and the sound of her voice gets completely absorbed in the loud music the pub is playing, the bubble of people's laughter and chatter. The woman next to her looks irritated, probably because of Hannah bellowing in her ear, and wincing, she gives up the thought of a drink and makes her way out of the bar queue, to where Grace is standing, her repeated requests for the man in front of her to move falling on deaf ears.

Hannah catches her by the arm.

"Grace?"

She spins, and the sight of her face up close shocks Hannah. She is pale, and Hannah notices that she is sort of quivering, her body vibrating against hers very slightly, almost imperceptible if you weren't one of her oldest friends, if you didn't know her quite as well as Hannah does. Beads of glistening sweat line her top lip, her anxiety physically pushing itself out of her body.

"Where are you going?" Hannah says, confused, and Grace makes a face at her.

"Sorry," she says, "I'm actually not feeling well. I think I'm going to head home." Her eyes look watery, as if she has been crying.

Hannah blinks at her, one hand on her stomach. It's instinctive, somehow, even though she knows it's pointless now.

"To Peckham? But, Grace, that will take you ages. I thought you were going to stay over at mine. You and Allie."

She doesn't say anything, Hannah can almost see her mind frantically trying to think of something to say, another excuse. She touches her nose, licks her lips. She can tell when Grace is lying; always has been able to, right from when they were young. A vein stands out in her forehead, a fine blue line bisecting the skin.

"Come over here," Hannah says, concerned, trying to push her own problems aside for a minute, leading Grace over to the corner, near the fire, where it's a little bit quieter. Someone has just put a log on; the flames crackle and spit, and Hannah watches as an ember lands on the scuffed wooden floorboards, flares briefly, then dies.

"What's the matter?" she asks Grace, her voice low, trying to maintain eye contact even though she seems to deliberately be looking anywhere but at Hannah.

"I don't feel well, Han, I told you. Sorry, sorry to be a downer but I think I'm coming down with something."

"Really?" Hannah puts a hand to her forehead; she does feel a bit cold and clammy. "Well, look, shall I give you my keys? Chris is in anyway, he can let you in if you like?"

The thought of Grace and Chris making awkward small talk in her kitchen almost makes Hannah laugh, but she pushes the idea away. She hasn't made up the sofa or the camp bed yet, was planning to do it when they all got in, but she could text Chris and ask him to do it. Not that he will be in the mood after what's happened, but he's bound to play along, sort her out.

"No," Grace says quickly, and Hannah feels momentarily rebuffed—is the thought of spending time with her partner really that bad?

"Sorry," Grace says, "I just really need to be at home, Han. Could you do me a favor? Could you get my handbag? I left it outside with the others."

Hannah stares at her, incredulous. "What? Why don't you

just come and get it quickly, it'll take two seconds? Don't you want your phone, your stuff?"

Grace shrugs, and when Hannah peers more closely at her, to her horror she sees that her friend is almost on the verge of tears. Droplets glisten on her eyelashes, threatening to spill down her cheeks. There is definitely something Grace isn't telling her.

Hannah feels a wave of sympathy for her, despite her own feelings tonight, and she puts out a hand and touches Grace's arm, trying to pull her toward her.

"Oh, Grace, what is it? You can tell me, really, you know you can. What's up?" It's almost exactly what Hannah is longing one of them to ask her, but none of them has.

"Nothing," she mumbles, but it's pointless; her face is ashen, coated now with a sheen of perspiration. Hannah has never seen her like this.

"Well, then, don't go," Hannah says, smiling at her, trying another technique. Tough love, as her grandmother used to call it. "Felicity wants us all here, you know she does. You haven't even talked to her new boyfriend yet. You know, the sexy doctor." A pause. She waits.

"Come on, you know she'd do it for you," Hannah says, and she can see the guilt in Grace's face, the struggle between doing what she wants and being there for one of her best friends. As Hannah waits a sound begins behind her, and she looks to see a young mother, a baby in her arms, her face harassed as she rocks her child, whispering to him, begging him to stop crying, to please stop crying. Hannah's insides tighten, and around her, the pub seems to blur a little bit so that all she can see is this woman, this woman and her child, as if the two of them are the only people in the entire bar. The beams of the pub seem to close in around her, the space growing smaller and smaller. The baby in the stranger's arms stiffens and for a moment is silent, but just as Hannah sees her features begin to relax, the child begins again, his mouth a gaping dark wound in his face. Wet tears are puddling on his little yellow Babygro; his cheeks are soaked. The woman catches Hannah staring at her and mouths an apology, then freezes as she sees her expression. She's expecting Hannah to wave it away, no doubt, to smile reassuringly and tell her they've all been there, that universal understanding between women with screaming babies, but Hannah doesn't. Instead, she glares at the stranger, furious. What is she doing, bringing her newborn to a crowded, dank London pub? She should be at home, looking after it, rejoicing in her luck.

Something inside Hannah unlocks.

She needs a drink.

She seizes her chance as Grace hesitates, taking her arm and beginning to tug her back toward the bar. Hannah wants all at once to drown out the sound of the incessant crying, and the relentless buzz of her own thoughts that are growing louder and louder the more the child screams.

Grace looks defeated and small as Hannah drags her to the bar, but she ignores it, beaming at Grace as she whips out her credit card.

"Two gin and tonics?" Hannah says, and Grace nods mutely as Hannah flashes a smile at the barman. It's a relief to be away from the mother; she feels her shoulders loosen. She shouldn't have looked at her like that. Judged her so quickly. She's probably a wonderful mum. It isn't her fault that she has everything Hannah wants but hasn't got. It isn't anyone's fault but her own.

The gin and tonics arrive and Grace takes hers immediately, her fingers grasping the bowl of the glass like a child picking up a sippy cup.

"Blimey," Hannah says, as Grace tips back her neck and drinks, in long, urgent gulps, and she sees Hannah looking and frowns.

"The only way I can stay is by getting really drunk," she says, and Hannah thinks she's joking, but then sees that her mouth is set in a straight, grim line, and she's already flagging down the barman, asking for a refill even though Hannah herself hasn't had the chance to even take a sip of her drink.

Hannah's phone buzzes in her pocket and she fishes it out, sees Chris's name lighting up the screen.

Are you OK? Please can we talk about it?

And then another text, straight afterward.

This is happening to me too. You can't just shut me out, Hannah.

And a third, this time with only a singular word.

Please.

Hannah ignores them all and reaches for her glass.

"Well," she says to Grace, "cheers to that, eh?"

Chapter Sixteen

Alice

Nathaniel and Tom are sitting next to each other, with Flick and Alice opposite, laughing away together as if they are all on some big, fun double date. It would only be if you looked closely that you'd see the chinks in their armor, the cracks in the picture. The way Tom won't really meet Alice's eye; the way Nathaniel laughs at her jokes but her own boyfriend doesn't; the way Felicity keeps checking to see whether Nate and Alice are getting along. The speed at which Alice drinks her glass of wine, and then another, and then another, until the edges of the world rub off. Nate brought a bottle back from the bar, which was probably a mistake, though very generous of him; Felicity beamed when he brandished it.

At some point, Felicity and Nathaniel get up to go to the bar again—though God knows why they both need to go, perhaps their oxygen runs out if they happen to get separated—and Tom and Alice are left alone. He's still on his first pint, sipping it miserably, and Alice feels a rush of spitefulness toward him.

"Are you ever going to look at me properly?" she says to him, hating the way her voice sounds, and he lets out a little laugh, short and sharp like a bark.

"I don't need to look at you to know that you're pissed."

She blinks at him, slow and stupid. "I'm not," she says, but the words are pointless; she knows it, he knows it. He looks up at her then, finally meets her eye, and Alice feels the anger deflate out of her like a balloon, sadness settling heavily on her in its place.

How did they get here, the two of them?

Tom and Alice have been together, on and off, since they were twenty-five. She met him on a night out, fell for his acerbic sense of humor, his bright, beady eyes, the way his face grew all animated when he talked about hockey. He used to play at a pretty high level, but a knee injury put paid to that about eighteen months ago. Sometimes, Alice wonders if that's when their problems started, but other times, darker times, 3 a.m. times, she wonders if the problem is just him: the way he is built. The nasty streak that she knows is always there, but tries to pretend to herself is a figment of her imagination.

She didn't notice it at first, obviously. The plea of all women, everywhere. And a lot of the time, Alice thinks it *is* her fault—she is too annoying, too loud, too earnest, too much. Too, too, too. A superlative sort of person. But when he tells her this, or rather, insinuates it, it confuses her—she'd thought he liked the fact that she is a teacher; when they first met he told her a story about how much he'd loved his teachers as a boy; the PE teacher who first handed him a hockey stick, the math teacher who told him he was smarter than 90 percent of the rest of the class. Little things that stuck in his mind. *Someday, the kids you teach will be remembering you to their partners like this,* he said one night, his fingers playing with Alice's dark hair, and she'd smiled at the thought of it, felt proud. He told her he liked that she cared about things, that she wasn't a pushover.

Now, the funny thing is that she *is* a pushover—to him, at least. Alice spends a lot of time walking on eggshells, scared to call him out on the things that bother her—the fact that he's late tonight, the fact that he has stopped visiting her parents with her, the fact that he deliberately doesn't laugh at her jokes, choosing instead to press his lips together, determined not to let a drop of approval out. But she knows what will happen if she does speak up—he will tell her she is being oversensitive, demanding, unfair. He will say he's been working all day and that she doesn't understand that because her school day finishes at half past three in the afternoon and so she has bags of time to while away, of course she does. And then Alice gets to the stage where she thinks he is probably right—he does work hard, she is a needy girlfriend, she does make his life harder than it needs to be. He has told her he loves her—why doesn't she believe him?

And then there is the flat. They currently rent a flat together in Hackney, and for ages now they have been discussing the idea of buying somewhere. Renting is throwing your money away, Alice's dad says disapprovingly, which is easy for him to say because her parents bought their Richmond house in the eighties then sold it last year for triple the original price. It's easy for her dad to tell her that renting is pointless when he and her mother now live down in Cornwall, where a three-bedroom cottage costs less than a grotty little one bed in Hackney Wick. Still, Alice had listened to them—she badgered Tom about it, repeated her dad's words, told him that they ought to think about buying somewhere. We. It wasn't as if she could afford it on her own.

So they look at flats and they hate them and they make pros and cons lists and they continue to live in their rented flat, throwing away almost £1,000 a month because they can't find anywhere decent to live that is remotely within their price bracket. It continues, on and on in an endless loop of snarky comments and subtle words, until sometimes, in the early dawn hours, Alice dares to ask herself why she is thinking of buying a flat with this man anyway, when so often she feels like he hates her.

But she doesn't say any of these thoughts out loud—she can't. She loves him. That is the thing, always the thing.

"Alice?" Tom is staring at her now, still nursing the last few dregs of his beer, and Alice shakes her head to clear it, like a dog getting water out of its ears.

She decides to be a grown-up; forces herself to smile.

"How was work?" she says to him, and he shrugs morosely.

"It was fine, I guess."

Alice waits for him to ask her how school was, but he doesn't.

"It's nice to see the girls," she says, and then, meekly, "thank you for making time to come."

"I said I would, didn't I?" he says, and she nods; he did, after all. He's only stating a fact.

"Felicity seems keen on the new guy," he says, and Alice is momentarily surprised; he isn't one to comment on her friends' love lives very often. But it's good, it's good he's showing an interest. Isn't it?

"Mmm," she says, a bit hesitant, unsure where the conversation is going but relieved that they aren't snapping at each other, at least. She wants to take another sip of her drink but worries about what he will say. She should've just drunk more before he got here, she thinks sourly. She'll know for next time.

"You seem quite keen on him too," Tom says, and the words hit her with a dull, disappointing thud: ah, so *that's* where this is going. He isn't looking at her as he says it, he's looking down into his drink, churlishly swirling the remnants of beer around. Alice watches the amber liquid churn, counting from one to ten in her head, willing herself not to get upset, not to say anything that might make this situation worse. Sometimes, she can snap him out of these moods, remind him why he loves her, make him laugh, or just soften. Occasionally, that happens without her realizing; something in him will alter and Alice won't quite know why, she will just breathe an inward sigh of relief that it has.

"Tom," she says gently, and she lays her fingers flat on the table, feels the tiny splinters of the damp wood under her fingers. She could slide her hand across to his, unwrap his fingers from around the glass, squeeze them in hers. She thinks about doing this, but doesn't.

"The way you're looking at him. It's embarrassing. I don't know why you were so desperate for me to come here tonight if you'd planned to spend the whole evening flirting with your best friend's boyfriend. A man you've literally only just met."

His lip curls slightly as he speaks, and he emphasizes the word *literally*.

Alice says nothing, trying to think. She wants Grace and Hannah to appear back at the table, with their smiles and their warmth, but neither of them does, and everyone else in the courtyard is too far away from them to be able to hear what they are saying. *You're being ridiculous*, Alice thinks, *you don't need* witnesses, *nothing bad is happening to you. It's just your boyfriend, being a little bit jealous, that's all. It's because he loves you. It's all because he cares.*

But she can't shake the feeling that she wishes someone else was around.

"Are you not even going to deny it?" Tom asks her, and this time he does look up, he brushes his hair out of his eyes—it's getting long, Alice thinks absentmindedly, her brain frantically scrambling for something else to think about other than this conversation—and his eyes when they meet hers are like hard, sharp flints in his face. Emotionless.

"Tom," she says, "there's nothing to deny. Of course I'm not flirting with Nathaniel." She pauses, watching his face, waiting for the moment the lines in his forehead ease up and his features settle. "Don't be ridiculous."

It's those words that push him over the edge. *Don't be ridiculous.* She should have known; the minute they are out she is frantically wishing she could retract them, cursing herself for being so stupid—Tom hates to be criticized, and more than anything he hates his intelligence being questioned. *Ridiculous* was a bad choice of word, a very bad choice of word.

"I am not," he hisses, and he leans toward Alice, so that their faces are close together across the pub table, so close that she can see the little dots of red in the corners of his eyes, smell the beer on his breath. "I am not—being—ridiculous."

She doesn't know what it is, whether it's the horrible scent of the alcohol on him, the hint of violence in his words, or the last sips of wine finally hitting her bloodstream, but something inside Alice pushes back at this, a small resistance that forms behind her eyes and takes over her mouth.

"Oh, Tom," she says, "you're being worse than ridiculous now. You're being *stupid*."

Anger flashes in his eyes and before Alice can do anything about it, he reaches out a hand across the table and grabs hold of her upper arm, squeezes it tight, tighter. She gasps, the blood rushing from her face at the shock of it—Tom's never laid a hand on her before, no matter how bad things between them have gotten, words are always his weapon of choice. He's never touched her like this before, and so the feeling of his fingers digging into her flesh is both painful and surprising. Alice looks down at his hand; his knuckles are whitening, and for a second it is as if she is floating, above the table, above the smoky, cold courtyard, above the Red Lion pub and all the memories it holds, and she is looking down on herself and Tom, watching them from the inky, starry sky.

Alice can see the gleam of her hair, the glow of the heaters, and Tom's dark slick of a head, the bagginess of his hoodie on the arm that is outstretched, gripping onto her. Hurting her. *So this is where it starts*, she thinks. The question is, where will it end?

And then she is back in her body and her whole arm is throbbing, and hot, embarrassing tears are pricking at her eyes and Tom is letting go, he has bowed his head, he is muttering something under his breath.

Alice thinks he's saying sorry.

But she is not listening to him now, she is getting to her feet and standing up, a bit wobbly but determined; she doesn't want to be near him, she wants to be on her own.

"Alice," he says, but she doesn't answer, she turns away from him, shaky in her stupid new boots that aren't impressing anyone, and she walks toward the pub, back to the toilets, her arm sore and painful from where he dug his fingers in as hard as he possibly could.

And that's when Alice bumps into Nathaniel.

Grace

"Where have you two been?" Felicity pounces on us at the bar, chinking her glass of prosecco against our G and Ts with a flourish. Trust her to be drinking fizz—for her, tonight is a celebration. The moment when her lover collides with her oldest friends. She doesn't know that I've been plunged into a nightmare—she doesn't know the man she's dating at all.

"There was a long queue for the bar," Hannah says quickly, and I nod, my mouth dry. It seems easier to go along with it than do anything else. My tongue feels too big for my mouth, as though I can't swallow properly, and I am overwhelmed by the absurd feeling that I might choke. I put a hand on the sticky wooden bar, trying to steady myself.

"Are you okay now, Grace?" Felicity asks, peering at me worriedly. "You went a bit weird outside when Nate arrived. Did you feel dizzy? Too much gin?" She laughs, a high, tinkling sound that grates on me.

"She's fine now," Hannah says firmly, and I think about protesting but cannot quite find the energy. I feel as though I am drowning, as if inside I am screaming as loud as I possibly can, but nobody in this entire, packed pub can hear me. Sweat breaks out on my skin.

"So." Felicity leans into us, her expression conspiratorial. Her blond hair falls prettily in front of her face and she pushes it back impatiently. "What do you think of him, Grace? Hannah, are you going to come out and meet him?" She pouts, like a child, and Hannah grins.

"Lead the way."

I am saved from answering the question. I don't know how I would begin to answer it. As we walk to the back door of the pub, I feel as though I'm marching toward my execution; dread makes my legs heavy, but I cannot think of an escape. I have to find a way to talk to Felicity, to tell her the truth. Or perhaps I should tell one of the other girls first, get them on my side? An image of my mother glaring at me comes to my mind—*what will I do if they don't believe me either?*

When we get outside, though, to my intense relief there is no sign of Nathaniel. Instead, we find Tom sitting moodily at the bench on his own, an empty pint glass in front of him, his hood up so that the sight of him is slightly threatening; for a second, it distracts me from the dilemma in my head. He looks up when he sees us, pushes the hood back off his face, and there is something odd in his gaze, a sense of guilt, as though we have just caught him doing something he shouldn't have. I go to my handbag, reassured to find it intact, my hands shaking slightly as I pull it over my shoulder. Hannah can't make me stay here, not with what I know. I need to get away. I have an urge to be back down in my houseshare in Peckham, the duvet pulled firmly over my head, blocking out the world in the way I have tried to do ever since that day, the day I met Nathaniel Archer for the very first time.

"Grace, sit down!" Hannah says, reaching out and grabbing my hand, pulling me down onto the bench next to her. Felicity is looking around anxiously, clearly in search of Nathaniel, and Tom is barely speaking, grunting when Flick asks him where Alice is.

"You're supposed to be my drinking buddy, remember?" Hannah is acting strangely; the alcohol has loosened her and her usually sensible attitude seems to have been laid to rest for the night. Whatever was bothering her earlier has clearly been put to one side; either that, or she is drinking to forget.

I know what that feels like.

"Actually, ladies, I think I'm going to call it a night," Tom says abruptly, standing up and pulling the hood of his sweater back up over his head, the sleeves down over his hands. With his face partially obscured, he looks menacing, and even though I know that this is Tom, Alice's Tom who wouldn't hurt a fly, something stirs within me; a little spin of unease.

Felicity makes a face at him, a sort of pout, tells him not to be silly, that he must stay and catch up with us all. She's always been able to wrap men around her little finger, has Flick, but Tom's face is set, stony. I wonder where Alice is, whether perhaps they've had a row. I've never properly warmed to Tom in the way that Flick and Hannah have, I find there is a kind of darkness to his humor that doesn't sit well with me—a harmless darkness, but there nonetheless. When I picture myself with a man—which I don't do very often now, a sort of shadowy blank appears in my mind when I attempt to—I don't picture myself with someone like Tom. Still, Alice loves him, clearly, and that's all that matters. My opinion of men is no doubt irretrievably warped; Tom is probably lovely and it's just me that can't see it. So what if he's wearing a hoodie—it's a cold night, after all.

"Where's Allie?" Hannah asks drunkenly, and to our surprise Tom just shrugs.

"She'll want to stay out with you guys. Just tell her I've gone, will you?"

"I thought you were going to stay at mine," says Hannah, and Tom ducks his head, doesn't meet her gaze.

"Alice will. Tell her I'll see her in the morning." He pauses, and then as if it's an afterthought, says, "Have fun. Look after her for me, right?"

There is gravel in his voice. And then he is gone, vanishing into the night, and the three of us are left staring at each other.

"Well, he seems a bit pissed off," Felicity says, breaking the silence, and Hannah makes a face, rolls her eyes.

"He can be a bit like that sometimes, I wouldn't worry about it. Allie knows how to handle him by now. She must be inside."

"You didn't tell me what you thought of Nate," Felicity says to me, a dog with a bone. "Quick, before he reappears." She sighs dreamily, like a girl out of a sitcom. "Isn't he gorgeous? Honestly, you guys, I like him so much, it scares me a little. He's so—well, he's just perfect. I can't believe it, really. I have to keep pinching myself." She's looking at me so expectantly, so hopefully, that I almost cannot bear it. My heart begins to accelerate in my chest, making my palms sweat even though the February air is cold, and the later it gets, the icier it feels.

I have to find a way to tell her.

"God, Flick, you really have got it bad," Hannah says, and for a second she looks wistful. "Make the most of it while it lasts, I'd say—once you get into it for the long haul you'll miss the headiness of the first few weeks; believe me, I know. Once you start farting in front of each other and discussing who's going to put the washing away, some of the passion starts to die—it's not me being mean, it's just a fact." Her words are beginning to run together a little bit, sliding into one another like rain into a puddle—drip, drip, drip.

Felicity looks a bit uncomfortable, as though safe in her bubble she doesn't want to hear any of this, but Hannah persists. "And then," she says, taking another sip of her drink, "when you start to talk about kids—well, once you get into that, it becomes a routine—mechanics, something to get through in order to bring about an outcome. The least sexy thing in the world. And then, when it doesn't work . . ."

She trails off, and I see the moment that she realizes, the point at which she remembers who she is talking to, picks up on her terrible mistake.

"Shit," she says, uncharacteristically—Hannah never swears—"I'm so sorry, Flick. I wasn't thinking."

The air between us feels frozen, time suspended until Felicity replies. I let out a breath as she gives a quick, tight smile; I hadn't realized I'd been holding it.

"It's fine," she says, "really, it's fine."

"No," Hannah says, "I shouldn't've—God, what an idiot. Me and my big mouth. I'm sorry, Flick."

She looks duly mortified, and Felicity keeps smiling, even though I can see it in her eyes: the vulnerability, the sadness.

It was last year when she told us she wouldn't be able to have children, and why.

Felicity's mother, Diane, died when the four of us were fifteen; babies, really. Ovarian cancer, long and drawn-out. The year after, Felicity had some time off school—none of us knew where she was, only that she was off sick. The teachers told us it was stress, the shock of the bereavement.

It was only later that we found out the truth.

Ovarian cancer is hereditary; it carries a risk. After Diane's death, Felicity's father, Michael, took it upon himself to take that risk away. Felicity's operation, illegal without her consent in the UK, removed the possibility of it happening to her too.

None of us could believe she'd gone along with it; nor that her father had done such a thing. She was far too young to understand the implications of what her consent actually meant.

She told us over brunch one day, as we sipped coffee with foam artwork on the top and ate avocado toast before moving on to mimosas. It was a sunny day, I remember, and we were in the window of a café in West London. The cherry blossom was out on the trees, pink and joyful, and I recall how unfair the whole thing felt—that Felicity, our beautiful, generous friend—not a flawless person, but a fundamentally good one—should be handed this card by life, without her having any say in the matter at all.

She'd said it quite matter-of-factly, as though it didn't matter in the slightest, but obviously, we all knew that it did.

"I couldn't let Dad risk losing me too," she'd told us calmly, but the three of us reeled in horror, and I knew that there was a darker side to what Mr. Denbigh had done. At fifteen, Felicity was a child with her whole future ahead of her. He had made a decision that was not his to make. The night she told us, we relayed the story to Chris over at Hannah's, whose expression told us everything we needed to know.

Felicity had as much right to want children as Hannah did—

Hannah had always been the most maternal of the group—but now there was no chance.

"No chance at all?" Alice had asked hesitantly, and Felicity had shaken her head, the sun bouncing off her hair, creating almost a halo effect around her blond head. We stared at her, unable to comprehend the enormity of the decision that had been taken out of her hands at such an early age. Chris showed us the laws a few days later, and for months I wondered whether to confront her, to show her the reality of what her father had done, the miscarriage of justice that had taken place. I never did; fear stopping me in my tracks, memories of Michael roaming around their old house.

"Anyway," she'd said, "I just wanted to let you all know. Shall we order more mimosas?"

We'd tried to talk to her about it again, a month or so later, the three of us conspiring frantically over WhatsApp, planning our approach—we didn't want to make her feel worse but we wanted her to know that we were there if she needed us, that whenever she wanted to discuss it—the unfairness of it, the way she felt, we would be here, ready and waiting. We whispered about her father, of course, about what he had done; speculating about the details, about how he'd gotten away with it. Alice thought we should tell someone, some sort of authority, but I'd pointed out that it was all too late. But when the time came, with Hannah, inevitably, leading the way, Felicity simply shut the conversation down as quickly as it had begun.

"I'd rather not discuss it," she'd said, her tone slightly clipped, "it is what it is, after all. And there are other ways to have children, you know. Biology isn't everything! I don't blame anyone for it. My father did it because he loves me."

"Oh God, of course!" We'd rushed to compensate her, ready to talk about adoption, surrogacy, the myriad options available to twenty-first-century women, but she didn't want to discuss those either.

"Maybe she just needs more time," Alice had wisely said later, and Hannah and I had nodded along, resolved not to mention it again unless Felicity herself brought it up. I haven't seen Michael Denbigh since she told us: I hope never to have to again.

What happened to Felicity prompted me to think about my own choices, too, forced me to look at the facts. Did I want children? I didn't have a partner to try with. My relationship with my own mother was, and always had been, fraught, made much worse by the events of the last eighteen months, and the thought of re-creating that filled me with a sort of dread, a terror even. I decided I'd think about it later—it wasn't as though I was even thirty yet. My future was wide open, still to be decided. All to play for, as Alice might say, although most days I found I couldn't think about the future at all; it had narrowed, darkened, after what happened when I met Nathaniel Archer. The girls were basically the only people I continued to see; I never dated, never hooked up with anyone. I couldn't. I didn't know how to anymore.

So it wasn't that we had forgotten about Felicity's infertility, no, but it hasn't been mentioned for so long that clearly, in the moment, Hannah has failed to remember. I feel horrible for them both—Hannah's guilt at her own crassness is written all over her face, and something in Felicity's eyes looks stricken. I wonder, briefly, whether Nathaniel knows—whether it is the sort of thing one announces straightaway to possible life partners, or whether it is something she prefers to keep under wraps until asked directly. The thought of her and Nathaniel having children makes me want to vomit—the permanency with which he would then be in our lives, even though it is, of course, an impossibility.

As if on cue, Felicity speaks, quietly, her voice serious. "He doesn't know, by the way. So please, don't mention it in front of him. I haven't found a way to tell him yet. It would be—bad—if he knew."

Hannah looks admonished. My gut twists.

I know I will have to speak to her, to warn her, but just as I am about to open my mouth, he reappears.

"Sorry I've been so long, it's mad in there."

As tall as I remember from my nightmares, he looms over us, then folds his long legs into the seat beside Felicity, pressing his lips against her cold, pale cheek. When he pulls away, there is a slight sucking sound; we all pretend not to notice.

"You must be Hannah," Nathaniel says, turning his smile onto her, blissfully unaware of the awkward exchange that has gone previously. She grins at him, clearly charmed, and then lets out a hiccup—a sure giveaway of her drunkenness, and an unfortunate side effect I have always been glad I am never subjected to. But he turns smoothly away from her, saving her embarrassment, and then it is happening, the moment I have dreaded—his eyes are on mine, clear and bright blue, his pupils small and focused, like laser beams.

I feel like an animal, trapped in the headlights. He is testing me, seeing if I'll run, or speak up. The old flight or fight instinct rises up and I have to force myself to sit still, moving my hands to underneath my belongings to prevent them all from seeing the tremor that has not stopped and is in fact getting worse.

I stare at him for one second, two, then shift my gaze down to the tabletop, unable to bear it any longer. Nobody else notices; it feels as though I am behind thick glass, that even if I stood up and screamed blue murder, my friends would carry on without paying the slightest bit of attention. What would I have to do, I think, to make them really listen to me? How far would I have to go?

Chapter Seventeen

Hannah

Hannah has drunk too much. The thought hits her all at once, slamming into her consciousness as she sloppily reaches for her phone, ignoring the three new messages from Chris asking her to call him, telling her to come home, checking more and more desperately if she's all right.

No, Chris, I'm not all right, she thinks angrily, even though she knows deep down that this is not his fault, that he doesn't want this to be happening any more than she does. Hannah's stomach clenches, and she reminds herself cruelly yet again that the inside of her is empty. Emptied, she should say.

She miscarried her second rainbow child two days ago.

It was worse than the last time—they were further along, and the awful thing is that Hannah had allowed herself to hope. To let those little glimmers of sunshine filter through her mind. She had believed the doctors when they'd told her, after the first miscarriage last year, that it was very common, that it happened to a lot of women, and that one miscarriage was no reason to think she would have another, no reason at all to think that she wouldn't be able to carry a baby to full term.

But they were wrong.

It has happened again, and inside her, underneath the haze of alcohol making its way around her bloodstream, is a tidal wave of sadness, a sadness that she thought she could control but that perhaps she cannot. She is out tonight with her closest friends and yet the thought of telling them what she is going through makes her feel sick—somehow, the revelation that once again, her body has failed her, is more than she can take. She has always been sensible, reliable, strong Hannah. Calm in a crisis. There for her friends. To weep and moan about the fact that she has lost this child, especially when Felicity herself cannot have children, due to such horrific circumstances, would be out of keeping, unjust. So Hannah keeps it to herself. She's already said something she shouldn't this evening—that blundering remark to Felicity, so she must keep her mouth shut. It's the safest thing to do.

And so, instead of talking, she drinks. And she drinks.

It's approaching 10 p.m. now, and the pub will be closing its doors within the hour. Richmond pubs aren't Soho pubs—the streets here are largely residential, the people who come here are well-behaved. The Red Lion is a friendly place, not a debauched one. There will be no lingering on the streets, no lock-ins after hours.

Hannah doesn't want to go back home.

She invited Alice and Grace to stay over because she can't bear the thought of being alone with her thoughts, or of crawling into bed beside Chris, having to deal with his hand stroking her back, his sympathy. *It isn't the same for you*, she wants to scream at him. These babies weren't inside you. It's not your body that is letting go of your own children. He thinks they are in the same boat, but they aren't. He steers the boat, while she begins to drown, barely clinging to the side.

"Who's for one more?" she says loudly, only realizing how loudly when Felicity stops speaking and stares at her, her mouth twitching up at the sides, a pretty red bow.

"I think Drunk Hannah's coming out to play tonight!" she says, laughing, pearly teeth gleaming, and Nathaniel looks at Hannah, amused. She feels a flicker of fury in her stomach; she doesn't want them to laugh at her. Why is she not allowed to be drunk? She has seen Felicity drunk thousands of times, and never felt the need to comment. Hannah doesn't like it when Felicity gets like this, it feels like she's playing games. They aren't teenagers in the attic anymore.

"I need to get home," Grace says. Hannah looks sideways at her and blinks; she's being very weird tonight. All that business about leaving earlier. And she's barely made any effort with Nathaniel, which Hannah thinks is a bit rude. Felicity's bound to notice. As Hannah stares, Grace's face seems to melt and shift until there are two of her; God, she really is a bit out of it.

Have a glass of water, the grown-up, sensible Hannah inside her says, but she ignores her, pushes her to the back of her brain. Sensible Hannah has let her down. She's done what she wants for years and look where it's got her. Clots of blood in her underwear. Two lost babies. A boyfriend she can't face going home to.

"Come on," Hannah slurs, "just one more." An idea makes its way through the fog of her brain.

"I know, let's go to The Upper Vault!" As soon as the idea takes hold, Hannah knows it's the right one—The Upper Vault bar is just what she needs right now. Noise, darkness, heat, dancing—she can forget about everything for a couple of hours, and put off seeing Chris.

Alice laughs, a big, throaty laugh.

"The Upper Vault! Christ, Han, we haven't been there in years!"

"All the more reason to go," Hannah tries to say, but it comes out differently, the words running together. She giggles, then hiccups, clapping a hand to her mouth. She can feel her phone vibrating against her hip again, but she ignores it. She will ignore everything, just for tonight. She is allowed one night, isn't she? Tomorrow, Hannah will grieve. She will talk to Chris, she will book an appointment at the clinic, she will make plans and be reasonable and decide that yes, they can try again, they can have another go at making a baby. But for now, she just wants to lose herself.

What's so wrong with that?

Alice

Inside The Upper Vault, it's exactly as Alice remembers it. They go up the carpeted flight of stairs, the bouncer on the door nodding them through—clearly, they're all past their prime—and into the top floor of the warehouse. The bar isn't that busy yet—it's February, after all, but the high, tall stools are exactly as they used to be, and the low lighting is flattering; Alice tosses her hair, runs her finger across her lips, tries not to think about the throbbing that persists in her arm, the imprint Tom's grip will have left. She wonders if it will bruise, a little ring of purple that fades to green like a fairy ring, found deep in the forest. A secret: shameful and dark. She wonders if he will do it again, now that a line has been crossed.

Music plays, a low, thumping bass, and beside Alice, Hannah

is laughing giddily, clamoring for another drink. Alice doesn't know what's gotten into her tonight but she doesn't mind it—it is cute, in a way. She never lets her hair down, does Han. Alice sees Felicity look over at her, whisper something to Nate. They both laugh, and she feels suddenly protective of Hannah. So what if she's had a few? Living with Chris—well, it must be a bit boring. She's probably glad to be out of the house.

"Tequila!" she is proclaiming, and Alice shrugs and tells her, *sure*. Grace has disappeared to the Ladies, but Alice orders her one anyway. God knows, she needs something to liven her up—she's no fun at all tonight. It's strange, she thinks, out of all of them, surely she is the only one with something to feel sad about tonight. She's the one whose boyfriend hates her. She's the one who will wake up tomorrow with a bruise—not to mention a hangover, at this rate. But the girls are all behaving oddly, even though they've got nothing to be fed up about.

Least of all Felicity. She and Nathaniel are at the bar, but Alice can see the way his head is turned slightly away from her, and as she watches, Nate swivels around, meets her eye. For some reason, Alice can feel herself blushing—thank God it's dark in there, and Hannah can't see.

Stop it! Alice tells herself. Christ, the last thing she needs is to develop some sort of hideously inappropriate crush on Felicity's brand-new boyfriend. He *is* attractive, though, and it's so nice to have a man look at her without seeing the horrible, weird scorn she is now so accustomed to seeing in Tom's eyes. He gestures at her now, and Alice goes over.

"Three tequilas, I think," she says, trying to sound jaunty, and Nate whistles, raises an eyebrow.

"Tequila, the good stuff, hey. Felicity didn't tell me that her friends were so much fun. Well, one of them, anyway."

Next to him, Felicity squeals, elbows him in the ribs. He's well-built; he probably barely felt a thing. *Stop it.* Why is she thinking about his body, for God's sake?

"Are you having fun, Al?" Felicity says, leaning around him on the bar, her other arm snaking around Nathaniel, a woman claiming her possession. Her eyes are bright, her cheeks flushed—Alice realizes with a jolt that she looks happier than she has seen her in months—since Diane died, even, though it was so long ago now. For years afterward, it was as if the light inside Felicity had been dimmed, but now it seems that it's back. Nate must be a pretty special guy.

"Remember the last time we came to The Upper Vault?" Felicity is having to shout slightly, the thrum of the music feels as though it's getting louder. A gaggle of girls appear on the other side of Alice, laughing and shrieking. Alice looks at them quickly—they must be at least five years younger than her and the girls. One of them catches her eye and grins; Alice sees her gaze flicker to Nathaniel and the almost imperceptible widening of her eyes. Her head turns, long hair flicking, and Alice sees her whisper something to her friends, followed by fresh peals of laughter. She'd bet money on the fact that she's told them how hot he is.

"Alice?" Felicity is still looking at her, and she forces herself to pay attention.

"God, well, it's been ages, hasn't it? I think it was after that birthday thing, you know, what's-her-name's." Alice is struggling, now, for her name—a girl they'd grown up with had hired the whole place out for her twenty-fifth birthday, decked it out in gold and silver metallic balloons. They'd been mocking, at the time, secure in their foursome, with no real need to keep ties to the wider hangers-on. *Balloons*, Alice remembers Felicity hissing bitchily, *what is she, five years old?*

"Tequilas coming up," Nathaniel interrupts, taking a tray from the barmaid, who is also looking at him almost hungrily. Alice sees Felicity notice and the way her arm tightens around his waist like a spring.

"Bottoms up," Alice says, tipping salt into the space between her thumb and her index finger, looking around for Hannah. She is, hilariously, dancing by herself, bopping away to the music with her eyes closed, a strange, faraway expression on her face.

"Han!" Alice calls, but the music is too loud, and besides, perhaps she doesn't really need a shot of tequila anyway, not by the looks of it. Alice hasn't seen her this hammered in ages. She never handles it well; she'll feel awful tomorrow, bless her.

Alice downs the shot quickly, feeling the adrenaline hit her, and along with it the thought of Tom, simmering on his way home, hood obscuring his face. All that anger. And what for? She hasn't looked at her phone since he left, nor does she want to. She needs to decide what to do, she knows she does; things cannot go on the way they are, and tonight has proved that, once and for all. She bites into the slice of lime Nate has given her, the acidic taste making her momentarily close her eyes and purse her lips. When she opens them, Nate is watching her, his eyes on her mouth.

Alice is about to suggest another shot, she likes the sharp, potent taste of it on her tongue, but suddenly Grace appears by her side. Her face is white, even in the softer lighting of the bar, and her expression is stony. Alice squints at her tipsily, smiles, and offers her the spare tequila shot. She doesn't smile back.

"I need to talk to Felicity," she says in Alice's ear, leaning close to her, her breath warm against Alice's cheek. At first Alice thinks she's just leaning close because of the noise of the bar, but then she realizes that she doesn't want anyone to hear—she's looking around cautiously, as if they're on a covert spy mission, not in a busy bar on a Friday night.

"Well, all right," Alice says, not understanding. "Go for it, then. She's just there, with Nate." The two of them have moved slightly away, are huddled over one of the trendy little tables, laughing at something or nothing.

Tom and Alice never laugh like that.

"I can't go over there," Grace says, and then mutters something under her breath that Alice doesn't catch.

"What?" she says, but Grace isn't looking at her anymore, she's looking past her to Felicity.

"Can you help me?" she says, still not meeting Alice's eye.

"Help you what?" Alice asks, confused, but Grace just shakes her head impatiently. Behind her, the younger girls are clinking glasses, their long, lithe limbs moving in unison.

"Talk to him for a bit, I need to speak to Felicity on her own. If I don't do it now I'll lose my nerve," she says.

"What are you talking about?" Alice says, really confused now, and then Grace leans in close to her again, wraps her fingers around Alice's wrist. Her hands are cold, surprisingly so.

"Keep Nathaniel in here, where people can see you," she

says. "I need you to do this for me, Alice." A pause. "I never ask for much from this friendship, do I, Alice, but I'm asking now." She reaches for the tequila shot, downs it in one, her expression never changing.

Alice doesn't know if it's the steeliness in Grace's tone, or the strange, hunted look in her eyes, but in the end she gives in and does as she says, obeying her as she gives her a tiny shove to where Felicity and Nate stand. What does she mean, *I never ask for much from this friendship*? She makes it sound like Alice doesn't care about her at all, which is completely unfair.

To Alice's horror, as they approach, Felicity and Nate move together and begin kissing, properly kissing, but Grace doesn't flinch; she moves forward like a bird of prey with its eye on the target.

"Grace!" Alice hisses at her, but she just carries on until she's standing right in front of them, unmoving, still with the same weird, fixed look on her face. Christ, is she pissed?

Obviously, they break apart. Alice feels embarrassed for Grace—what the hell is she playing at? But Nathaniel has that amused glint on his face again, as if her odd behavior doesn't bother him at all.

"Felicity, can I talk to you?" Grace says, and Alice sees a flicker of annoyance cross Flick's face, which, to be honest, is pretty understandable given that Grace is being so weird. They are standing so close to Nathaniel that she can smell his aftershave; a deep, musky smell that somehow manages to set Alice's nerve endings on fire, even though she is willing her body, her stupid, treacherous body, not to react.

"What about?" Flick says, but she's a good friend, and clearly she can see that Grace is upset. Casting an apologetic look at Nathaniel, she obediently follows Grace away from the table, toward the back of the room, where the neon green sign of the fire exit lights up the doorway. It flickers, just briefly, like a warning.

And then Nate and Alice are alone.

Chapter Eighteen

Hannah

Hannah doesn't know how long they've been at The Upper Vault; time has become elastic, the way it does when you're very, very drunk. She knows she's been dancing, but now one of her shoes has come off, and for some reason she finds that very, very funny. One foot is completely bare, she's not even wearing any socks and her toenails are painted red, a bright, frivolous red that makes her want to laugh. So she does.

She laughs and laughs, and she doesn't think about the bloodstains on her sheets, or the look on the nurse's face, or the way Chris's eyes blurred over when they confirmed what both of them already knew, their expressions soft but firm. Loss was part of their everyday lives; Hannah didn't want it to be part of hers. She doesn't think about the tiny pair of knitted baby bootees she bought herself in a stupid, selfish, happy moment last week, that are sitting in the bottom drawer of their dresser, that she wishes she had burned or thrown out with the rubbish. After all, they are worthless to her now. Aren't they?

She is stumbling, and she feels a bit sick. The room is so loud, pulsing music and bodies, it has filled up so quickly, this place, and all of a sudden there are too many people, too many strangers, all crowding around her, but none of them has noticed that she can't find her shoe and none of them cares that she's just lost her baby.

And then Hannah feels a hand on her arm.

She looks up, and it's Felicity's new boyfriend, the one with the big hands, Ned, Nick? Her brain gropes around for his name; she can't remember.

"It's okay, I've got you," he says, and he's got an arm around Hannah's back. He's helping her to the side of the dance floor, even though she didn't ask for help and she doesn't need it. She's a grown-up, isn't she? Grown-up Hannah. Sensible Hannah. *Oh, Han will be the first one to get married. The first one to have kids. She's a mother to us all already!* She remembers Grace saying that, she doesn't know when. When they were young. They're not young anymore. Her body isn't young, not young enough. This wouldn't be happening if it was.

"You're all right," he says, and it's Nathaniel, that's it, she has remembered now, handsome Nathaniel, the doctor, the one Felicity's so excited about. The one Grace doesn't seem to like, for some unfathomable reason that she isn't prepared to explain. Why will none of them open up to each other? When did life become about keeping their cards close to their chests?

"We need to get you some air, some water," Nathaniel is saying, and Hannah laughs again, because he sounds like a real doctor now, and because he probably came out tonight to get away from work, not to have to look after a drunk, sad woman who doesn't know her limits. And then the laughter has turned to crying, and suddenly she is sobbing, big, sloppy tears that splash down her cheeks and onto her shirt. One of her buttons has come undone, exposing a sliver of skin, and Hannah reaches up to try to do it up but she can't see properly through her tears and so she just leaves it and lets herself cry, snotty, ugly sobs that clog up her throat and make her head ache.

"Hey, hey," Nathaniel is saying, and then there's a bump and a rush and Hannah realizes they're outside, they've come outside onto the street downstairs and he still has an arm around her waist. "What's the matter, hey? What's wrong?"

Her cheeks are cold, the tears freezing on her skin, and she lets him guide her to a little low wall outside the bar. Hannah's bare foot tenses at the harsh texture of the pavement; she is hobbling slightly, like an old woman. There are cigarette butts on the ground, lots of them, and someone's left a glass out here too, the dregs of something in the bottom of it. She feels her stomach churn. There is something dark in the air, something she can't put her finger on but she can sense it, closing in around them. It is the same sense of darkness she used to feel when they were younger, when Felicity's father was around—a sort of creeping dread. She doesn't know why she's feeling it now.

"We need to get you home," Nathaniel says, and he looks worried, his blue eyes swim in front of her, intense with concern. At the thought of going home, of sobering up and dealing with it all, a fresh wave of tears assaults Hannah and she pitches forward into his shirt, never mind that he is a man she has only just met, that she doesn't know him at all, and that she is making a colossal fool of herself. In the moment, all she can do is cry.

Hannah expects him to push her off, but all he does is place a hand on her back, a large, gentle hand, and rub it in small slow circles, allowing her to sob. After a minute or two, she sits up, feeling pathetically grateful for his kindness.

"God," she says, when she can speak, "I'm so sorry. I'm so sorry, I . . ."

"No problem," he is saying, "really, it's fine. Are you all right? Is there anything I can do? I'll go get the girls, but I don't want you to be . . ." He trails off.

Hannah forces herself to take deep breaths, in through the nose and out through the mouth, makes herself look up at the crystal black of the night sky above them, focus on the stars, weak, but just about visible even in London.

"I'm sorry," she says again, trying harder to articulate the words. "I'm just—" She looks at him, into his eyes. He's obviously a kind man, and she feels a jab of happiness, that Felicity has someone who might finally look after her, that she has, for once, chosen somebody good. She thinks how it would feel to say the words aloud, to unburden herself.

"I lost a baby," Hannah says, "yesterday. I miscarried at eleven weeks." She says the sentence without breaking down, speaking matter-of-factly, and somehow, it isn't as bad as she'd thought. It even helps, the acknowledgment, the sense of relief at saying the thing that has been inside her all night, the only thing she has been able to think about. The reason she has drunk so much, got herself into this state. It is because she lost her baby.

Not because she's a bad person.

"I'm so sorry," he says, very gently, and he reaches out, puts a hand on hers, leaves it there. There is such comfort in it, and in the simplicity of his words, that tears threaten to take over again and Hannah has to force them back down. He doesn't deserve her crying all over him. Felicity will probably be furious. But even as Hannah thinks this, she knows that she is doing her friend a disservice, that she won't be furious, she will be sad. She will be sad for Hannah, and for Chris, and she will understand. She will realize the loss, perhaps the most of them all, because it is a loss she has already experienced, albeit in a different way.

"She's done it already," Hannah says aloud. "She's lost all the children she was ever going to have."

Nathaniel's hand grows stiller on her own.

"What?" he says then, and his voice is different, more stilted.

"Felicity," Hannah says, and the grief blooms again in her chest, unstoppable this time, for now she is crying not just for herself and this baby, but for Felicity, the hand life has dealt her, the crushing loss she too must have felt when she woke up from the operation, too young and confused to know what her father had done to her. "She can't have children. She will know how it feels."

Hannah thinks of her, stoic and brave, being coerced into a decision that would alter the path of her life forever, and then she thinks of how selfish she herself is, sitting here sobbing because her baby has been taken. She can try again, can't she? But Felicity can't. Hannah should have told someone, she should have reported Felicity's father when she had the chance. She knows she should. They all feel guilty about it.

"It's not fair," Hannah says aloud, stupidly, into the empty night sky, and she doesn't realize what she has done, what she has said to Nathaniel, until it is too late, far, far too late. She has told a secret that was never hers to tell, but in the early hours of the morning, her body loose and slack with alcohol, she doesn't realize the impact of her words.

"I didn't know," Nathaniel says hoarsely, and Hannah tries to reach out to him, wanting to comfort him in the way he has comforted her, but instead she pitches forward, her stomach lurches, and she throws up, all over the cigarette butts, all over the floor, and all over her one remaining shoe.

Grace

Felicity doesn't believe me. The force of that fact hits me full-on, square in the face, a blow to the stomach. The pain feels that way; almost physical. I have told her what happened, and Felicity, one of my closest friends in the world, simply does not believe me.

It is the same thing as with my mother—it is happening all over again.

I can see it in her eyes, even before she says the words.

"Are you sure, Grace?"

Am I sure?

Am I sure that the man inside the bar, her new boyfriend of two months, Nathaniel Archer, is the man who raped me last year on a hot summer's day, at a garden party hosted by my parents?

"Yes, Felicity," I say, slowly, as though talking to a child. "Yes, I'm sure. It's the worst thing that has ever happened to me. I've spent the whole night trying to find a way to tell you, a way to warn you. I couldn't not tell you, Flick—he's dangerous. Tonight has to be the last you see of him."

My legs are shaking slightly; we're out at the back of The Upper Vault, on the fire escape, and neither of us has a coat. I am gripping onto the iron handrail to keep myself steady; the metal is freezing beneath my fingers. The music from the club can still be heard from behind the thick fire door, but it's faint, as if someone has turned the volume down on the rest of the world and it's only the two of us now, Felicity and me, out on the corrugated iron steps, the concrete below us. I am telling her the truth—not *my version of it*, as my mother cruelly said, and not Nate's version of it, the one everyone believed, but the truth. The indisputable fact that Nate Archer, a client of my father's business, raped me in my childhood bedroom in the middle of the afternoon on a hot July day, for no reason at all other than because he could.

I have been trying to put that day to the back of my mind ever since. I have buried it, deep within me, after the initial shock and shame and the awful, life-altering days afterward; the days in which I tried to talk to my parents and had them disbelieve me. My own mother refused to believe what had happened, and my father wouldn't dare speak up against Nathaniel; the son of the man who owns one of the biggest private hospitals in England and thereby pays my dad's wages. My parents and I had never been close, but this was the final straw.

After that, I didn't tell anyone. Not even the girls. So when they ask why I am alone, when they try to cajole me into dating, when they ask why I never want to be set up with anyone, I lie. I tell them I am happy alone, when the reality is that what Nate did to me has left me terrified of men, of what they might do. It has shown me that the truth is irrelevant—no matter what happened between us, the fact is that there were no witnesses, there was only the two of us, and that when it came to his word against mine, the people I told chose to believe him over me.

I didn't report it, of course. I couldn't bear the idea of another person looking me in the eye and telling me I was lying. I simply didn't think I could take it.

And so I shut it down, locked it away, pretended, at times, that it had never even happened. I never spoke his name again, I didn't look him up online, I didn't seek him out to try to get some form of justice, retribution for what he did. I simply erased it. Continued to live my life, as best I could. But I shut myself down, slowly, bit by bit—as the weeks and then months went by, I distanced myself from my colleagues, I alienated my parents; the only people I could be a version of myself with were the girls, the three of them. I told myself that was enough, that I'd carry on, get through it. Nobody would know, and so nobody would think any less of me. And I'd never have to see the man who did this to me again—despite the fact that he wouldn't leave me alone.

In the weeks and months afterward, Nathaniel called me. I'd given him my number that day, stupidly, before what happened, and he abused it—ringing me at all times of the day and night, even trying to pass on messages through my father. He emailed me, multiple times, as though nothing had happened, asking me to come out for dinner, telling me he couldn't stop thinking about me. That I'd put a spell on him. To my parents, it was further proof that he was telling the truth—he just liked me! He was a handsome, successful doctor—the undertone of their words was that I ought to be grateful.

Eventually, I blocked his email address, changed my phone number. It worked; the calls stopped. It took months for me to finally allow myself to relax, to accept that it was over. He couldn't get to me—whatever game he was trying to play with me was finished, dead. Perhaps, I thought, he'd gotten bored, moved on. I gave my new number to the girls, told them I'd had to switch it for work reasons. I thought the man who haunted my dreams was gone.

But now Nathaniel Archer is back. He is here, and Felicity is in love with him. It is obvious, so obvious. She is my friend, and she is in danger.

That's why I had to tell her the truth.

I didn't think, not for one second, that she wouldn't want to hear it.

Alice

Alice is on her own, texting Tom, sitting on one of the velvet sofas in the back when Nate slides up beside her again, to where they had been talking together on the low soft seats that line the back wall of the bar. He's looking a bit odd, shaken almost, says Hannah got sick outside and that he's called her a cab home.

"I saw her as I was on the way to the bar," he says. "She was on her own, dancing like a lunatic, missing one of her shoes. Sorry, in all the palaver I forgot to get our drinks."

Immediately, Alice goes to get up, concerned for Hannah, but he puts a hand on her arm, just like he did back in the pub. Just for a moment, but it is enough for Alice to feel the spark of electricity between them. How different his touch is from Tom's aggressive grip.

"She'll be gone already, I think," he says. "She was out of it; I didn't want to leave her alone to come and fetch one of you guys. I didn't know where Felicity and Grace had got to—have you seen them at all?"

Alice shakes her head. Something seems to flash across Nate's face, and she worries that he wants to be with Felicity, is fed up of being stuck here talking to her. But then he continues, "Well, Flick said Hannah lives around the corner, right? And her boyfriend's at home?"

Alice nods. "Chris will be home, yep. God, poor Han. I did think she was a bit out of character tonight. She's not normally such a boozehound."

She laughs a little at her own words, then feels guilty. She fires off a quick message to Hannah, asking her to call her in the morning, and texts Chris too, just to be on the safe side.

H in cab home—too much to drink. Look out for her, will you? Won't stay tonight. X

"I was meant to be staying at theirs," Alice says morosely, realizing that now she'll have to go home—she can hardly wake Hannah up later if she's already in such a state, she'll just pass out the minute she gets home. Her phone flashes up in her hand and Alice think it's Chris but it's Tom, three words: *I'm so sorry.* And then, *Come home. Please. Xx*

She sees Nate's eyes darting to her screen, and when she catches him, he looks a bit sheepish.

"Sorry, didn't mean to read your texts." He colors a bit, Alice thinks, but it's so dark over here that she can't really tell.

"Boyfriend trouble? The guy earlier?"

She sighs, takes a sip of her drink. She'd gotten herself another wine, assuming Nate had found Felicity, but actually she doesn't really want it now; she thinks she's had enough, and it takes quite a lot for her to say that.

"Tom, yes." Alice nods, her voice thick.

"I can't believe any guy would be foolish enough to mess

you around," Nathaniel says quietly, and Alice is suddenly aware of how close he is to her, the press of his leg against her thigh. She goes hot all over. There is a line, a very clear line here, and she cannot let herself cross it.

"Well," she says, "you know. It is what it is. We've"—she coughs, feeling awkward—"we've been together a long time. A few years now."

"People change," Nate says, and he lifts up a hand, brushes a strand of hair from Alice's face where it has fallen forward as she hunched over her phone. His skin is warm and dry, unlike hers, which is beginning to feel sticky with sweat. Alice lifts her head, just slightly, scanning the club for Felicity and Grace, but there are far more people here now, their bodies writhing and bucking to the music, blocking the two of them from view. They are alone on the sofas. The strangers mask them, and the line feels blurrier now, less and less clear.

"You're so beautiful, Alice," Nate murmurs in her ear, and he slowly moves his other hand so that it is at the very top of Alice's thigh, his fingers almost reaching her crotch, and she can't help it—she knows how wrong this is, how awful, but she lets out a tiny little moan, the sound escaping her almost without her realizing. She can feel the rigidity of his body, the anticipation of her own. The music is throbbing around them, and it's so dark, and his lips are inches away from hers. There is a sickening pulse between her legs that she cannot stop no matter how hard she tries, and Alice thinks of Tom at home, of his fingers sinking into her arm, the shock and the pain of it. She thinks of Felicity, laughing, smiling brightly, her hand in Nate's, and she thinks of her giggling, both of them doubled over, bound together in friendship, and then his body shifts so that his fingers touch Alice's crotch and she gives in, his lips finding hers, both of them leaning forward, a soft groan, her body yielding to his.

And then Alice opens her eyes because there is a bright white flash, the sound of a camera phone clicking, up close, and then out of the corner of her eye she sees the shadowy figure of a woman, moving away from them, unspeaking, the evidence captured forever. She blinks frantically, springs away from Nate, but it is too late—the body of strangers continues to heave and writhe, and whoever it was is lost in the crowd, in the music, swallowed up in the bar. The sound seems to swell around her as the panic rises in her throat—Alice stands and spins around, trying to see who it was, whether it was Felicity herself or one of the others. But it's useless.

She is gone.

PART THREE

Chapter Nineteen

March 30
Botswana

Grace

My throat is dry and parched. I have been following the river for what must be close to an hour now, forcing myself to keep going, slowing my pace from a run to a walk when the heat began to overcome me. Overhead, the sky is blue, almost obscenely so, a brilliant, cloudless color that seems to mock me. I wish I had had the foresight to bring something from the lodge—water, fruit to eat, but I was so frightened, so terrified after seeing Hannah, dead at the dining-room table, the blood congealing beneath her, the steady drip of it onto the floor. My mouth feels like sandpaper, and I try not to think about what could happen if I don't reach safety—the thought of dehydration makes my chest tighten, and I need to stay calm, to be able to think as clearly and rationally as I can.

The river water glimmers up at me, but I have no idea if it's safe to drink—it seems unlikely, although in some ways now the thought of plunging in, immersing myself in it, is strangely tempting. A frog glistens greedily on the bank, belching quietly;

above me, swallows dip and glide as though nothing is wrong. The water feels like it is calling to me, inviting me in, reaching out dangerous hands that will pull me under. No. I must keep going. I picture the lodge—Alice's body rotting beneath the towel, the eerie sight of Hannah propped up at the table. The blood, the smell, the death. I imagine flies finding them, crawling all over their eyelids, my once-beautiful friends becoming fodder for insects. The thought makes me feel sick, and I momentarily pause, crouch down, touch my palms to the hot dry earth beneath me. It is scorched, red; it goes on for miles. The cut on my finger has dried now, a thin sliver of rust the only reminder.

Hannah's phone has 7 percent battery life.

I must keep going.

I get to my feet, brushing the dirt from the ground off my hands, and continue walking, determined not to look back or to look out toward the plains, for fear of what I might see. As I do so, I think about my friends, and the myriad ways in which I have let them down.

Why did I not tell them about the rape when it happened? Why did I not entrust them with it, this thing that had happened to me and had thrown my life off course? Perhaps if I had, things would be different; the four of us might never have fallen out in the way that we did. If I had found a better way of telling Felicity about Nate that night at The Upper Vault, I might have been able to show him for what he was.

If I had trusted Alice and Hannah with the truth, too, they might have felt able to share their truths with me, because mine wasn't the only secret that night, I know it wasn't. None of us is blameless.

As I round the corner, exhaustion filling every limb, I see

that to my relief the river has led me to a dirt track; empty, and run-down, but indisputably there. I feel a lift inside me and run toward it, ignoring the way my muscles are screaming in protest and the raw dryness of my throat. My feet find the road and I push myself harder, away from the river and the plains now, propelling myself forward, desperate to see a sign of life. Instead, I am confronted with death—a donkey lies prone on the verge, its hooves still and cracked with the heat, its skin crawling with maggots. Tears prick my eyes as I stare at it, helpless. I've never felt farther from home.

And then I hear it. A car.

The sound of it ignites something within me and I begin to run faster, leaving the poor donkey behind, terrified that the vehicle will come and go, pass me by before I can flag it down. Abruptly, the track splits and I reach a crossroads, just in time to see the dark blue car slowing, its wheels crunching on the hot road. The sight of it is like an oasis; relief swells in my chest.

I raise my arms, one sweaty hand still clutching Hannah's phone, and begin to limp toward it, breathing hard. I cannot see who is inside; the sun is glaring onto the windows, making them appear black, and I squint, hold a hand to my brow in an attempt to shade my eyes from the light. *Let it be a woman*, I think, *please let it be a woman.*

The car slows to a stop, and the driver cuts the engine. I am mere meters away now.

"Please," I say, "you have to help me. I'm British, I'm here on holiday, and there's been a terrible—"

My words dry up as I see his face.

Nathaniel.

"Grace," he says, smiling at me, as if all this is totally normal, as if we're not in the middle of absolutely nowhere in Botswana, and that instead we're back at my parents' garden party, and he's introducing himself over the barbecue, like he did on that fateful day, the very first time we met. "How are you?"

It takes me a few seconds to find my voice, and when I do, it comes out as a croak. Weak and exhausted.

"What are you—how are you here?"

He frowns at me.

"I'm here to see you."

I step back from him, almost tripping in my haste. My head is spinning. I want help—I need help, but I don't want it to come from this man. This monster. I told myself that I had to face my fears, but those didn't include seeing Nathaniel. I knew that if I wanted the girls back in my life, Felicity's disbelief was a price I would have to pay. I told myself that what happened to me was in the past, that it wasn't worth losing all three of my closest friends over. I had tried to tell Felicity the truth, and it hadn't worked. Therefore, I had to accept her reaction, and if I wanted to be a part of the group again, I would have to live with it. I had never planned to find myself alone with him—never. I thought they had broken up.

"Where's Felicity?" I say to him, clutching Hannah's phone so tightly that I feel the plastic casing slip underneath my fingers. My eyes flicker down, quickly checking the battery: 5 percent. I need to have a phone, I need to be able to call for help.

"Don't come near me," I shout, as he takes a step forward, his hands outstretched, but he laughs, holds them up by his head, a peace gesture.

"Where's Felicity?" I say again, when he doesn't reply, but

he simply shakes his head, gives a little tut as though I am a naughty child and he's putting me in my place.

"Felicity . . ." he says, as if pondering her name. He's standing with his arm resting on the car door, casually, as if completely relaxed. Anxiety twists inside me. I remember his face above mine, the tears on my own as I begged him to stop. The look in his eyes when he finished. The way he zipped up his jeans, afterward, and went back out to the party, shook hands with my father. The way he rang me obsessively afterward, the messages he sent. I have put myself at risk, yet again—I can't believe I came out here without having full confirmation that they'd split up, that I thought I was brave enough to handle anything. That I *should* have been brave enough to handle it—why should I? What he did to me was wrong, and no matter what my parents think, or what Felicity thinks, it happened.

I will not let this man beat me.

"Alice and Hannah are dead," I say, matter-of-factly. "The lodge we were invited to was empty on arrival. Felicity wasn't there." I take a deep breath. "Did you do this to them?"

He recoils from me, and a strange expression flits across his face; disgust, or shock. "Of course I didn't," he says, spreading his hands, palms raised to the blue sky above, the picture of reason. "God, Grace, what do you take me for? I mean, Jesus, I know you were . . . hurt by what happened between us, but . . . how long have you been out in the sun?" He looks concerned now, and reaches into the car, pulls out a bottle of water from the side pocket of the driver's seat. I look behind him—there is nobody else there.

"Here," he says, "you look like you need this. Do you feel

dizzy at all, confused? You might have got sunstroke, you know. The heat's a lot stronger out here than it is back home."

He holds the water bottle out to me, and I can't help it—I grab it, take a long drink before I can worry about whether he might have put something in it. I am so thirsty, and I gulp it down quickly, finish the bottle in seconds.

"Told you you were thirsty," he says, smiling as if I haven't just told him that my friends have been killed, and I watch him in horror, wondering if he really is more unhinged than I ever thought, even back then, when he had my friends under his spell, when only I could see the truth.

"Come on, Grace, get in the car," he says, and his voice is gentler now. "Let me drive you back to the lodge."

"I can't go back there!" I say. "We need to go to a police station, we need to report their deaths! Didn't you hear me? Two of my friends are lying dead—someone out here has murdered them."

"Look," Nathaniel says, "I don't know what Felicity has told you, Grace, but the two of us broke up months ago. In New York. I was never meant to be here. I don't know anything about your friends, but I'd say Felicity probably does. She isn't . . . she isn't the woman I thought she was. She sent me a strange message last night, saying you were all out here, and that she was going to get her revenge for that night at The Upper Vault. That you'd betrayed her. I got worried when she wasn't replying to any of my messages—worried about her state of mind, and about you as well. I just want to make sure you're safe, that's all. You know how much I care about you, Grace, how much I've always cared. I've told you so many times now. If we go back to where you were all staying, I can help you look around. Felicity must be there, I'm sure of it."

I'm still holding the bottle of water; the cool drink has helped, a little, and I stare at him, my mind racing, trying desperately to process what he is saying. Felicity and he broke up in New York—we were right, then? My mind spools back, thinking about her messages—she'd never mentioned him at all. If what he is saying is true, Felicity really had been out here, alone—had we all walked into her trap?

Unless he's lying, of course.

He's watching me, his head tilted slightly to one side. He can see me weighing up the risks. I look up and down the road; nothing. No one. How long would it be before another car came along here? How long can I keep walking, before the day turns to night? In my left hand, Hannah's phone vibrates, and I look down to see the battery icon flash up on the screen before it turns black. Dead. I have no way of phoning anyone now.

"Grace? Come on, let me help you. I know you don't like me, and I want to change that, to talk to you about what you think happened between us, but look, I'm not a killer. I'm here to find Felicity, and to make sure you're okay. I care about her welfare too, just as much as you do. We were together for years, remember? But I know she's not well—in the last few months in New York it became more . . . obvious. Even your friend Hannah, she rang me yesterday, telling me she suspected something. She wanted me to help you. She knew something wasn't right." He pauses, sighs as though remembering something unpleasant. "Look, I don't know who attacked your friends, but I will help you find out."

A pause. I can't believe that Hannah would have called

Nate; she told us she didn't have his number, but then I think of her strangeness when we were trying to get hold of him, the expression on her face. Perhaps she didn't want us to know. Another secret.

"C'mon," he says, "what else are you going to do? You can't stay out here on your own, it isn't safe. You must know that, Grace."

His eyes meet mine and he attempts a smile.

"No," I say, "I'm not going anywhere with you. I don't trust you."

"Grace," he says, and he is genial again, spreading his palms as if trying to show me how harmless he is, how easygoing. He would fool anyone. He fooled Felicity. He fooled me.

But he won't fool me again.

"Come on," he says, and this time there is an edge of impatience in his tone; almost imperceptible, but there. He takes a step toward me, reaches out a hand as if to take mine. I stand stock-still, like an animal, trying to assess whether I can possibly run. But I can't outrun a car. Not without food, not without water. I could try to retrace my steps to the lodges, but he will come after me.

He takes another step forward.

I know I have no choice.

"No, no, come around the front," he says when I eventually put a hand on the back seat door handle. The metal is boiling hot, and reluctantly I do as he says, going around to the passenger side. My heart is thudding, and fear knots in my stomach, but I know I cannot go on as I am, running through the wilderness with no sense of direction, and, crucially, no food or drink. At least if I am inside the car, I can find a way to get water, and I can work out some sort of plan. If I can find a way to appease him, I might be able to get what I want. I might be able to outwit him at his own game, if I am very, very careful.

I slide Hannah's phone into my pocket, and as I do so, I feel the hard, cold sliver of the shard of glass I put there this morning. I run my finger over it, gently, and take a deep breath, forcing myself to go against my instincts, to keep calm. A plan is forming in my mind.

Inside Nathaniel's car, it is blissfully cool; the air-conditioning blasts my legs and my torso, and the seat is soft and yielding underneath me. In spite of everything, I feel a strange sense of relief at being in a familiar environment. All I want is to get back home. I can't stop going over what Nathaniel has said: if he and Felicity really had broken up months ago, it explained why he wasn't on any of her social channels, why she didn't mention him in any messages. But why hadn't she told us? And why did they break up? Could it be that she finally saw through him after all?

"Seat belt on," Nate says, smiling at me, as if we are a couple heading off for a picnic, not two virtual strangers with a horrible, dark past. He puts on his own, his hand brushing against my leg as he buckles himself in, and not knowing what else to do, I follow suit. I hear a clunking sound, and realize he's activated the automatic locking system. I am trapped.

The engine starts, and Nate checks the road behind us as we pull out from the side of the verge, even though it is empty. Not a single other vehicle has passed us this entire time.

"Do you know where we are?" I ask him hesitantly. "My GPS hasn't been working, I—I just want to get a sense of how far we might be from the airport."

He doesn't answer straightaway, and for a moment I think he hasn't heard me. There is a frown on his face, as if he's concentrating on the road, and his hands on the steering wheel are growing white at the knuckles.

"What happened to the girls?" he says eventually, ignoring my question, and I tense up, my fingers digging into each other. I hadn't realized my fists were clenched.

"I told you, they're both dead," I say rigidly, unwilling to go into details with him. The word sounds strange in my mouth: *dead*. I still can't believe it, cannot bear that they are gone.

"Please, Nate, can you just take us to the nearest town? Felicity isn't at the lodge, we've searched. Please."

He looks sideways at me, sliding his eyes toward mine.

"I know you don't trust me, Grace," he says then, the words surprising me, and I say nothing, simply look straight ahead as the car turns a corner and we begin to head south, back in the direction of the river. My mind is turning over his words, and suddenly I realize—I need to play along with this. To get what I want, I have to be clever.

I have to give this man what he wants.

"What do you mean?" I say, licking my lips; they are dry and cracked.

He is still facing forward, looking at the road ahead. I want to open the window, feel the air on my skin—the car feels as though it is sealed, locking us both inside. We pass more empty, flat space; a cluster of goats, scraggly and thin; a group of tin huts, the sides sagging in defeat. Nathaniel is oblivious, focused only on the track. The car bumps, and my seat belt tightens automatically around me. The roads here are potholed, poor.

"I could tell," he says, "that night at the pub two years ago. With Felicity. You looked as though you'd seen a ghost."

I can hardly believe what he is saying.

"How did you—how did you expect me to react?" I say eventually, finding the words, but he just shakes his head, makes a little tutting noise.

"Grace," he says, "I liked you, don't you see that?"

You raped me, I want to scream, but I cannot—for now, Nathaniel is my only hope of getting to safety, the only option I can see other than sit and starve to death on the roadside while the bodies of my friends rot, forgotten, back at the lodge.

I don't respond, and a flash of agitation passes across his face.

"When you reacted like that, Grace, I was confused, really confused," he says, swinging the car abruptly to the left as the road ahead bends. I look at the time on the dashboard, the red illuminated figures ticking slowly onward. We must be nearly there. I didn't run far, but I am disoriented; this morning feels so long ago, and I can't work out where the lodge must be in relation to where we are now. Inwardly, I am furious with myself for being so stupid, for putting myself in this position, for blindly running from the lodge without a map or a working phone. But that won't help me now.

"I wanted to see you, so badly, after the afternoon at your parents'," he continues, and this time he glances over at me, a quick, sideways glance, and he takes one hand off the steering wheel. I stare at it, hovering in the air between us, above the gear stick, and the muscles in my legs contract. I can't bear the thought of him touching me, even though a part of me is already steeling myself for it; a part of me knows that I may have to bear it if that is the way out of this dreadful situation. But I don't want to accept that, not yet. Not while I still have a chance.

"Why did you want to see me, Nate?" I say at last. I use his abbreviated name in an effort to appear friendly, to show him that he doesn't scare me, even though my heart is thudding so fast inside my chest that I almost feel sure he must be able to hear it.

The air-conditioning is cold on my legs, and I wrap my arms around my torso, feeling the pressure of my palms against my body, trying to reassure myself. If I can just get through this car ride, if I can just make it out of the car, if I can get him to ring for help . . . surely once he sees what has happened, once he knows I'm telling the truth, he will help me, no matter what?

Despite how I feel about him, he is the only person I have right now. A rapist doesn't mean a killer, I tell myself, trying to stay calm, it doesn't mean he did this to them. He could be telling the truth about Felicity—besides, how well do I really know her now anyway? After these years apart. How well do any of us really know anyone?

The harsh bark of his laughter makes me jump. His hand moves back to the steering wheel, grips it tight. His hands are large, strong. Unwittingly, an image of them wrapped around my neck comes to me and I have to turn away, craning myself toward the passenger-seat window until the thought subsides.

"I told you, Grace," he says, and a hint of exasperation is beginning to creep into his voice; the sound of it makes the hairs on the back of my neck stand up. I must keep him calm, keep him comfortable. I cannot anger him. I know that now.

"I wanted to see you because I liked you, for *fuck's* sake!" Without warning, he bangs his hands on the wheel as he swears, momentarily causing the car to jerk over to one side, and I let out an involuntary yelp of fear. Sweat is pooling at the base of my spine, and already I am regretting the decision to get into the car, to trust him as my only option. My eyes slide to the locking system, but he sees me looking and the corners of his mouth turn up very slightly. He knows what I am thinking. He isn't going to let me out.

"I liked you so much, Grace. That afternoon we had together . . ." He trails off, and I try to keep the look of disbelief off my face. How can he really think that what happened between us was consensual, enjoyable even?

Although I don't want to, I force myself to go back, to unspool the last few years to that boiling summer afternoon. The feel of his breath on mine, hot and raw like an animal, the pressure around my skull that intensified every time he thrust himself into me. The way my body burned afterward in the shower, the temperature of the water turned up as high as it could possibly go. The way I scrubbed and scoured at my skin afterward, desperate to feel clean again. The way none of it worked.

He is shaking his head, muttering to himself. I worry that he isn't concentrating on the road, but we have yet to pass a single other car. I try to think what I would do if we did—how could I alert them? Would there be a way to get their attention? The thought of it makes my heart rate speed up again; we're going too fast for me to flag anyone down.

"Slow down a bit, Nate," I say, keeping my voice neutral, calm. Perhaps if I can get him to decelerate, I might stand more of a chance if we do pass someone. I think about rolling the window down, screaming at the top of my lungs, or leaning over and pressing the horn, grabbing the wheel, anything someone might pick up on, remember. But he ignores my suggestion and instead puts his foot down harder on the accelerator. The car jolts and we speed up; my stomach rolls over with fear.

"I tried to call you," he says suddenly, "after that day. I wanted to see you. I rang you, I wrote to you. Christ, I even asked your father. But you just cut me out of your life, of everything, like I didn't matter, like that day had never happened."

He is talking as though I am an ex-girlfriend, a person that meant something to him rather than a young woman he forced into sex at her parents' house. I look at him in profile—his straight, roman nose, the dark curling lashes, the smooth skin. Can it really be that his memory of that terrible afternoon is so different from mine? Does he actually believe the words he is saying? *Delusional.* The word comes to me—the same word Felicity flung in my face that night at The Upper Vault. I remember the pain in her eyes, the spittle from her mouth as it landed on my cheek. She couldn't bear to hear what I was saying, couldn't stand to hear Nathaniel defiled. *We believe what we want to believe*, my mother used to say. We all alter our own versions of events, we spin our own histories, smoothing things over and playing things up, exaggerating and minimizing as we see fit. We are flawed, we humans. If it were to be Nate's word against mine in a court of law, which of us would be believed?

"What do you remember about that day?" I ask, as if I'm asking him if he wants a cup of tea; my tone is light, conversational, even though it is costing me everything to keep up the charade.

He smiles; it splits his face open wide, and this time he does put a hand out, so quickly that I cannot even shift away. It lands on my right leg, his palm over my kneecap, his long fingers gripping the flesh of my lower thigh, the join in my bones. There is nothing I can do. I stay very still, like a fly waiting to be hit, the shadow of him falling across me. Helpless.

"I remember how you looked," he says, "that short little dress. Red. Your lipstick, the way your hair fell. You were gorgeous." To my horror, he gives my knee a squeeze—short, sharp, almost painful.

"You still are," he continues, "the most beautiful woman I've ever seen. Far more beautiful than the others, those so-called friends of yours."

"What about Felicity?" I squeak out, my voice coming out tiny and frightened, but he doesn't seem to notice; he scoffs, shakes his head.

"Felicity!" he says. "She's got nothing on you, Grace. Never did have. You must know that, you must be able to see the way the three of them kept you down? Criticized you, demeaned you, deliberately tried to outshine you. It was obvious to me that night. The way you all were together. I hated it. I hated seeing you like that."

"But," I say, and my mind is racing now, trying to make sense of what he is saying, "you and Felicity—you . . ."

"Grace," he says, "surely you can see—I only ever wanted Felicity to get closer to you. I knew you wouldn't let me into your life any other way—you wouldn't accept my calls, you wouldn't see me after our afternoon together, it was hell for me. I thought the only way you might realize who I was, who I really was, would be if you got to know me naturally—through someone you trusted. I thought if Felicity trusted me, you would too." He laughs bitterly. "After I thought you might have lied to her, told her your version of things in the bar that night, I tried getting closer to Alice and Hannah. I wasn't going to give up on you—I just needed a way to get you to trust me, and I thought if one of them did, you would as well. It would be my way back to you." He grits his teeth, his jawline tight, as though he's angry with himself. "But it didn't work. It only made things worse. It drove a wedge between us."

Us. *There is no us!* I want to tell him; I want to rip his hand off my leg and shout it in his face, to tear my fingernails down his handsome, symmetrical features, the features that have let him get away with anything and everything for his entire life, and I want to destroy him, the same way he has destroyed me. I think about what it has done to me, that one afternoon—the way I went into myself, accepted a smaller life, a safer life, let my friends carry on without me, moving forward and upward while I stayed on the ground, buried in shame and sadness and fear. He did that to me.

And now I am alone with him in a locked car.

"I spoke to Felicity's father," Nathaniel says suddenly. "To Michael. He was the one who told me what to do, who told me that what happened between us was a sign of love. That the only way I'd feel better about it was if we were together, you and I. If everything came full circle."

I stare at him, shock coursing through me.

"You spoke to Michael Denbigh about me?"

He nods animatedly. "Yes, yes. He was the one who—he reassured me. You see, you got to me, Grace. The way you ignored me, it made me feel like I had done something wrong, something bad to you that day. You made me doubt myself. But Michael listened to me, he told me I hadn't done anything wrong, that I just needed to bring you around to my way of thinking. I needed to find you, make you see that we should be together. That way everyone would know I'd done nothing wrong. It was all his idea." He glances over at me, assessing my reaction. "Michael knew I wasn't right for his little girl. Besides, he wanted her to himself. It's such a shame about his passing."

The words send a chill down my spine. Nausea swirls in my stomach. I picture Michael's face, his poison infiltrating Nathaniel, convincing him of such a twisted version of events. Evil, spreading its tendrils from one man to the other.

"Michael died?" I say woodenly, and Nate nods, frowning into the distance as we drive.

"Only recently," he says, "poor Flick. She took it badly."

I stare through the windscreen, the landscape blurring by— we are going fast, too fast now, and fleetingly I wonder if this is all part of his plan, whether he is going to run us off the road, deliberately crash the car with both of us inside.

And then I see them—the gates to the lodge. Relief surges up inside me at the sight of them, and I quickly point, shifting in my seat so that the hand on my leg slides off.

"Here!" I say. "This is it, the lodge complex. This is where the girls are. Please, Nate, you have to help me."

He does slow down, and for a few seconds I think it will be okay, that he's going to let me out, he's going to see their bodies and realize the situation—a situation that is much more serious than what happened between the two of us. It's only as we slow that I realize—he has taken us directly to the gates. In my panic, I didn't give him any directions.

How did he know where to come?

He couldn't, I realize, *unless he'd been here before.*

We are slowed, but not stopping, and as the gates grow closer I see that Nate is accelerating again, rather than pulling over to the right.

"Nate!" I say. "Please, that's the lodge, that's where Alice and Hannah are. We have to call the police, we have to get someone to come out here. I thought you wanted to look for Felicity."

He has a strange expression on his face; colder than before, as though a mask has slipped down over his features.

"I don't think so, Grace," he says, and when he looks at me, I feel the blood in my veins turn to ice. He sees the expression on my face and chuckles, the coldness disappearing again, replaced by his handsome smile. White teeth gleam at me; his blue eyes flash.

"It's admirable, your loyalty," he tells me, and now we're speeding up again, and the gates to the lodges are growing smaller and smaller, vanishing as they recede into the distance.

"My loyalty?" I say weakly, and he nods, as though satisfied that I am engaging with him properly at last.

"Yes," he says, "your loyalty to your friends. Can't you see, Grace, that the way they treated you wasn't good enough? That to them you were a laughingstock—meek little Grace, pushover Grace, everyone's least favorite member of the group? It was clear to me immediately. You deserve better, Grace, you deserve to be looked after. You need someone that really cares about you—someone like me."

There is a silence; the words hang between us in the air, like tiny daggers waiting to strike me. I wait for the pain of what he is saying to slice into me, but strangely, that moment never comes.

It's not true, I think. *What he's saying isn't true.* Yes, there were moments where I felt inferior. Yes, sometimes Alice had a sharp tongue. But they loved me. We loved each other. Nate's view of reality is not the same as mine.

"Felicity used to talk about you so disparagingly, Grace," Nate says. "She had so little respect for you. I couldn't stand it. You're worth ten of each of them. I just want you to know that—I wanted to open your eyes."

We're miles from the lodge now, and I can see a main road up ahead—the track we've been on is widening out. Colors blur past me—the tired browning fields, the red flashes of succulent flowers, the green clumps of gum trees.

"Where are we going?" I ask him, but he just grins at me. He seems more relaxed, now that we're past the lodge, now that he's shown me he isn't going back there. We pull up to a junction, and to my relief there are signs, pointing to various towns and sights that I have never heard of.

As we slow to a set of traffic lights, Nate turns to me and smiles. "We're going to the airport," he says. "This is our chance, Grace, don't you see? With everyone else out of the way, you and I can do what we should have done two years ago. We can make a life together. Just the two of us, somewhere else. You'll see."

Horror fills me as I stare at him; his face is deadly serious.

"The airport?" I repeat back to him, stupidly, trying to buy time so that I can think; it is so hard to, but I know that I must, that the only way of escaping is to think logically, calmly, to outwit him at his own game. I slide my left hand into my pocket, feel it tighten around the shard of glass, but his eyes shift toward me and I freeze, not wanting to alert him to the fact that I have a potential weapon.

"Yes," he says, "and the best part is, Grace, that we can go anywhere. Anywhere at all. You and me together, the way I've always wanted it to be, the way it should have been ever since I first saw you that afternoon." He can't keep the excitement from his voice, and the sound of it sickens me.

I look out of the window, turning away from him so that he cannot see the despair on my face, the tears that are threatening to spill from my eyes. I dig my fingernails into the palms of my hands, forming crevices in my skin, harder and harder until the pain forces me to pay attention to it. I must find a way to keep strong, to stay ahead of him. He has already ruined a part of my life, and I cannot let him ruin any more.

I have to find a way out of this, for the sake of my friends. Dead or alive.

We pull away from the junction, and to my relief I see we're now out on a busier highway. Cars are flowing to and from the direction of the airport, and the sight of them is so refreshingly normal after the last few days of isolation in the lodges that I can feel my brain clearing a little, the fog of panic lifting slightly. Perhaps if we're around other people at the airport, I will be able to get somebody's attention—surely, I will be able to slip away and ask somebody for help. Ask to use someone's phone. It is only here in the car that I cannot get away from him—once he unlocks the doors I will stand more of a chance.

"Grace?" His voice is snappy, and I jump; it's a shift in tone from the dreaminess that came into his voice when he was talking about our future together. I haven't responded in the way that he hoped.

"I thought you'd be excited," he says, and now he sounds almost petulant, like a child who has been told he cannot have what he wants. "I've done so much for you already, Grace," he says softly, and I feel the fear creep up my throat. I can't put it off any longer. I have to ask him again.

"Nate," I say, "you know I told you about my friends, Hannah and—"

"They're not your friends." The snarl interrupts me. I hesitate, frightened of making him angry.

"Well," I continue, my voice trembling slightly, "Hannah and Alice, the—what happened to them. Do you know who—who might have done it? Do you know where Felicity is?"

He ignores me for a second, his eyes darting up at the signs above our heads, the little white airplane images showing that we're going toward the airport. Cars are sliding past us regularly now; a black Jeep overtakes, and a motorbike roars past us, leaving a thick, smoky trail, the smell of petrol leaking into the air. Everyone is going so fast—there is no way I could flag anyone down. My only hope is to wait until we're out of the car.

"Grace," he says eventually, "now isn't the time to think about the past. Now is the time for us to look to the future— together. You know that. I'm not telling you again. You and I—we have to be together. Michael said. It will make everything right."

With horror, I realize his rationality—if he and I are a couple, it somehow absolves him of his crime. Suddenly, my rape isn't a rape at all—it's the start of a relationship. Us being together, in his twisted mind, would legitimize what he did.

As if on cue, we enter a roundabout and swing off to the left, and the sight of the airport comes into view, the huge gray terminals rising into the bright blue sky. I blink—it feels like a lifetime ago when the three of us landed here, but in reality it has only been days. I think of us sitting at the champagne bar in London, the dark drowsiness of the flight, the touchdown here—how excited I was. How much I hoped that this would be a new start.

Nate drives in silence. I see a sign for a multistory car park, but instead of taking the turn, we swing off the road again, around behind the airport. The circular movement of the twisty roads makes me feel sick, and for a moment I feel as if this might go on forever; us moving around and around on a terrible, unstoppable roller coaster, me with no way of getting off.

"Where are we going?" I say, but he ignores me. He looks agitated now, as if something has gone wrong. We're moving farther from the airport, and I twist around in my seat, confused. He's taking us down a track that runs along a field at the back of the runways; I see planes lined up ready for takeoff, and hear the dull roar of an engine ascending into the sky, a white trail billowing out behind it, cutting through the air. But he does stop, parking us just out of sight of the airport, deftly and precisely, and cutting the engine.

That's when I hear the noise.

Chapter Twenty

Grace

A scraping, first of all, and for a moment I wonder if it's the exhaust, if something has happened to the car itself; we've been driving so fast, perhaps he has damaged it somehow. But then it becomes louder, a scratching sound coming from behind us, and now it is unmistakable: it is as if there is something—or someone—in the back of the car.

"What's that?" I say, but Nathaniel ignores me. He is muttering to himself now, reaching into the back of the car, where I see, with a thud of dread, a suitcase, zipped and packed.

"Your passport," he says to me, reaching out a hand, and with a drop in my stomach I realize that I do have it—I brought it with me, and it's in my shirt pocket, the maroon edge clearly visible to him. He must have seen it straightaway—that's why we didn't need to go back to the lodges after all.

"I can keep it, can't I, Nate?" I say, and I smile at him, trying desperately for a real, warm smile, although it takes every ounce of effort in my body to keep it up. With my left hand, I close my fingers around the glass, feel the point of it, deadly sharp against the tip of my finger. He reaches out, leaning over to me, his fingers brushing my chest as he takes the passport from my shirt pocket, flips to the photo page, and smiles.

"So beautiful," he says, touching it gently, and as he does so there is a bang from the boot of the car, a thudding sound that is impossible to ignore.

I swallow, hard. If I do it now there will be no going back.

"Nathaniel," I say, "will you please let me go to the police about my friends? I want to go home, Nate. I want to be with my family. You know my parents, my father. You can understand."

But he's shaking his head, agitated now. The banging sound from the boot grows louder, and he lets out a sudden groan, bowing his head to the steering wheel, grasping his hair in his hands. I look around; we are isolated, despite the aircraft flying overhead nobody can see the car—exactly his intention, I realize. He has managed to make me feel even more vulnerable than I already do.

"What's that noise, Nate?" I say to him again, but he shakes his head, as if I am a fly to be swatted, a distraction that he doesn't need. "Please," I say to him, "listen to me, Nate, I just—"

But he whips toward me, and I can tell that I have angered him now. My mouth is dry, salty with my mistake. There is nobody around to hear me scream as he reaches out toward me, grips my hair between his knuckles, tipping my head back painfully. I wince, the tears springing to my eyes quickly and easily. He is leaning over, his breath hot on my face; it is slightly sour somehow, as though he hasn't washed for a while. Panic pulses through me, hot and unchecked. I squeeze my eyes shut, and all at once I am back there, at my parents' house, and his hands are tight around my neck. I know what this man is capable of. I know what he is prepared to do. It doesn't matter whether I play his game or not, whether I go along with everything he wants—he is still stronger than me, he will still beat me no matter what.

"You will do what I say, Grace," he mutters, and I whimper in fear, feel something give inside me. After all this, I am here once again—powerless to stop him from doing what he likes.

He grunts, and I cannot stop him moving across the car, pulling me toward him. I feel the gear stick sharp against my body, the strength of his arms as he manhandles me like a rag doll. The heat of the car is stifling; surely, I think, I will suffocate in here, with this man who professes to love me but hates me on a deep, intense level—the level at which all women sit in his mind. For this is a man who has to have power, who is used to exercising it, who doesn't care who he hurts to get what he wants. I imagine him driving the knife into Hannah, kind, caring, responsible Hannah who has only ever wanted to help people, who put her friends first at all times, who made one mistake one night, and one alone. He is unbuckling his jeans, the snap of the belt flies across my stomach, and I think of him grappling with Alice, forcing her head under the water, of how powerless she must have felt beneath his strong, wide hands. Did he enjoy it, as he held her down? Did he relish the sensation of her body giving in, of her lungs filling with water like sponges, of her breath becoming air? Did he feel pleased with himself, as he conquered and dominated, again and again?

Because I know now: he killed them too. He is capable of violence—of course he is. Rape isn't murder, but a man like Nathaniel Archer will stop at nothing to get his way. All he's had to do is escalate things.

He's kissing me now, his lips wet and vile, pressing against my cheek and my skin like a dirty stamp that I will never be able to erase. I am on top of him, my limbs unwillingly dragged into the driver's seat, my crotch against his. He reaches up a hand

and rips my T-shirt, exposing my chest, and I feel a hot spurt of shame, my skin recoiling from his touch. His breathing is loud, an animalistic pant, just as it was before, just as it is in my nightmares. I couldn't stop him then, and I can't stop him now.

"You want this too," he says, just as he said the first time, and I feel the sharp pain in between my legs, raw and inevitable. My hair has come loose from its ponytail, the strands hang limply around my face, dangling down onto him, helpless. He is holding both my wrists, his fingers tight as a handcuff, and I struggle desperately, thinking of the only weapon I have. As he thrusts himself forward, there is another sound—louder than before, a banging from the back of the car, and then the sound of something unlocking, and just for a second, his grip relaxes on my wrists as he strains to listen, unease etched suddenly and shockingly across his face. I know this is my chance.

My fingers disengage from his and I feel inside my pocket, close them around the shard of glass and bring it back up before I can lose my nerve. I see the surprise flash across his features, and in that second he is rendered something else—not a grown man inflicting harm on a woman, but a child, a child who has been caught out and who doesn't have time to react. I raise the glass in the air, the back of my hand brushing against the soft felt of the car roof, and then I bring it down hard, driving the point of it into the side of his neck, feeling the dense resistance against my hand as the shard cuts through his skin and into his flesh.

The blood is much worse than I thought—a stream of it, dark and sticky, staining the car seats and my torn top, running down his thick, veined neck, snaking along his torso in a trickle that fast becomes a river. His eyes, dark blue, those eyes that have fooled people for so long, are wide and staring, as if he cannot quite believe what is happening to him, as if he can't believe what I have done. Even now, he doubts me, and the thought gives me the energy to push the jagged edge into him once again, harder this time. I think of Felicity, of her father, of the horrible suspicions that Nate has just confirmed. *Michael's special little girl.* Legitimizing a crime. I think of Alice and Hannah, the three of us holding hands, laughing together, of the friendship ties that bind us, even after everything that has happened, even from beyond the grave. They give me power, and they set me free.

There is a horrible gurgling sound coming from Nate's throat, but I don't stop to listen to it. I swing my left leg backward, away from him, and I fumble at the door, unlocking the car and stumbling out into the sunshine. I am breathing fast, and there is pain between my legs, dark spots dance in front of my eyes, but I steady myself with a hand on the side of the car and lurch around to the boot, my legs trembling. I am still holding the shard of glass in one hand and I drop it in horror, letting the bloodstained splinter fall to the hot, scorched earth beneath my feet.

The metal of the lock is blazing when I touch it, but it gives easily, loose already, and I step backward, afraid of what I will see, as the boot swings upward, revealing the body inside.

Felicity is lying in the trunk, curled up like an animal, her blond hair dirty and matted to her head. Her hands, her beautiful, manicured hands, are red and sore-looking, her fingernails ripped, fresh beads of blood springing up from the skin. She has obviously been clawing at the metal lock on the boot for quite some time, has exhausted herself with one last effort. Her eyes are half-closed, her lids heavy, but when I put out a hand to touch her face she is still warm, and relief courses through me.

"Felicity!" I say, and at the sound of her name she opens her eyes fully, directly into mine. I see something flash across her face, quick and unreadable, then dissipate when she sees it is me, and not Nate.

"Grace," she says, the sound a croak, and I wonder how long it has been since she's had any water, whether he fed her, or just left her to boil to nothing in the metal coffin of the car.

"You're all right," I say weakly, "you're all right, you're all right." I repeat the words until the fear leaves her eyes, and she begins to cry softly, still curled in the boot, her body curving in on itself as she sobs.

"Thank God, oh thank God," she whispers, as I reach down to help her, lifting her poor, fragile body from the car—it feels light as a bird, a bag of skin and bones. Her skin feels papery beneath my touch, and in that moment, I would kill Nathaniel again, over and over, drive the shard into his throat as many times as it would take to stop him hurting women like this.

As her feet touch the ground, the tears spill from my own eyes—tears of relief that she is alive, that we have made it, and tears of grief for the other half of our friendship group, for Hannah and for Alice, lying alone back at the lodges, at the mercy of Botswana now, the unlucky girls.

Felicity puts her skinny arms around my neck, winding them close to me, and I feel her sadness soft on my skin, her tears mingling with my own.

"It's over," I say. "It's over now, Flick, it's over. You're safe now. We both are. He's gone." At that, she cries harder, and we cling together, the survivors, as the hot sun beats down on our backs. Above us, the planes soar, their engines loud and unstoppable; the passengers looking down wouldn't see us at all.

Chapter Twenty-One

Two days later
London, England

Felicity

The interview room is cool, the coffee cup in front of me drained. Dregs cling to the bottom; I think about asking for another one but don't.

The policewoman has a Yorkshire accent, it is comforting somehow, the friendly flat vowels make me feel at ease. Perhaps she knows that. I have a sudden, bizarre urge to burrow myself against her chest, feel her hand stroke the top of my head, flatten down my hair as though I am a child again. I don't, of course. I cannot make this woman stand in for my mother. Nobody can do that.

"Can you walk us through it again, please, Felicity, just one more time?" she is saying, even though I have told them my story, stuttering through it, terrified of getting it wrong. Not a word out of place, I told myself, this story has to match the one I began to tell Grace as we sat in the airport at Botswana, wrapped in blankets that covered our bloodstained limbs, as the airport security staff telephoned for the police. Both of us slept on the flight home, our heads bent together, wearing strangers' clothes. Grace held my hand the entire way, our fingers linked as if we were children again. The last two pieces of the chain.

"Nathaniel and I broke up almost four months ago," I say again, wearily, rubbing a hand across my features as if I am exhausted, as if the relentless questioning is breaking me down. "Our relationship had become . . . difficult."

"You said before that he was abusive toward you?"

I nod, keep my eyes on the coffee cup. There's a chip in the side of it, stark white against the black. I wonder how it got there, whether someone lost their temper, hurled it across a room.

"That's right, yes. He would inflict both verbal and physical abuse on me, more and more regularly. At first I thought it was the stress of moving to New York—it started in America, the physical side of things. He had a new job—that's why we'd gone there—it was a lot more money, a great hospital, but he was under pressure. I told myself it must be that."

Tears glimmer in my eyes, but I reach up a hand to brush them away. Too soon, I think. The policewoman's face is devoid of emotion, though I see the way her eyes crease as I speak. Does she feel sorry for me? Is she trying to trip me up?

"And the abuse was what led your relationship to disintegrate?"

Disintegrate, I think, it's an interesting choice of word. Nate and I didn't disintegrate, we blew up. He had an explosive temper, and I suppose so did I.

"Yes," I say, "I didn't think I could take it anymore. I ended things, went to stay with a colleague in Brooklyn. I didn't know many other people out there—I had no family left. My father had recently passed away. I'd left my friends behind in London."

I think of them, Grace, Hannah, and Alice. Hannah sent me flowers when we left for the US, heavy-headed white lilies, as though I was dying, not moving. I put them in the bin—I don't like the way the little yellow pods stain your clothes. I didn't think lilies made up for the fact that she'd tried to ruin my future with Nate, told him that I was barren as if the fact was hers to tell.

It turned out he hadn't cared in the way I'd thought he would—I know now that he never wanted my children anyway. It was Grace he wanted. Grace's children he pictured when he lay awake at night. Grace's future.

"And after that, did Nathaniel attempt to contact you, track you down at all?"

I pause, bite my lip. The seconds tick by in my head, three, two, one.

"Yes," I say, and then I do allow myself to cry, just a little bit, a tear snaking down my cheek. I'm not wearing any makeup, I know I look younger without it. I rub my eyes; an eyelash disengages, comes off painlessly on the back of my hand. *Make a wish*, I think ludicrously, but it's too late—I've used up all my wishes now.

"He wouldn't accept the breakup," I say. "He didn't want things to end between us, he said he was sorry, that he was in the wrong. I suppose—I suppose I didn't believe that he'd change. He was obsessed with going back to London, he kept talking about it, said he never should have taken the New York job, that it had stressed him out, brought him to the edge of burnout." I pause.

"I realize now he wanted to go back for Grace, that he'd been unable to make the break he'd thought he could. His—focus on her, it hadn't gone away. Being across the ocean had in fact made it worse."

The woman nods, her face sympathetic. I wonder whether she feels sorry for me—the spurned girlfriend, standing in for the one he really wanted. The police found a folder on his computer—images upon images of Grace. He'd taken some from outside her flat in Peckham, zooming in on the upstairs windows. He even had one of her at home with her parents, and a few from the night in the Red Lion, too, of her sitting at the pub table out in the courtyard. He must have taken them from the doorway of the pub. None of us noticed, of course.

I hope they burn them along with his body, but I know that they won't. They'll be filed away as evidence. *The Botswana case.*

Underneath the table, I pull at the skin around my fingernails, ripping off tiny white shreds, leaving little tracks, red and raw. Minuscule jabs of pain, but it is nothing compared to when I think of him lying there in the front seat of the car, blood dripping down his neck. His beautiful neck.

She shouldn't have done that.

"Yes," the policewoman says, and she notes something down on the pad in front of her. I can't see what it is, and I can't strain forward to look—they'd think it was strange, a sign that I am worried.

"Did it upset you, his fascination with your friend?" Her question surprises me, I hadn't thought they'd go down that track. Perhaps she doesn't feel sorry for me after all.

"I mean . . ." I trail off, allowing her question to linger in the air between us. "I think it was about control," I say slowly. "He wanted control over all of us. That's why he did what he did, that night—he tried to cause a rift between the four of us, it was a game to him. Controlling women."

"The night you're referring to is the night at The Upper Vault in Richmond, correct?"

I nod, then realize she wants me to speak for the tape.

"Yes, that's right. It's the night he came on to Alice. The night Grace told me about the rape."

I don't tell her about the photograph I took, that awful image of Alice kissing him, his hands in her hair. They might think it strange. They might think it was a motive.

"You didn't believe Grace when she told you about the alleged rape, did you?"

The policewoman has folded her arms now, crossed them tightly against her chest. Her shirt is a little too tight for her; it strains across her breasts. Alleged rape. I still hate that word.

"I didn't want to believe it," I tell her firmly. "I loved Nate, in spite of the way he became toward me. I didn't think he was capable of it. I wouldn't hear a word against him."

She nods, apparently satisfied, uncrosses her arms.

"And so after the breakup with Nathaniel, you decided to get back in touch with your friends."

It's a statement, not a question, and I swallow, nod.

"Yes. I had missed them—dreadfully. I was feeling low, you know, after what had happened with Nate, the breakup: I wanted to treat myself. And my friends. I realized they'd been right about him; I wanted to talk to Grace about it in person. I knew I needed to do something big, something drastic, to bring us all back together. My birthday was coming up." I smile, almost by accident. "I've always liked my birthday."

Another note on the pad; perhaps I shouldn't have said that. It sounds frivolous, childish.

"And did you tell them that you and Nathaniel had split up?"

I shake my head, anticipating the question. "I didn't tell them because we hadn't shared details of our lives for two years. But I thought they probably had guessed—they knew I was coming to Botswana alone, and I no longer posted about Nate on any social media. In fact, I deleted a lot of it; I was so hurt. It would have been odd for me to have called them crying about Nate. We hadn't properly spoken after the night at the Red Lion—don't forget, I felt betrayed by them all." I raise my fingers, checking them off. "Hannah had told him about my infertility. Grace had accused him of rape. And Alice had come on to him—that's what he said."

I hold my three fingers aloft: the sins of my friends.

"It would have been weird to go into it all with them," I carry on, "but I planned on telling them in Botswana, discussing it all, making peace with it, with them. I planned to ask Grace to forgive me. For not believing her about who Nate really was. I figured Hannah had just been drunk, and that he might have lied about Alice, too. I now think he probably came on to her, not the other way around."

"Can you tell us about what happened when you got to Botswana? You'd booked the Deception Valley Lodges, the whole complex."

I swallow, dig my nails into my skin.

"Yes—it was meant to be a treat, a surprise for them. I felt I needed forgiveness—after how wrong I'd been. I'd cut them out of my life; I wasn't sure if they'd want to see me again, so I thought I'd be able to show them how much I cared by paying for it all, getting somewhere really luxurious, you know. Proving how much they meant to me."

"It must have been expensive, paying for all that."

The words make me feel defensive, I don't know why.

"I inherited money," I tell her, "firstly when my mother died. She had cancer. And then more, just recently, when my father passed away." No harm in reminding them of that, of what I've already been through. They'd do well to pay attention to it. Be a bit more sympathetic.

"Right," she says. "Of course."

I wait, but she just nods at me, gesturing for me to go on.

"I flew out there earlier in the week," I say. "I wanted a break from it all—to get out of New York. I thought I'd take a few days to myself, lick my wounds as it were, then everyone would come join me at the weekend, and we'd celebrate my birthday."

I swallow, my throat suddenly dry.

"Nate followed me out there, to Botswana, without my knowledge. He had my passwords, he found the details in my emails. He came to the lodges on the Thursday evening, the night before the others were due to arrive. I was terrified. He forced me to stay away from them, held a knife to my throat. He wrote those text messages to the girls, pretending I was sick, acting as if everything was normal. He canceled all the other invitations to the party—I'd invited other people, too—everything I said about the event was true. You can check. The girls were going to come early, so we'd have a chance to talk things through on the Friday night, and then on the Saturday we were going to celebrate. I was going to get my life back, turn things around."

She is making more notes now, her pen moving quickly across the page, making a tiny scratching sound that reminds me of my own nails against the car boot. A shudder passes through me, cold and unpleasant.

"Nate locked me inside Zebra Lodge," I say. "He stayed in there with me, that first evening. He—he wouldn't let me out to see the girls, he had my phone the entire time. I could hear them calling out to me, but he kept the blinds shut and the door bolted. He removed the locks from all the other girls' lodges. He wanted to be able to get inside.

"On the Saturday," I say, my voice breaking a little, cracking as I speak, "he drugged me. He left me alone in Zebra Lodge, that's the last thing I remember. When I woke up, I was in the boot of the hire car. He'd left Hannah and Alice for dead, tidied up the lodge so that it looked as though I'd never even been there. He was playing a game with us all."

"Why do you think he kept you alive?" The policewoman is sitting up straighter now, focusing on me more intently, unless I am imagining it. She seems to be leaning forward slightly, her eyes burning into mine. I close my eyes, just briefly, and bright colors flash inside my head: the blue of the plunge pools, the green of the cacti. I must keep going. I am almost at the end, now.

"I think he lost control," I say. "I think things went wrong. He wasn't expecting Grace to run from the lodge. He wanted to look like a hero in front of her, rescue her from whoever was attacking our friends." I inhale, exhale, one, two, three.

"He planned to blame the whole thing on me."

If I close my eyes, I am back there, away from this small police interview room in London, back in the heat of Botswana, the air cloying and sticky, the blue sky illuminating the lodge complex in front of me. The grasses are swaying in the light, subtle breeze, and the sun is burning my scalp, my shoulders, hot as fire on my face. The wooden decking is solid beneath my feet, and the sound of the running water is soothing, a constant stream of it, bubbling beneath us all, just waiting for the right moment to swallow us up. I can feel the old panic rising inside me, blurring the corners of my vision, and I have to place both hands down flat on the cold gray table, bow my head slightly to keep myself calm.

"Do you need a break?" the policewoman asks, concern in her voice, and I nod gratefully, gasp out a yes.

"A break would be great," I say. "Yes, please."

She leads me out of the room, presses another coffee into my hands. I smile at her.

"Thank you," I say.

Most of what I told the police is true, but not all of it.

Nate and I didn't break up in New York, but he wanted to. I couldn't stand it. I'd never loved anyone like I loved Nate Archer. I still can't imagine that I ever will. That kind of love only happens once in a lifetime, and you have to do everything you can to hold on to it. That's what my father told me; that's what I believe.

I couldn't bear the thought of Nate with anyone else.

I planned the trip to Botswana, organized everything. I knew he'd come if Grace was going to be there; I knew he was still obsessed with her, that New York hadn't been enough.

We flew over together, barely speaking on the plane. He was pretending, of course, pretending he was giving our relationship one last chance, a holiday together, the act of a desperate couple, but I knew the real reason he'd agreed so readily.

That night, I drugged him in Zebra Lodge, crushed *gifblaar* in a glass of champagne. An ingenious plant, known in English as poison leaf, found in abundance in Botswana and easy to source. I knew I had to make it look like an attack on all three of them—sacrifice Hannah and Alice for the sake of killing Grace. The only way Nate would ever be mine is if I removed the object of his obsession—got her out of the picture once and for all. Crossing continents didn't work—this was the final solution. I'd tried lesser tactics, pulling strings with the hospital chain to get him the New York job offer, threatening to sue them for allowing the operation that left me infertile, when in reality I was too young to make the choice. Most people think hospitals operate in isolation—but the private sector is owned by a select few. Once I'd spoken to them, they were happy to make Nate an offer he couldn't refuse, rather than have what happened to me splashed all over the papers. It was a small price to pay; after all, Nate was good at his job. He was initially reluctant, but when they told him he had no choice, he went with it. And of course, I went with him. But it all continued—the Google searches, the pictures of her on his phone, the phone calls to her parents. His obsession was just as strong, and the only way to stop it was to cut off the source. Remove Grace, remove the problem. Just like my father removed the problem when I was fifteen years old.

It's what my father taught me, growing up. At night, when he visited my room, my father told me how much he loved me, over and over again. I was his special girl. That's why I've kept his secret, and why I couldn't listen to Grace. Daddy often used to say that rape isn't always a sign of evil, it can be a sign of love. I knew Nate loved Grace. But I couldn't lose him, not after I'd lost my dad.

The difficult part was Grace herself, who utterly ruined the key part of the plan by escaping; typical Grace, messing things up. Really, it's her fault the others died, if you think about it properly, distill it right down.

It wasn't hard to drown Alice. I only had to think about her kissing him that night, putting her hands all over him as if he was hers, not mine. I pictured them together as the water closed over her head; the memory of it spurred me on. She deserved it, really. I had the photo to prove it, for times when I felt weak.

Hannah was harder. Poor Hannah. I almost didn't go through with it, but she started asking questions about Alice when I surprised her in the kitchen; I could tell she suspected me. She cried a bit, apologized for what she did that night, her drunken slip of the tongue. I didn't bother telling her that Nate hadn't cared that much anyway, I didn't really see the point. She apologized, too, for not reporting my father, for not acting on her suspicions and concerns. That was what really pushed me over the edge.

Grace was going to be last. I had it all planned out. I'd frame Nate for all three murders, then go to the police, tell them how he'd drugged me in the lodge. My messages would all match up—they'd see how excited I'd been for the girls to come, how I'd not felt well on that very first night. Everyone knew we were friends—we'd been friends since school. Nate would take the blame; his prints were on the knife. I wore his surgical gloves to kill Hannah; he'd brought his medical bag with us, in case of emergencies.

I'd forgive him, naturally. Just like I forgave my father.

I imagined myself visiting him in prison, whispering promises into his ear, his only savior. There would be no other women in prison—and above all, no Grace. Nobody to tempt him—he would be mine, and mine alone.

Only of course, it didn't work out like that.

Chapter Twenty-Two

Botswana

Felicity

I watch as the girls enter Zebra Lodge. They're anxious now, I can see it in their faces. Grace in particular; squirming with tension. Alice's face is paler than usual; she's exasperated with Grace, but she's uneasy too—she wants to know where I am, why the complex is so eerily empty. Hannah is being her sensible self, but even she is starting to feel unnerved.

They knock before going inside—Grace first, a mousy little tap, then Alice who does it properly. I tidied up as best I could, removing any traces of myself, making it look brand-new. It was too risky, being in there; we'd had a close shave when Hannah had come looking late last night after their dinner; I'd held my breath as her footsteps hesitated outside. Braver than I thought—perhaps she'd have been better off in Lion Lodge after all.

I've had fun writing those notes. Just my little game. I miss the ones we played as children. No harm in re-creating some of the magic. Now that my father is dead, I have found that fragments of my childhood have begun to come back to me, little slivers that have been buried in my mind for a very long time.

We are better in the car than the lodge. Parked a few meters down the track, the headlights off, I sit watching and waiting. It is easy for me to slip in and out while Nate lies comatose in the back; the girls never think to leave the complex—either that, or they're too scared to. I bet Hannah has brought a guidebook with her, warned them all about the snakes and the lions and the things that go bump in the night. Predictable to the end. I enjoy myself filling up the champagne glasses, laying out their food. One last treat—how generous I am. The main lodge is so large and I am so familiar with it now that it's easy to slip into another room at the sound of their voices, play an endless game of hide and seek. I've always liked a game, and this is my best yet. There is only one moment where I almost get caught—after I've slipped the fortune-teller between the pages of *The Jungle Book*, when Grace comes into the drinks room for a new bottle of champagne. I escape through the window and forget to close it behind me. Still, I don't think any of them actually notice—too busy lamenting the puddle of fizz on the floor.

"Not much longer, my love," I whisper to Nate as the first rays of dawn light filter through the windscreen on Sunday morning; of course, he doesn't reply. I gave him just enough of the *gifblaar* to ensure he'd stay comatose for as long as I needed, but not enough to kill him. There's no way I want that.

I ease myself out of the hire car, closing the door gently behind me. The sun is casting an orange glow on the lodges as I make my way in, the dew of the night brushing against my ankles.

Hannah is in the kitchen; clearly, she has barely slept; Alice's untimely passing has obviously hit her hard. Her hair is in a lank ponytail, pulled back from her face, and she doesn't struggle, not really, but I do feel a sense of sadness as the light goes out of her eyes. She is the least guilty of the three of them, but I know I have to stick to the plan above all else. At least the kitchen knives here are sharp—it's over quite quickly, and afterward, I close her eyelids. I try not to think about her baby back at home—there is no point, really. It is too young still to remember her properly; I made sure to check.

The door to Lion Lodge is closed when I approach it, the knife still in my hand, treading softly and silently on the wooden walkways. I picture Grace inside—will she be sleeping, or wide awake, terrified? I can't help but hope it's the latter. The game is reaching its denouement: the end is in sight.

It's the last thought I have before Nate's hand covers my mouth. The last thing I see is the knife soaring through the air, landing in the plunge pool with a soft splash, sinking beneath the blue. After that, everything goes black.

When I awake, I don't know where I am. The space is small and dark; it reminds me of being a child, hiding deep in a wardrobe from my parents. Playing a game, even then. Only this time, I'm on the wrong side, and I don't like it at all. I feel my way around—my wrists are not bound, and my palm hits the curve of a wheel, the soft felt of a parcel-shelf.

Panic washes over me; I curl my hands into fists, bang on the lid of the car boot. Nobody answers. Nobody can hear me. My father isn't coming to find me, this time.

It feels like hours before the car begins to move. I have no way of knowing who is driving, though I presume it must be

Nate, and I shout his name, as loudly as I can, beg him to stop the car, to let me out. I tell him I am sorry, that I love him, more than anything. He will never know how much—what I have sacrificed to keep him. He doesn't reply to me—I don't know whether he can even hear what I'm saying. I go over and over everything in my head—I must have given him the wrong dosage, he has woken up too soon.

Eventually, we do stop; I hear the metallic, dull sound of the car door opening and closing, the muffled strains of a conversation, then an additional weight as two people get back into the car, one on either side. I have lost track of time—I don't have my phone, and it feels as though I have been locked up for hours, though it might be much less. My mouth is dry, my fingernails bleeding. I have been trying to break the metal lock on the boot to no avail. When I close my eyes, I imagine water, cool and clear, flowing down my throat.

Tears fill my eyes as I hear Nate telling Grace how he feels about her; it has all been for nothing, then. All of it. The air in the boot feels like it is lessening; it is becoming harder and harder to breathe.

I hear him lie through his teeth about me, telling Grace he doesn't know where I am, telling her that I am unstable. Anger builds in my chest as I realize in horror that he means to leave me in here, let me rot away to nothing—no one will know I was ever in here at all. And then I hear him tell her about my father, about how he gave him advice. Tears start to form in my eyes, they slide helplessly down my cheeks, puddle at my chin. Daddy didn't want anyone else to love me. But he's gone, and soon I will have lost Nate too.

Desperately, I gather all of my energy and try again, hitting the boot with my hands and my feet, despite the weakness that is overtaking my limbs, despite the ache in my joints that gets worse by the second.

The car stops. I can't make out what they're saying anymore; there is the sound of planes overhead, loud and unmistakable. And then I hear the noise—a terrible, guttural scream—Nate, my Nate, and I feel horror rising up through me—Grace, oh Grace, what have you done?

And then she is there, above me, blinking in the sunlight, and I open my eyes, slowly, as though I have been in a daze. She's telling me that it's over, that everything is going to be all right now, and I start to cry as I realize what she's done, that my Nate, my beautiful Nate, has gone. My sobs become uncontrollable, and she reaches down to lift me up, hugging me to her body, my treacherous friend. I wrap my arms around her neck, bury my face in her hair, trying to think as quickly as I can, fighting the urge to squeeze her tighter and tighter until her throat closes up and her body goes limp.

She rubs my back with a small, firm hand, and we stand there in the blazing Botswana heat, the sun burning down on us, bleaching away the past. I cannot look at Nate, at his body in the front seat of the car, still and unseeing. It breaks my heart, splinters it to pieces.

I hold Grace's hand as we stagger to the airport, make our way through the automatic doors like two survivors of a massacre.

There are voices and people, they envelop us all at once, and I know time is up. I have to get my story straight. One last hand left to play.

Chapter Twenty-Three

Three weeks later
London, England

Grace

Felicity and I sit together in the church. The morning sun is filtering softly through the stained glass; I watch as it dapples the pews. It's so much weaker here than the sun in Botswana; milky white instead of burning fire. Before us, the two coffins stand side by side; Hannah's has white flowers, Alice's has yellow. Our hands are clasped together; in front of us, Tom and Chris sit white-faced. The baby, Max, is not here—too young to understand, too painful to endure. At the end of the service, a woman approaches Chris, puts her arms around him for what looks like a moment too long. They look closer than friends, and my mind snags on the image briefly before pushing it aside. Tom doesn't speak, he is silent with shock. Perhaps he is only just realizing what he has lost, and what he took for granted.

Afterward at the wake, I hug their parents, press my cheek against theirs. They are cold, stiff, numb with grief. Felicity follows suit; I watch as she kisses Alice's father, puts a reassuring hand against Hannah's mother's back. She is dressed beautifully;

a black shawl over her slim shoulders. Despite everything that has happened, she still has the power to make me feel inferior, less than. My own jacket is shabby, a little bit too big.

Seeing me watching her, she comes over to me, watery-eyed. I open my arms, feel her familiar body angle against mine, breathe in the scent of her hair. It is just the two of us now, together with our memories.

"Let's go for a drink," she says softly, "somewhere quiet, just the two of us. We can toast them both."

I nod, take a deep breath. The last few weeks have been exhausting—the police interviews about Nate, relaying everything that happened out in Botswana. Felicity has been a rock throughout, despite what she went through herself, the horror of it, and the truth about her father, what he did to her growing up. I have told her how sorry I am for never daring to question it—the suspicions we all had. They will not charge me for Nate's death—it is marked down as self-defense. He is found guilty of both the girls' murders, their parents will not have to sit through a trial. Out of it all, I realize, has come forgiveness, and understanding—Nate was found guilty of my rape posthumously, and finally, finally, I feel a sense of peace. The gap in our lives where Hannah and Alice once were will never be filled, of course, but at least there is a sense of justice having been done.

We leave the wake together, arm in arm, our footsteps the only sound in the quiet lane. It is April, now, the hedgerows are becoming cloudy with cow parsley, white fronds like broccoli stretching upward to the sky. A butterfly flits in front of us; a red admiral, its wings fluttering rapidly before it disappears out of sight. Felicity squeezes me to her, warm and tight.

"We're the only ones left now," she says. "We have to look after each other."

"Of course," I say. "That's what friends are for."

She smiles, her golden hair glowing in the sunlight. "I'll buy you a drink," she says.

And I follow her into the pub.

Acknowledgments

I wrote most of *The Wild Girls* in the 2020 lockdown. This year has been an incredibly hard one for so many people, but writing has provided a huge source of comfort to me and I feel very grateful to have been able to write this book—during a time when the world felt (and still feels) very scary, it was a privilege to be able to escape into Botswana, if only in my imagination. So, thank you to everyone at my publisher HQ for allowing me to write this and giving me the security of a book contract.

Thank you to my new editor, Kate Mills, for helping to shape this book, for having so much enthusiasm about it from the beginning, and for making it such an easy and collaborative process. Thanks to Charlotte Phillips at HQ for designing such a fabulous cover, and to everybody at HarperCollins both in the UK and abroad for their support. Particular thanks to Becky Heeley for all of your help, to Jon Appleton for your copyedits, and to my dad for pulling me up on my grammar and dubious geography, some of which is still dubious, but I had to take artistic license! Thank you as ever to Camilla Bolton, Jade Kavanagh, Mary Darby, and all at Darley Anderson for your energy, kindness, and belief and for selling my books around the world.

Thank you to Alex for putting up with me during lockdown

and letting us get kittens (got to get Sooty and Smudge in here somehow!), and thank you to my amazing family for always championing my novels.

And as always thank you to my readers; I found an old draft of *The Doll House* (my debut) the other day and I really can't believe I'm now on book four. Every week I get messages from people telling me they've enjoyed my books, and it makes my day every time. If you want to get in touch with me, please do so on www.phoebemorganauthor.com, or find me on Twitter @Phoebe_A_Morgan, Instagram @phoebeannmorgan, or Facebook @PhoebeMorganAuthor. Thank you for buying my books, for reading and reviewing them, and for telling others about them too—it really helps and makes all the pain of the first draft worth it!

P.S.

Insights,
Interviews
& More . . .

About the author

About the book

Read on

Meet Phoebe Morgan

HarperCollins UK

PHOEBE MORGAN is an author and Editorial Director at HarperCollins UK. She studied English at Leeds University after growing up in the Suffolk countryside. She lives in London, England.

phoebemorganauthor.com
🐦 @Phoebe_A_Morgan ෴

Q&A with Phoebe Morgan

Q: What inspired you to write The Wild Girls?

A: I knew I wanted to write a novel set somewhere other than the UK, and my agent and I had a brainstorm to try to think of locations. I suggested the idea of a safari, and at first I thought it was too far-fetched, but actually after I did some research and found this amazing website showcasing luxury lodges, the idea started to take shape in my mind and I realized it could be a really perfect escapist setting. I wrote most of this book during the first lockdown of 2020, so sadly travel was banned and I didn't get to see Botswana myself (hence it is an imagining in the novel, and mistakes are my own!)—but it did save my sanity for those months as I felt as though I was traveling there in my mind and that's what I hope readers experience too.

Q: The four women, "the wild girls," in the book are a very close-knit group of friends who love each other but also keep a lot of secrets, criticisms, and jealousy to themselves. How do you hope readers will feel about their friendship by the end?

A: I loved writing these four women; female friendship is something I hold very dear and I think it's a fascinating topic. All the women in *The Wild Girls* are flawed and imperfect, but I want the reader to realize that they do love each other (possibly with the exception of one, which I won't mention in case of spoilers!) underneath everything and that sadly, sometimes life and other circumstances really do get in the way of once-beautiful friendships. As a reader, you certainly don't have to like all of my characters ▶

3

(I often write fairly horrible ones!), but I do hope that you will at least be able to understand one of them, and empathize with some of the feelings they have toward one another.

Q: Botswana is such an inspiring setting, especially for a heart-pounding thriller. Are there any other places outside of the UK that you feel inspired to set a book in?

A: My next book actually takes a brief foray into Thailand (but only brief!). I'd love to set a novel in Europe—Italy is one of my favorite places on the planet—but it feels so far away right now given we're all still in lockdown (I'm writing this in March 2021 . . .). My first three novels were set in places I knew—London, Essex, and then Suffolk, my home county where I grew up—so I am definitely open to exploring other places. It's a lot of fun!

Q: What did you enjoy about writing The Wild Girls most, and what do you hope readers will get from it?

A: I enjoyed writing from a few different points of view; I always like to switch things up and keep the reader on their toes by changing points of view relatively regularly. I liked getting inside the mindset of each of the women—to me, Grace was the "main character" if there has to be one, but I will be really interested to hear from readers as to which woman they connected with the most. I hope readers above all get a sense of escapism from my book, that it provides a few hours of distraction from the world, and that they'll enjoy my writing style enough to pick up my other books, too! ∾

Reading Group Guide

1. Who is your favorite character in the book? Who is your least favorite?

2. Which of the four women do you sympathize with most: Hannah, Alice, Grace, or Felicity?

3. Hannah, Alice, Grace, and Felicity are very close, and they care deeply about one another, but they also had a falling out and have their own secrets and judgments about one another. What do you think this says about female friendship?

4. How does the Botswana setting add to the impact of the story?

5. Have you ever been to a reunion or on a trip with friends you hadn't seen in years? Would you or would you not recommend it and why?

6. Why do you think the friends find Nathan so compelling?

7. Which character do you think is the most to blame?

8. Did the novel end the way you expected it to? Why or why not? ◠

Don't miss these addictive thrillers from Phoebe Morgan

THE BABYSITTER

A heart-pounding psychological thriller about betrayal, loyalty, and the lengths people will go to hide their darkest secrets

THE GIRL NEXT DOOR

A gripping thriller about little white lies in a marriage that spiral into a deadly web when a teenage girl is found murdered

THE DOLL HOUSE

A haunting and tense debut about a woman who discovers someone is making doll-sized re-creations of her home and the deadly secrets lurking inside ∾

Discover great authors, exclusive offers, and more at hc.com.